The Sound of Murder

by

JOHN AND EMERY BONETT

The Sound of Murder

by

JOHN AND EMERY BONETT

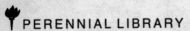
PERENNIAL LIBRARY
Harper & Row, Publishers
New York, Cambridge, Philadelphia, San Francisco
London, Mexico City, São Paulo, Sydney

Library of Congress Cataloging in Publication Data

Bonett, John, 1906-
    The sound of murder.

    Reprint. Originally published: New York : Walker, 1971, c1970.
    "P642."
    I. Bonett, Emery, 1906-   . II. Title.
[PR6005.079S6   1983]   823'.914   82-48809
ISBN 0-06-080642-7 (pbk.)

83 84 85 86 10 9 8 7 6 5 4 3 2 1

The Sound of Murder

The Chief Characters in the Story

Halberd Corsair	*A successful businessman*
Netta Corsair	*His wife*
Keith Antrim	*Halberd's nephew*
Lieut.-Col. Bertie Summersby	*Halberd's brother-in-law*
Claire Summersby	*His wife*
Julian Killigrew	*Editor of "Bookman's Weekly"*
Anthea Merrow	*A young actress*
Pamela Ducayne	*A widow*
Roddie	*An electrician*
Lennie Buxton	*A night caretaker*
Miss Purslane	*Halberd's secretary*
Miss Brind	*Julian's secretary*
Minnie Butterworth	*The Corsairs' maid*
Sid Butterworth	*A farmer; Minnie's brother*
Sir Otto Graffham	*An old friend of Inspector Borges*
Detective Chief Superintendent Mallick	
and	
Inspector Borges	

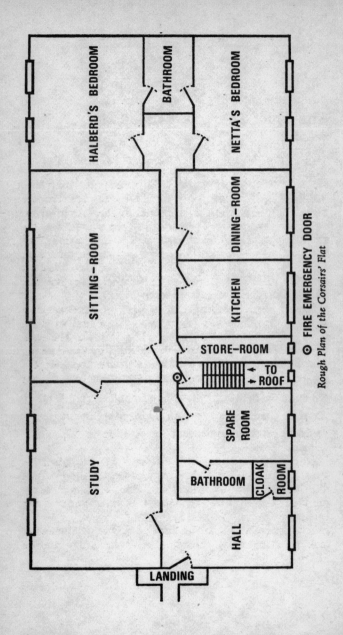

Rough Plan of the Corsairs' Flat

◉ FIRE EMERGENCY DOOR

Chapter One

IT was twenty to six when Sid drove into the courtyard. Backing the lorry into place beside a dark-green Humber parked by the portico, he clambered out and stretched his limbs. On the way into London he had run straight into the strangling grip of the Friday-night rush hour. The traffic had lurched, stopped, lurched all the way until he turned off Gray's Inn Road. There was one comfort—he hadn't lost his way; nor, once within sight of that whopping big sky-sign, had it been possible to miss Termini House.

Mighty queer, he thought, how quiet the place was now that the office folk had gone home. Not a soul in sight, scarcely a sound except the muted drone of traffic. The evening was dark, but the courtyard, shadowed by the towering mass of concrete, held the blackness of a later hour. Bit of a graveyard, he muttered, but if Minnie's happy here it's not for others to worry. He took a parcel from the cab of the lorry and, following her directions, made his way to the side entrance. Finding it open, he went in and gave four resounding blows on the door at the end of the passage. "Open up," he called. "Police. Open up."

He was grinning hugely at his own humour when his sister opened the door. "I knew it was you," she said. "You don't have to break the door down." She gave him a smacking kiss. "Come on in, lad, and tell us what you're doing here. I didn't expect you till next week."

"I sold some calves to Jim Sutter over by Maidstone and took 'em along today. Thought I'd give you a nice surprise

7

on the way back. Ma's sent you a cake." He handed over the parcel. "Careful when you open it. There's a pot of strawberry there too."

While the kettle boiled they exchanged family news. Then, as Minnie poured out his second cup of tea, she said, "I'll just take Lennie his cuppa—he's the caretaker here. Now you get on with yours." She bustled out, returning a few moments later to tuck into the cake with exclamations of appreciation.

"I'd best be off in a few minutes," Sid said at ten-past six. "Want to come part way with me in the Rolls? I'll drop you where you can get a bus on to Finchley."

"Course I'll come." Minnie tidied up briskly, changed her shoes, and was soon ready to leave. She was about to climb into the lorry when she exclaimed, "Lor, I've forgotten that jumper I was knitting for Ma. Shan't be a brace of ticks, Sid," and she ran back into the building.

"Sure you've forgotten nothing else?" he asked good-humouredly as she sat down breathless beside him. "Cor lumme!" As his boot slipped from the clutch pedal a shattering thump came from the rear of the lorry and the engine died.

"Ruddy foot's all thumbs," he commented, pressing the starter again. "Hope I haven't bust the lot." The engine roared, he let the clutch in slowly, and, as the lorry moved off, sighed in relief. "Nothing to worry about," he said, easing out into the street and turning towards Euston Road. "Give us an acid drop, Minnie—the bag's just in front of you—and have one yourself."

An hour and a quarter later Sid reached the farm, drove the lorry into a barn, and decided not to muck it out that night. On Saturday he rose as usual at five o'clock and, after a snatched cup of scalding tea, was busy in byre and stable until eight, when he came in for a substantial breakfast and a quick look at the morning paper. Going out afterwards to the barn, he took off his jacket, hung it on a nail, and lowered the tailboard of the lorry. It was with very considerable surprise that he saw a large, well-dressed, bespectacled man apparently fast asleep on the trampled straw. A polite cough, followed by a heavy hand on the shoulder, failed to rouse the sleeper. A further resultless shake, a closer look, two calloused fingers on a pulse that was not there, and Sid realized that the stranger was dead.

Going over to his jacket, he packed a pipe and sat down on an upturned bucket to think. He could get into the lorry and take it down to the village; but somehow he didn't fancy delivering a corpse at the cottage where the police constable lived. Bob might be out, and his wife wouldn't be overpleased at the idea of turning her parlour into a temporary mortuary. Sid got up and, crossing the yard, put his head into the dairy, where his son was cleaning the separator. "Get your bike out, Bill," he said, "and nip down to the police station. Say that Bob had better be along as soon as he can make it."

During the next twenty minutes Sid heaved out the dead man, placed him on an unused tarpaulin, covered him with new sacks, and cleaned out the lorry. This done, he stood outside the barn smoking until his son, tearing up some fifty yards ahead of the constable, asked excitedly what was happening and had to be packed off firmly to finish his work in the dairy.

"Took your time, didn't you?" Sid greeted the policeman, leading him into the barn and removing the sacks. "I found him a while back in the lorry. He's a goner."

"How d'you know?" Bob bent over the body.

"Well, he ain't breathing," Sid replied shortly.

A minute passed before the constable straightened himself and, removing his helmet, asked, "Who is he?"

"Search me. Never set eyes on him before."

"Then what was he doing in your lorry?" Bob produced a notebook and a stub of pencil.

"He wasn't answering questions when I found him," Sid said drily. "But I reckon he must have fallen in last night.

9

Suppose you put that ruddy notebook away and I'll tell you." He told him.

"Must have landed with a rare thump, Sid. Seems to me that if I'd been driving I'd have got out to have a look."

"Maybe you would. But I didn't."

Bob grunted. After a short pause for thought he said, "You didn't ought to have moved the body."

"Oh, didn't I? I suppose you'd have left the poor beggar lying in all that mucky straw. Not me—I've some respect for the dead. 'Sides," Sid went on firmly so that there should be no misunderstanding about the matter, "I'll be needing to use the lorry after I've had my dinner."

Chapter Two

"IT sounds like a block of flats for tarts," Halberd Corsair had said without a smile.

He was referring to Fayre Court, the ten-storey building in Scott Street of which his Company had bought a long lease. Although Scott Street lay to the south of Euston Road and was separated by that busy thoroughfare from the three main-line stations to the North, Halberd, brushing aside the murmured suggestions of his co-directors, had insisted on re-naming the building Termini House.

"For tarts," he repeated with emphasis. "Ours is a Company of national reputation. The Head Office must bear a name that immediately conveys importance and solidity. It should also indicate the central nature of this locality. Everyone knows King's Cross, Euston, and St Pancras. No-one has —as yet—heard of Scott Street. We're going to make Termini House a landmark." He paused for a bare half-second and, turning his slate-grey eyes on a harassed-looking man who sat halfway down the long mahogany table, went on: "Chambers, please see that a sky-sign is put in hand immediately and erected by the end of the month. If any point has to be cleared with the authorities I'm sure you'll be able to deal with it yourself."

That had been ten years ago. The beckoning sky-sign still shone, even though it had served its original purpose. Now every taxi-driver in London knew Termini House, and the great glass doors under the pillared portico swung open a thousand and more times each working day. Between these self-closing doors and the monogrammed glass inner doors lay a rectangular foyer to the walls of which were affixed forty-one polished brass plates, each bearing the name of a limited liability company, followed in smaller type by the words "Registered Offices." Topping them, a considerably larger plate carried the name of Wydspred Investments Ltd. This was the master company which controlled a diversity of enterprises ranging from earth-moving machinery to the manufacture of brass brads, from disposable nappies to pipettes. This was the company of which Halberd Corsair was Chairman and Managing Director, and which had grown from acorn to spreading oak during his tenure of office. Shareholders had seen the value of their holdings multiplied many times. Those who had sold their shares in earlier days tried to assuage their regrets by assuring themselves and their friends that one day the bubble would burst. But the skin of the bubble had proved tough and seemed indefinitely expansile.

On this Thursday the silently jerking minute hand of the electric clock in the Directors' luncheon-room was five minutes short of two o'clock when Halberd rose from the table, squaring his heavy shoulders. Below the deep chest a paunch curved above surprisingly thin legs. The figure was that of an actor whose upper half had been made up as Falstaff while the lower half remained that of Petruchio. The pale, unlined face, slightly shadowed under the eyes, proclaimed a man who judged his fellows shrewdly and kept his own counsel. He waited unmoving while the silver-haired banker who was his guest folded his spectacles and slipped them into a case.

"I'll put the figures before my Board on Tuesday," the banker said as they walked along the passage to the lift. "While obviously I can't commit us to any specific undertaking. . . ." The tone of voice of the uncompleted sentence left no doubt that the proposals would be approved.

"You'll give me a ring, then?"

"As soon as the meeting is over—probably about four o'clock." The banker paused to look out of a wide, metal-framed window, observing in a casual tone that indicated completion of the business discussion, "Magnificent view. Are we on the top floor?"

"Of the office block, yes. I had the floor above converted into quite a pleasant little flat and put in a private lift from the side entrance. It has certain tax advantages," Halberd observed. "If one doesn't look after oneself these days the revenue people skim off all the cream." He made a gesture of irritation. "Every Budget, every new Chancellor, creates problem after problem." United in criticism of Government interference and short-sightedness, the two men entered the lift.

Three minutes later, having sped the banker on his way, Halberd went into his office on the ground floor. The white-panelled room looked out on to a small patio in which a bronze rhomboid, punched irregularly with holes the size of a sixpence, stood a little aslant on a marble base bearing the legend "Contemplation". Behind a walnut desk, bare except for three telephones, a blotting-pad, and a copper ashtray, hung a Canaletto riverscape. Thus Halberd, while modestly disclaiming connoisseurship in art, was able silently to bare the soul beneath the business carapace.

Sitting at the desk, he pressed a button that activated a green light-bulb in his secretary's room. Miss Purslane came in, seated herself at his signal, and began to take down his rapidly dictated notes of the lunch-time conversation. When he stopped speaking she looked up. She was the perfect secretary, middle-aged, intelligent, efficient, trustworthy, and neuter. It had never occurred to her employer that he knew little more of her than he had learned when he engaged her some fifteen years ago.

"One carbon only—for the Private File," he said. "Please let Mr Antrim know that I'm free."

Keith Antrim was Halberd's nephew. He had come down

from Cambridge with a good Arts degree and joined the firm shortly before both his parents were killed in a motoring accident. After two years Halberd had made him his Personal Assistant. Tall, pleasant-looking, quiet, and able, Keith had proved himself an invaluable *aide* to whom, as time went on, his uncle was happy to delegate many of the problems of an ever-growing financial empire. When Keith came in Halberd said, "I'll have most of the final figures tomorrow. I'd like you to look at them over the weekend. Let me have them with your comments on Monday. Then we can make a start on the report. Meantime, will you rough out something for the Chairman's speech? You know the sort of thing I say each year. Turnover well up, trading exceedingly satisfactory, profits higher for the Xth year running, dividend maintained despite remorseless and ill-advised taxation, prospects for the coming months excellent. A trumpet voluntary full of optimism. Keep it short, but work in a couple of jokes that the papers can quote. I came across something the other day about the world being full of screwballs trying to unscrew it." He produced the hint of a smile. "You might be able to work that in."

Keith laughed. "I certainly will." After a moment's thought he ventured, "You don't think we should be a little —conservative about future prospects?"

Halberd shook his head. "No, my boy. I've got something up my sleeve which I'll tell you about as soon as the final 'i' has been dotted. By the way, I hear that you took Sylvia Hallam out to dinner the other night. Anything in the wind there?"

Keith grinned. "I don't know."

"Well, you've picked the right sort of girl, my boy. Roderick Hallam's a power in the City. I suppose you've met him."

"I've dined at his house a couple of times." Before the words were out of his mouth Keith felt certain what his uncle's next remarks would be.

14

"I hope you got on well. He's the kind of man I'd like to see on our Board." Halberd stroked his chin thoughtfully. "Why not bring your young woman along one evening? We might take her to the Caprice. I'll have a word with your aunt and get her to suggest a day."

"I'm sure she'd love to come," Keith said dutifully as he turned to leave.

As the door closed Halberd picked up the internal telephone and spoke to his secretary. "Ring my wife, will you, Miss Purslane, and remind her that we have to be at the Coburg Rooms by seven-fifteen. I don't want to be late."

He put on his reading glasses and was glancing at a memorandum when Miss Purslane rang back. "Mrs Corsair's out shopping," she reported. "Minnie will give her your message as soon as she comes in."

Netta Corsair, like many other women in London with well-to-do husbands, spent a great deal of her time in Harrods. There she was assured of meeting a number of acquaintances with whom she could exchange gossip and confidences while they strolled through the dress salons, investigated the cosmetic counters, placed orders for food "to be delivered today" and quizzed the sales staff with a total unconsciousness of ill manners. In tailored suits or fur coats, youthfully hatted, elegantly shod, scented and a little over-powdered, with busy tongues and penetrating voices, these ladies found in Harrods something of the healing atmosphere which their husbands breathed in clubs where women, if they were allowed to enter, were confined to the side staircase and the less cosy rooms. A former director of the stores had christened them "The Old Harrodians" and, with tongue so well in cheek that for a moment his fellow directors thought he was speaking in all seriousness, had suggested that a scarf be designed and presented to all those who could produce evidence that they had used the powder-rooms not less than a thousand times.

Today Netta had arranged to meet Claire Summersby in the Banking Hall. Claire was Halberd's sister and a woman of a wider world than Netta's. They had met only spasmodically until Claire and her husband Bertie returned from service abroad just over a year ago. Now they met regularly, each pleased to have a companion who would help to fill the unoccupied hours. If in their friendship Claire was always on the receiving end, Netta was only too happy to treat her sister-in-law to luxuries which the latter could not afford.

The Banking Hall shrilled like an aviary of love-birds when Netta tripped in from the street, her small, round countenance showing regretful awareness that she was, as usual, late. In one of the leather club chairs Claire lay back, watching the smoke from her cigarette float upward. With her prominently boned, haggard face, her long thinly-fleshed legs and expression of disdainful discontent, she had something of the air of a Borzoi condemned to live in the servants' hall.

"Don't worry, darling," she interrupted the fluttering apologies. "I've been very comfortable here. I'm sure you had a lot to do before you left home." If there was a note of irony in her voice it was lost on Netta, who had a simple and literal mind.

The bill for a delicious lunch was, Claire's keen eyes noted, almost as large as the allowance that Bertie was able to give her for a week's housekeeping. Afterwards Netta bought some marrons glacés for herself and an expensive jar of skin-beautifying cream for Claire. A window-shopping stroll was followed by a visit to St James's, where they made a few purchases before taking a taxi to Termini House.

Going in by the side entrance and passing a metal door which opened into the offices and was marked "Staff Only", they came to the bronze latticed gates of the private lift beside which hung a flat-topped box with a rectangular slit in the lid. To prevent any doubt as to its purpose the box was

16

labelled "Letters—Mr and Mrs Halberd Corsair". At the end of the short passage a buxom, country-faced young woman was about to open a door. She turned at the sound of voices. "I'll be up in a minute to make the tea, madam," she said. "And there's a message from Mr Corsair." Repeating the message, she drew back the lift gates and held them while the two ladies entered.

"So you've still got Minnie," said Claire as the lift rose. "I thought Halberd said he didn't want a maid occupying the spare room."

"She lives downstairs—where you saw her just now. There was some sort of little store-room there, and Halberd had it converted into a flatlet for her."

"Lovely to have a successful husband," exclaimed Claire lightly. "Lovely to have so many clothes," she said an hour later as she knotted string round a substantial parcel. "Are you sure that you'll never wear any of these things again?" She was looking into an open jewel-box on the dressing-table when the telephone rang and Netta, picking up the receiver, said "Hello." In a moment she exclaimed, "Oh, it's you, Roddie. Yes, tomorrow then. Any time before six will be safe."

"Sounds as if you had a boy-friend," Claire commented when the receiver had been replaced. There was amusement in her voice and in the quirk of her thin eyebrows. Could it be tit-for-tat, she was wondering. For Bertie had recently heard a rumour that, as he expressed it, Halberd had a little bit of fluff tucked away somewhere.

"Oh, don't be ridiculous." Netta blushed under the other woman's ironical gaze.

"Good luck to you if you have." Claire picked up an enamelled brooch and held it against her dress. "Isn't this one of mother's?"

Netta made an assenting sound. Her mother-in-law had given it to her shortly before her death. It was a Victorian piece, set with a number of yellowish Brazilian

17

diamonds and worth, at present-day prices, considerably more than a hundred pounds. Seized with one of her moments of generosity, she said impulsively, "Please keep it, dear. I'd like you to have it."

Claire spoke a few words of moderate gratitude as she put the brooch into her handbag. In her heart she was thinking that the gift was something that Netta did not want for herself and would never miss. Netta had so much more than she needed, and would one day be a wealthy widow. "Which is more than I shall ever be," Claire murmured to herself—though Halberd had once said that there would be a "little something" for her when he died. A "little something" while he lived would be welcome; for in Bertie's hands money was transmuted into quicksilver, and nowadays an Army pension seemed scarcely to keep them out of the breadline.

When they moved into the sitting-room Claire began to talk about Bertie's unavailing efforts to find a permanent job. "No-one wants to employ a man of over sixty," she said bitterly. "Bertie gets an occasional day's work with a firm who do market research. He calls on housewives to ask them what kind of floor polish or pudding mix they use. He says he quite enjoys the job—though it always seems to be raining when he does it." She gave a shrug of disdain. "It's not a job for a gentleman, is it?"

"No job's a job for a gentleman." Halberd had come into the room unnoticed. "The days when you walked into a soft seat in the family business are gone. If Bertie's happy in his work, why be ashamed of it?" A tight, amused smile narrowed his mouth as he met Claire's eyes. He neither liked nor disliked his sister. Theirs was, in fact, an acquaintanceship rather than a close relationship. He had been ten years old at the time of her birth. A year later his mother had left home, taking the baby with her. Their father, a mildly successful estate agent whose rigid vocabulary excluded the word "divorce" had, with the help of a widowed sister, brought up Halberd and his elder sister, Charlotte. The

18

children had not come together again until, after their father's death, they assembled at a lawyer's office over the distribution of his small estate. When some years later their mother died Claire was in Austria and Charlotte, with her husband Hadley and their son Keith, on holiday in Spain. Four years ago Hadley and Charlotte had been killed when a lorry went out of control and crushed their car against a wall. Bertie was at that time stationed in Germany, and it was not until he retired and Claire found them a home in London that she and Netta became friends.

Halberd, who judged his sister's motives shrewdly, looked on the friendship with an objective and tolerant eye, but himself took care not to be drawn into too many meetings. He was fully aware that Claire expected him to provide some employment for Bertie in one of the companies he controlled; but, though he found Bertie a pleasant enough fellow and a useful mixer at parties, he had no intention of creating a sinecure for a man whose business ability was non-existent. There was, in his opinion, no earthly reason why Claire should not take a job. She was in her early forties, healthy, intelligent, and childless. It was no good her thinking that, because she was a Colonel's lady, the world owed her a living. By an occasional permanent 'loan' to Bertie and a reasonable legacy to Claire in his will he felt that he was adequately discharging such responsibility as a blood relationship might be thought to entail.

"I'm not ashamed of it," Claire replied tartly. "I'm ashamed that a man who's served his country for most of his life should have to beg for work to augment a pittance of a pension."

Halberd's eyebrows rose. "Surely one serves one's country equally well in commerce—and no Government gives one a substantial pension for that."

"Oh, you *know* what Claire means, and I'm sure that. . . ." Netta threw herself into the discussion before Claire could frame a reply, then, finding that the thread of whatever she might have been going to say eluded her, turned to Claire. "I know you're in a hurry, dear. I'll give you a ring and we'll arrange our next meeting." She fluttered while Claire collected handbag and parcel, and trotted ahead to give her a reassuring embrace in the hall.

Claire's resentment was fading by the time she left the Tube at Mornington Crescent and made her way to the somewhat depressing neighbourhood in which she and Bertie had lived for the past year. Bertie, who would have preferred to spend his latter years in the countryside among people of his own kind and purse, had yielded, after an uneven struggle, to her wish to be in London. Their flat was on the ground floor of the last house on the north side of Sycamore Terrace. The rooms was small, but since, like many an ex-Army couple, they did not possess a great deal of furniture, the lack of space was not a major problem, though Bertie, a tall, well-built man, found it constricting.

He was sitting in an armchair before the television set when Claire came in. At once he rose and, switching off the programme, turned a florid face to say, "Hello, old girl. Had a good day?"

She gave a non-committal shrug. "Good lunch. Netta chattered away. She's given me some of her cast-offs, and—" Claire had been about to mention the enamelled brooch, but if Bertie did not know about it he couldn't suggest selling it when the next emergency arose. Looking round for somewhere to put down her parcel, she was unable to find an uncluttered space. "Where on earth did all those books come from?" she inquired testily.

"Chap next door's moving and gave them to me." Bertie began to collect the books and stack them on the floor against a wall. "Some good stuff there—Surtees, Mason, and that Ruritania fellow. He's got an old bookcase he says we can have. I'll pick it up in the morning and it can go in that alcove— just fit nicely." He moved over to the mantelpiece and picked up some papers from behind the clock. "'Fraid there's a stiff notice here from the rates people. Don't suppose you've got any money, have you, old girl?"

Claire had three pounds in her handbag. She was a good and successful bridge-player and, at the twice-weekly sessions with well-to-do friends, seldom came away a loser. But she was not going to disclose her reserve until calamity hit. It was always possible that she would have a losing day tomorrow and, in any case, the money would almost certainly be needed to keep the household going until they could pay something off their overdraft. She shook her head.

"Didn't expect you had," Bertie said equably. This was not the moment—in fact it was difficult to imagine what would be the right moment—to confess that he owed a local book-maker twenty pounds and had promised to pay the debt this week. "But we'll manage. I'll squeeze a few quid out of the bank somehow and keep the rates people quiet. Think I might have a word with Halberd. He may come up with a pony. Wouldn't do him any good to see his relations in court—bad for his reputation." Bertie nodded wisely and squared his shoulders.

"You'd better ask him for fifty pounds." Claire's tone was decisive, almost imperative. Intuition told her that he was holding back some unwelcome information. Objectively she eyed her husband. He was still a handsome man. The clipped moustache diverted one's attention from the weakness of the mouth. Perhaps it was his innate helplessness that made him so easily likeable. She remembered a friend saying to her some years ago, "Bertie's such a fubsy man. I adore fubsy people." But fubsiness wasn't enough. She picked up the parcel and went towards the bedroom, saying, "I'm going to change out of my good suit. Peel some potatoes, Bertie, and put them on in cold water. There are sausages in the larder. I'll be along in a few minutes."

Chapter Three

AT four minutes to nine on the following morning Halberd left his flat and, taking the private lift down, walked round to the main entrance, pausing for a moment to breathe in the October air. One or two members of the staff, hurrying to reach their departments before a red line was ruled across the signing-on book, spied their Chairman and hastened their steps. His timing was as reliable as that of the clock in the great hall. At precisely nine o'clock he passed through his secretary's room with a "Good morning, Miss Purslane". At nine forty-five he finished dictating replies to those letters which required urgent attention, then, glancing through a letter from the Fidelis Assurance Company, he passed it across the desk.

"No need to send a reply," he said. "Give them a ring and say I'll come in at noon on Monday. And send someone reliable down to Somerset House to get copies of birth certificates for my wife and myself—the short kind. No need to go to the expense of detailed ones just to keep a pack of civil servants in tea." Like many wealthy men Halberd was close-fisted about trivial items of expenditure. "We'll deal with any other letters later."

Miss Purslane closed her shorthand notebook and rose. "Mr. Grace of Pan-Finance rang last night just after you'd left, to ask if you could look in for a few minutes before the meeting at Boswell House. It begins at four forty-five."

"Ring his secretary and say 'yes', and give me a reminder at four-fifteen, please."

"And Mr Antrim rang before nine to say he'd be a little late and would explain when he arrived."

"If he's here now ask him to come in. But first get me Mr Ravenscroft on the 'phone. I want to speak to him personally, not to anyone else."

He was talking into the mouthpiece as Miss Purslane showed in Keith, and he signed to them both to wait. "No, Ravenscroft, not a new one. A codicil's all that's needed. I don't want another of your fancy bills. Yes, I suppose you lawyers have to live, but not entirely at my expense. Right, next Tuesday then—half past two." Replacing the receiver, he said, "Miss Purslane, please tell Mr Coats to come and see me at four on Tuesday instead of two-thirty. Now, Keith, what's your trouble?"

"Sorry to be late," Keith apologized. "Part of the ceiling of my room fell down this morning as I was dressing. It took a little time to clear up the rubbish and to get away from my landlady."

Halberd gave one of his rare chuckles. "Ceiling down, eh! You've only got one room, haven't you?"

"Yes, and it's in a bit of a mess. But I'll manage until the damage is repaired."

"You'd better use our spare room for a few nights. Ring your aunt and tell her you're coming along. She'll be glad not to be alone in the flat this weekend. Ask her to send Minnie down to your office with the spare latchkeys." It was a command rather than an invitation, but one Keith was delighted to obey.

When he returned to his office he spoke to his aunt on the telephone. "Oh, my poor boy, you might have been killed," she cried. "It'll be so nice to have you here. But I'm going out at half-past six to dinner and the theatre, and it's Minnie's night off. Shall I get her to leave you something cold?"

Keith explained that he was dining out. "I'll bring my things along when I leave the office," he said, "if that's all right." It was not for a further few minutes that he was able

23

politely to disengage himself. Then, taking out a cigarette while he glanced through some of the day's post and finding that in the morning rush he had left his lighter behind in his digs, he opened a box of initialled book-matches, presumably a gift from some business contact, which his secretary had put on his desk, and settled down to work. Shortly Miss Bohun came in with the keys which Minnie had delivered, and remained to take dictation.

In his eighth-floor office overlooking the courtyard of Termini House, Julian Killigrew laid aside proofs of the next issue of the *Bookman's Weekly* and, rubbing a stiff right knee, rose to look out of the window.

A little less than a year ago his office had been a dark, narrow room above a printing works in Carter Lane, his view across a well nothing more than a grimy window through which he could dimly see heads bent over desks. Then had come the news that Bowe Printers were being taken over by one of the octopus City companies. Later that week had come his interview with Halberd Corsair, the tall, top-heavy Chairman of Wydspred Investments, who had already weeded out of the printing firm what he termed "the worm-eaten wood".

"Sit down, Mr Killigrew," Halberd had said when he came into the white-panelled room. "Smoke if you wish to." But the invitation was not one which he was meant to accept. "I find that in taking over a printing works I have also taken over a weekly paper. I understand that they both print and publish it."

"They've done so for fifty years," said Julian. "As you probably know, it's a literary weekly with a long list of distinguished contributors—"

"Yes, yes." A raised hand restrained further speech. "My father used to read it. Essays, short stories, book reviews, etc. Quite a good paper, I believe, in its period, but not the sort of thing that sells today."

"Sixty thousand circulation," Julian said quietly. "It shows a profit."

"Sixty." Halberd's eyebrows indicated his opinion of the figure as he placed elbows on the desk and rested his chin on clasped hands. "Well, Mr Killigrew, I'm in business to make profits—and good profits. Sentiment may be all right in literature, but one can't afford it in commerce. If your paper's still making a profit in twelve months time, well and good. If it's showing a loss. . . ." He made a chopping gesture. "Your salary stands. You'll have an office in this building and bear your share of the overheads—they may be rather higher than in Carter Lane. Let my secretary have a weekly note of the circulation figures. Don't bring your problems to me." He leaned back and looked penetratingly at the intelligent, long-jawed face across the desk. "You're not married, are you?"

"My wife died three years ago," Julian replied shortly.

"Sorry to hear that." He allowed the news a brief silence. "Glad to have met you. You'll have to work hard to keep your paper going—but that's up to you." He held out a well-cushioned hand as Miss Purslane opened the door.

Walking back to Carter Lane, Julian considered the situation. Wage rises in the printing industry were a continuing threat. Even a small increase in overheads and distribution costs would endanger the narrow profit margin. He came into his office to meet the kindly, gossipy face of his secretary raised in anxious inquiry.

"We've been given a year, Miss Brind," he told her. "Our new boss is very much as we thought, a Philistine and hard as nails. But I think he's fair-minded, and he hasn't told me to sack you." He smiled. "Well, not yet. I think we shall win through. We've damn well got to."

Today the twelve-month period of grace was nearly over, and in that time his sole meeting with Halberd, apart from occasional glimpses in corridor or hall, had been at the annual party for senior staff. There had been one or two moments of

25

anxiety, but no disaster. Standing now at the window, he felt the satisfaction of achievement. He turned as the door opened, to see Miss Brind looking almost rakish in a pink felt hat. "I'm off to my lunch, Mr Killigrew," she said in the tone of voice of one confiding a secret.

Miss Purslane and Miss Brind had lunched together every working day from the time they had met soon after Julian's arrival at Termini House. Usually Miss Purslane listened while her friend repeated the office gossip of the day and passed on the rumours which had come her way.

Today being Friday, the salary envelopes had been brought round in the morning by the head messenger and his assistant. It was thus the day when the two ladies deserted the steamy little Cockney-Italian restaurant round the corner and treated themselves to a dainty and rather more expensive lunch at Fuller's. They were enjoying a slice of iced walnut cake with their coffee when Miss Purslane put down her fork and, looking round for possible eavesdroppers, said in a low tone, "I think you might like to know that Mr Blanchford's secretary will be leaving very soon. She's going to have a baby."

Miss Brind nodded. "I was wondering. I noticed that her skirt was getting a bit tight. Mr Blanchford will be sorry to lose her." She paused thoughtfully. "I suppose you were thinking that I might know of someone to take her place. I don't think I do, but I'll make inquiries if you like."

"I was wondering if *you'd* like to work for Mr Blanchford," Miss Purslane said in a conspiratorial voice. "He's a very nice man—and a bird in the hand is worth two in the bush," she continued, with an apparent irrelevance which her friend had no difficulty in interpreting.

"You mean—you mean that you've heard something about the *Bookman's Weekly*? It's not going to be closed down, is it? Oh, poor Mr Killigrew. He's put so much into it. It's his life." The final word was breathed in capital letters.

"I don't actually know," Miss Purslane said cautiously.

"But it's been losing money—and you know what you told me Mr Corsair said to Mr Killigrew when he took over the Bowe Printers."

"But the circulation's going up," Miss Brind protested. "It's higher than it's been for ages at this time of year."

"So are overheads and other costs. I saw The Nose's report this morning. He says that it's been losing about fifty pounds a week for the past three months."

"The Nose!" Miss Brind repeated in the tone of mild contempt with which the female members of the staff were apt to refer to Mr Caddis, a skimpy little man with nicotine-stained fingers and bad breath who described himself as an internal auditor and whose job it was to dig out figures and provide memoranda for the Board's consideration. "And what's fifty pounds to a firm like ours?" she went on fiercely. "They ought to be proud of publishing a paper like the B.W." She enlarged on the prestige which it conferred on its owners and on its reputation in the literary world.

Miss Purslane allowed her friend to run on until she had unwound, then murmured, "I couldn't not let you know about this, dear. Of course it mayn't come to anything, but if it does I'm sure Mr Corsair wouldn't want to lose you and, if you didn't mind my putting a word in, I'm sure he'd see that you were the best person for the other job." She leaned across the table. "You'll keep what I've told you to yourself, won't you?"

"You know I never, never betray a confidence," Miss Brind assured her. "I'm ever so grateful to you for telling me. If you should happen to hear anything more you'll let me know, won't you, and we can have another little chat."

While she waited for Julian to come back from a late lunch Miss Brind found little difficulty in convincing herself that her duty to her immediate employer was at least as great as that which she owed her friend. Accordingly, within a few minutes of his return Julian was in possession of the information. He also became aware that Miss Brind's adoptive in-

27

stincts had been kindled, and determined that no blurring of their hitherto admirable relationship must be allowed. Lightly he assured her of his invincible faith in the future, dictated a warm letter to a contributor commissioning an article, then, when she left the room, picked up the telephone and, after a short conversation, took the lift down to the second floor and went to see his friend MacInnish.

Hector MacInnish was the Company's Chief Accountant, a man of wide financial experience and little sentiment. He listened in silence to Julian, nodding at intervals, and then said, "The first point is that, although you'll show a small profit for the year, you've been running at a loss during the summer. Second, Corsair doesn't care a tuppenny damn about literature—well, you know that. If he reads anything but the City pages it'll likely be a book on time and motion study. If he wants to close down your paper Caddis's memorandum gives him some sort of excuse to do so."

"But it doesn't give a fair picture of the situation," Julian protested. "And in any case the figures may not be correct."

"They'll be correct as far as they go. You need have no doubts—or hopes—about that. Caddis is Corsair's ferret, and Corsair wouldn't keep him around if he made mistakes. Mind you, I haven't seen this memorandum. Caddis's reports are supposed to be for the Board's eyes only. But"—he gave a rich chuckle—"one way and another I manage to see them, and I'm prepared to bet you a bottle of Scotch—it'll be the malted for me, by the way—that he's given the trading figures only and nothing else. Now, the *Bookman's Weekly* is printed by Bowe Printers, and I can tell you that the profit they make on your print order is quite a wee bit more than fifty pounds a time. In other words, the existence of your paper is worth a useful little weekly sum to Wydspred. No *Bookman's Weekly*, no print order, no profit. Are ye with me?"

"Happily so far." Julian smiled.

28

"But that's not the end of it. Here's a question for you. If Bowe lose your print order, why shouldn't they pick up another to replace it without any loss of profit?"

"I suppose the answer is that they will."

MacInnish wagged a bony finger. "They'll be damn lucky to get any new order. Their machinery'll be out of date before long—in fact it's pretty well out of date now. Unless and until Corsair's prepared to spend a tidy sum on new machines —and that's something I've already taken up with him— they'll need every job they can keep. So, provided your circulation doesn't drop too much and other costs don't escalate— now there's a nice fancy word for you—there'll still be something for the Company."

"Then it seems that there's really nothing to worry about. Thanks a lot, Mac. You've taken a load off my mind." Julian started to rise.

"Sit down, laddie. You can't let the future of your paper be decided without raising a finger yourself. I don't say that Corsair's going to make a snap decision to close it. However, he might, and if he does it's not going to be easy to argue him out of it. But whatever we do, we've got to be careful about it. We're not supposed to know about Caddis's memorandum. If Corsair learns that we do he won't rest until he finds out where the leak was. He'll sack that person—and we don't want that to happen, do we? So"—the shrewd eyes held Julian's—"what do we do?"

"I haven't the slightest idea."

"We use a bit of guile." MacInnish chuckled. "First you ask that secretary of yours to get Miss Purslane to put that memorandum at the bottom of Corsair's pile of papers. All being well, he won't get down to it until Monday. Second, you write a report and get it into Corsair's hands so that he can read it over the weekend. Say that as it's just on the end of the twelve-month period you're sending him a statement covering the facts he'll wish to have. Mention that you've consulted me and that I advised you to include relevant figures from Bowe Printers." He glanced at his watch. "Off you get now, and I'll let you have the figures you need within twenty minutes. And keep your report short. Corsair won't appreciate a literary masterpiece."

Back in his office Julian spoke to Miss Brind, who telephoned her friend only to find that Caddis's memorandum was now on the Chairman's desk. Miss Purslane promised she would do her best to place all incoming papers on top of it. Cheerfully Julian collected the appropriate files and began to assemble the materials for his report.

Sitting beside his uncle after lunch, Keith said, "Spurry rang me this morning to apologize for the delay in delivery of metal casings, and to say that he'd catch up within the next ten days and be ahead of schedule by the end of the month."

Halberd grunted. "Did he convince you?"

"He seemed absolutely certain. Said that his teething troubles were over and he was right on top of the job. I'm sure we can rely on him."

"And if we do and he lets us down, how do we satisfy our clients?" Halberd demanded. "Do we let them down? No, my boy, we don't. We find a supplier we can depend on. I've had a private word with Gunnings. They're a tip-top firm, they've got the capacity to spare, and I've no doubt they will meet us on price. As soon as we're able to start them on the job we terminate the contract with Spurry. Clause Six gives us the necessary power."

Keith was taken aback. "Yes, I suppose it does. But it's a standard clause to cover cases of gross negligence and so on. Isn't it rather—severe to apply it here? If we do, how's Spurry to carry on?"

"That's not our problem," Halberd said coldly.

"No?" There was a note of doubt in Keith's voice. "Surely we have some sort of responsibility? We entered into a long-term contract on the strength of which he borrowed the money to instal a new bank of machines. If he loses the contract he's sunk."

"Due to his own inefficiency," said Halberd stonily. "If a man can't run a business he's better out of it. When he goes bankrupt, as he will, we should be able to buy the factory at a break-up price." He opened a drawer and, flipping back the lid of a cedarwood box, extracted a cigar. Accepting with a nod the match-booklet that Keith proffered, he lit the cigar with care and examined the glowing tip. "Go and see Gunnings on Monday and as soon as you've reached agreement with them give Spurry a ring and tell him to come and see you. Say that we're terminating the contract and will accept no deliveries after the end of next month."

Keith sat temporarily bereft of speech. It had come to him suddenly and shatteringly while his uncle was speaking that from the outset it had been Halberd's intention to get hold of the Spurry factory. And Keith was to bring down the axe on Richard Spurry's neck. Admittedly the letter of the contract had not been fulfilled, but a two- or three-week delay in deliveries at this stage was of little importance, since the goods in which the Spurry items were incorporated would not have to be supplied until the beginning of next year. To enforce the contract conditions was perfectly within the law; but to do this to a man with whom one had dealt on a basis of friendship. . . . The words of protest were forming on Keith's lips when Miss Purslane came into the room.

"I'm sorry, sir, but Mr Livings is outside. He has an appointment with you and says he's rather pressed for time. And Colonel Summersby's on the 'phone and insists on speaking to you."

Halberd shrugged. "All right. Put him on—and come back, will you, and find me the Livings file. It's among those papers over there." He picked up the receiver, waited, and said as soon as the connection was made, "Hello, Bertie. Make it short. Yes, I'm very busy—as usual." He listened, smiling tightly. "All right, I'll help. No, not today. Got to be off at seven—business trip. I'll be back on Monday. Look in then. Yes, yes, yes, come in for a drink before dinner."

His voice sharpened as he concluded the conversation, and there was still an edge to it as he said to Keith, "I've told you what to do. Now run along and do it." Taking the file from his secretary, he drew a deep breath as the door closed behind Keith. "I've no patience with fools, Miss Purslane. Give me a minute before you show Mr Livings in."

Going out, Miss Purslane felt surprised that her employer had allowed himself to show exacerbation. He was probably worn out after a hard week. He should really give himself a rest at weekends. Halberd appeared, however, completely to have recovered his equanimity when she returned at four-fifteen to remind him of his appointment. Signing the last letter, he picked up his brief-case and with a "Have a pleasant weekend, Miss Purslane," went off. At a quarter to six he was strolling back by Coram's Fields, contemplating with satisfaction the verbal agreement reached with Pan-Finance. Coming to Termini House and passing the main entrance, he reached the side-door. There he stopped abruptly and his lips stiffened.

Chapter Four

KEITH went straight from the office to South Kensington Station and, turning off Harrington Gardens, let himself into a stucco-fronted house in Pearson Place. He was looking at the heap of plaster swept to one end of his room when his landlady knocked at the door.

"I've had the builder in, Mr Antrim," she told him, "and he says that the rest of the ceiling will hold up for now if no-one goes poking at it. He can't start pulling it down till Monday, and then he'll want the room empty for a day or two. I could let you have a shake-down in the box-room if you think you could manage there."

Explaining that he was going to stay with his aunt, Keith dusted a suitcase and began to collect what he needed for the next few days. "I'll give you a ring on Tuesday then, Mrs Biddle, to find out how things are going." Finishing his packing, he gave her the address and telephone number, detached himself from her verbal gladiator's net, and took a taxi to Termini House. Looking at his watch, he decided that to take the taxi on to Warwick Gardens where he was dining would be a stupid extravagance; there was time to go by Tube if he didn't dally. Paying the driver, he carried the case round to the side entrance. When hurry-hot, having run the last hundred yards from Earl's Court Station, he reached his friend's flat he was a quarter of an hour late. With rueful humour he explained what had happened to him during the day.

"Then you'll be staying with your aunt until the ceiling's

mended," said his friend Derek. "You know we can always put you up if you're not happy there."

"Thanks, but I'll be living in the lap of luxury—maid service and all that." Keith eyed the glass in his friend's hand. "What about offering me a drink—or can't you afford them for your guests?"

"This *is* yours," said Derek with dignity.

It was after midnight when in high spirits Keith vaulted the low wall into the courtyard of Termini House, let himself in by the side-door, and picked up a letter addressed to his uncle that had been left on top of the letter-box. Reaching the flat, he found his suitcase in the hall and, putting it down by the spare room door, went into the sitting-room. The standard lamp by the Chinese screen near the window was alight and the large casement window had been left wide open. A slight hum made him turn his head. The television set was on, though the blank screen showed that the last programme had ended. He had just switched it off when the telephone bell shrilled and he went into the study. The voice that answered his "Hello" was richly feminine and anxious. "Is Mr Corsair in?"

"No, he's gone away for the weekend," said Keith. "He'll be home on Monday. Can I give him a message?"

Seconds went by before the woman spoke again. "Are you sure he's gone?"

"He was leaving at seven."

"Then there's no message," she said dully and hung up.

Closing the window and seeing through the door of Aunt Netta's bedroom that she had not yet returned, Keith left on the passage lights and took his case into the spare room. It smelled pleasantly of clean linen, and on the silk-quilted bed the top sheet had been turned invitingly down. Within five minutes he was fast asleep.

Bertie picked a loose hair from the brush, dipped into the tin, squeezed off the surplus paint, and applied the brush to the bookcase which his departing neighbour had given him in the morning. One coat would have to be enough, he decided, and the paint would be dry, or so the instruction leaflet said, within a few hours. Claire had departed shortly after lunch for her regular Friday bridge game. While she was dressing he had telephoned Halberd and, following her into the bedroom, repeated the conversation.

"Well, that's that," she had said coolly. "We'll have to manage." Picking up her gloves, she went into the sitting-room. "If I get reasonable cards I should pick up a pound or two. Expect me back between seven-thirty and eight. Spread plenty of newspaper before you start painting." She turned in the doorway. "And don't make a mess of things."

"I'll be careful," he said shortly.

When she had gone he washed up the luncheon dishes, glanced for a few moments at the *Radio Times* and, fetching the tin of paint he had bought during the morning shopping-round set it aside while he covered the carpet with sheets of yesterday's *Daily Telegraph*. Soon he lit a cigarette, dismissed to the back of his mind the immediate financial problems, and, picking up a piece of coarse sandpaper, started to remove the thick varnish which covered the bookcase.

Shortly before a quarter to six Claire folded four pound notes, opened her handbag, and gave her hostess two and six-pence change. The after-tea rubber had lasted only two games, and, by general agreement, it was too late to start another. She was, in any case, glad to leave before the cards deserted her. The centrally-heated flat and the difficulty of achieving concentration in the face of her opponents' chatter had given her a headache. Bidding her friends goodbye, she let herself out and turned down Westmoreland Terrace towards the Embankment. Slowly she walked down-stream, enjoying the fresh breeze, content to think that she had plenty of time in hand.

Her headache had gone by the time she reached Mornington Crescent and, going into an off-licence, bought a bottle of claret. A pungent but not unpleasant smell of new paint greeted her as she opened the front door. In the sitting-room the now gleaming bookcase stood on folded paper in the alcove. Through the communicating door she could see Bertie moving around in the kitchen. There was a glow of accomplishment on his florid face as he came out.

"All completed—and no mess," he said, taking the bottle from her hand, unwrapping the paper, and looking at the label. "You must have had a nice little win, old girl." With a pocket knife he began carefully to cut round the top of the foil capsule. "We'll let it get *chambré* while the meat's cooking."

She looked at the well-shaped, grizzled head bent intently over the bottle, and the hard lines of her face momentarily softened. Like a dog-owner rewarding an obedient pet, she gave his shoulder a light pat.

Lennie swept up the pieces of a broken cup and emptying the dustpan into a piece of paper screwed it up with a vicious twist. When he had mopped up the spilt tea he went down to the basement. After a cursory glance at the dials of the heating system he went into his cubby-hole next door. A camp-bed, a cupboard, a table and chair were the sum total of furniture in the tiny room. From the cupboard he took out his work-box and an empty Dimple whisky-bottle and carried them up to the main hall. Putting them down on a table in front of the inner entrance doors, he felt for his cigarette packet, remembering almost at once that he had left it on a bench by the Staff Door. When he returned to the hall he sat down moodily at the table and lit a cigarette.

Soon he opened the work-box and carefully lifted out the nearly completed hull of a model ship, five inches long and a fraction narrower than the neck of the whisky bottle into which he would introduce it some time next week. Then would come the moment when, pulling lightly on the threads of coloured cotton dangling from the neck of the bottle, he would watch the masts rise—and slowly, oh so slowly, a fully-rigged schooner would appear, riding a painted ocean in a bubble of glass. A visit to the ship-chandler in Shaftesbury Avenue would follow. Lennie could not produce his ships-in-bottles fast enough to satisfy the demand.

But tonight he could do no work. His hands were shaky. He let a miniature mast drop to the table and passed a palm across the beardless patch of skin with which the plastic surgeon had endowed his otherwise bristle-rough face. "Nosy bastard," he muttered, and stood up.

"It's nearly five o'clock, Mr Killigrew."

Julian finished scribbling a phrase. "Is it, Miss Brind?" Then, "Good God, I haven't nearly finished this report." After a moment's thought he picked up the house telephone. "Oh, Miss Purslane, do you know what time Mr Corsair will be leaving tonight? He's gone, has he? I see. I'd hoped to get a report into his hands so that he could read it over the weekend."

Miss Brind saw his expression stiffen then soften, watched him nod, and heard him say, "Right, I'll do that. Many thanks." Replacing the receiver, he said, "Miss Purslane says he won't be returning to the office, but if I get the report round to the flat by seven he'll have it before he goes away for the weekend."

"I'll stay and type it up, Mr Killigrew." Miss Brind was agog to play her part in the rescue enterprise.

"No, you run along and enjoy yourself. As soon as I've finished the draft I can rattle it off myself on the typewriter. Thanks for the offer, and"—he grinned—"keep your fingers crossed."

Shortly before half-past six, the foolscap envelope containing the report in his hand, he switched off the desk light and hurried along the passage and down the stairs, to find Lennie installed at his table in front of the inner glass doors.

"Didn't know there was anyone working late," Lennie

observed, getting up and leisurely starting to move the table.

"Quickly, please," urged Julian. "I want Mr Corsair to have this before he leaves."

"You'll be all right, sir," Lennie reassured him. "He's not gone. There's his car outside and there's lights in the flat." In answer to Julian's question he gave him the time and was opening the doors with somewhat officious efficiency when a woman trotted diagonally across the courtyard and into the street. A few moments later the outer doors closed and Julian, passing the big Humber, walked round to the side-door. Deciding against going up to deliver the report, he considered leaving it in the lift, propped up on the casing of the press-button, but finally placed it on the lid of the letter-box, where it could not fail to be noticed by anyone going out. Shortly he crossed Gray's Inn Road on his way to his flat in Wren Street, stopping briefly at The Wren Arms to order and ingest a large whisky.

Minnie came into the sitting-room as the French ormolu clock over the fireplace struck five. "Is there anything else, madam?" she inquired.

Netta lowered the opera glasses through which she had been watching a boy on a flat roof trying vainly to catch a waddling but exasperatingly anticipatory pigeon. "I don't think so," she said vaguely. "Do you want to go out?"

"If there's nothing more." Minnie guessed rightly that her mistress had forgotten giving her the evening off. "I've got to be over in Finchley by seven. I've packed the master's suitcase and put it in the car—and here's his keys." She put them down on a table. "The spare room's made up for Mr Keith, and if he wants any meals other than breakfast I've got plenty in. So if that's all, madam, I'll go down and get myself ready."

When the doorbell sounded its discreet note half an hour later Netta was changing her dress. In bedroom slippers and silk dressing-gown flying she trotted down the passage. The young man to whom she opened the door gave her a

38

broad wink. "Whoo!" he exclaimed. "Caught you in your undies, love. Thought you might be out when I had to ring twice." He followed her into the sitting-room and put down the fibre case he was carrying. "You pop back into the bedroom now—and let me get on with the job. Reg'lar service on the dot. That's my motto, and that's what the customer wants, eh?" She's not a bad old bag, he said to himself: Pretty good for her age. 'Course she's had a soft life—never had to lift a finger for herself. Head on one side, hand in pocket, he stood looking at her with a half-smile on his boldly handsome face.

Netta hesitated before going. She was always conscious of a not unkind amusement in his manner and never knew how to respond to his good-humoured familiarity. Gripping the front edges of her dressing-gown, she gave a nervous laugh.

Some time later, fully dressed, she was watching the quick, assured movement of his hands as he knelt before the television set in his shirt-sleeves. A slight current of air from the windows he had opened wide stirred the fair hair that flopped over his forehead. Taking a somewhat soiled duster from the fibre case, he gave the set a brisk and thorough polish, then made some small adjustment of a tuning-knob.

"Right on the button, as the soldier said to the belly dancer," he commented, turning to her with a wink. "If there's nothing else I can do for you today, love, I'll be off. Be round again before you've forgotten me." He picked up the case, touched his forelock in mock salute, and was gone before she could muster any reply. Slamming the front door, he was about to press the button when he saw the lift coming up. "Night, night," he said to the tall, frowning man who got out.

"G'night," Halberd grunted, half recognizing the man's face but unable to put a name to it. Dropping his newspaper in the hall, he went into the sitting-room where Netta was still standing in front of the television set.

"Hello, dear. Minnie here?" he asked.

"She's downstairs. Do you want her? She's packed your bag and put it in the car."

"I'll have a word with her on Monday." He picked up the car keys and gestured at the television. "For heaven's sake, turn the volume down. I can hardly hear myself speak. That's better. I don't know how you can stand that constant noise. You're going out with the Bradnells tonight, aren't you—supper and theatre?"

"Yes, I'll be off quite soon. Did you say you were going to Manchester, dear—just in case someone rings?"

"No, not Manchester this time, thank the lord. Always gives me asthma. Bad enough having to make these trips instead of having a good rest at home. But there's something in the offing that needs the personal touch—Chairman to Chairman." Why on earth do I feel compelled, he asked himself, to give these long-winded explanations? "I'll be back on Monday morning. By the way, I want to take young Keith and his girl out to dinner one day next week. If we haven't got anything on next Thursday—" He stopped short as the telephone bell shrilled. "All right, I'll take it."

Striding into the study, he picked up the receiver. "Yes?" he said curtly. "Yes, naturally I need it. . . . No, of course you can't. . . . What? . . . . All right, then. . . . Before six-thirty." On his way into the sitting-room he heard a door close and almost immediately the faint sound of music. Netta must have gone to her bedroom and turned on the radio. Why did she have to have noise wherever she was? Opening the cocktail cabinet, he poured out a measure of whisky and was about to add soda when the front-doorbell chimed softly.

In her bedroom Netta screwed on the top of a small bottle and, getting up, pushed the dressing-table stool aside. Then, waving her arms in time to the music, she began to circle the room on tiptoe, watching herself in the several mirrors. When, some time later, she returned to the sitting-room Halberd was not there. Just before she turned up the volume of the television a cough indicated to her that he was elsewhere in the

40

flat. For a moment or two she listened to a man on the screen talking about architecture, wrinkled her nose, and began to look for something she felt sure was in the room. After two minutes she gave up the search, picked up her gloves and handbag, and went out. "Goodbye, Halberd," she called out as she passed the study door. Pulling the front door to, she pressed the lift-button. A cruising taxi picked her up before she reached Euston Road.

Chapter Five

KEITH looked up with a smile as Minnie came into the dining-room. "No, I couldn't eat another thing. Best breakfast I've had for years."

"Mrs Corsair's not awake yet," Minnie said as she collected plates and stacked them on a tray. "I 'spect she was late last night, so I'm letting her have a good lie-in." Putting the tray down in the kitchen, she collected some cleaning materials and, on her way down the passage, picked up Halberd's brief-case and placed it in the study by the side of his desk. Then she came into the sitting-room, where Keith had settled down in an armchair to read the morning paper. His eye was caught by a short paragraph on the front page reporting an electrical failure on the Piccadilly Line shortly after half-past six last night and mentioning that normal service had been restored in fifteen minutes. Wondering why such a comparatively frequent occurrence was considered worthy of inclusion, he turned the pages to read the financial columns.

In due course he put down the paper and took up an office folder. Work this morning, then down to Richmond for a game of Rugger and an evening with half a dozen friends. He was immersed in a detailed memorandum which his uncle had given him to study when Minnie, completing her dusting, inquired whether he would like the window open. At his assent she opened it wide and, leaning out to flick the duster, saw the postman enter the courtyard. She leaned out farther to see him stop almost below the window and pick up something from the concrete. The next moment he was holding a pair of opera glasses and looking upward. Observing Minnie, he called out something she could not hear and beckoned her to come down. It was then she noticed that the dark-green Humber was still standing by the main entrance. Waving acknowledgment, she turned back into the room. "It's the postman," she told Keith. "Looks as if he's found the mistress's theatre glasses in the yard. I'd better go down and see." As she crossed the room she added, "The master's car's down there. Seems he didn't take it after all." She was gone before Keith, deep in consideration of the memorandum, realized what she had said.

Shortly Minnie returned and, putting down some letters on a table, laid the opera glasses beside them. "They're hers all right," she told Keith. "They're a bit knocked about and one of the glasses is cracked. She won't be any too pleased."

Keith glanced at the opera glasses and agreed absent-mindedly. "I expect they can be repaired," he added as he looked through the letters. Going into the study, he put them on the desk and returned to work. At ten o'clock he heard Minnie take a breakfast tray into his aunt's room. At half-past ten the doorbell sounded, and a minute later Minnie showed in a solidly built man in police uniform. He waited until Minnie had closed the door before introducing himself as Sergeant Rollins from Holborn Police Station. "The maid tells me," he said, "that Mrs Corsair is still in her bedroom. I understand that you are Mr Corsair's nephew."

Keith assented. "Do you want to see my aunt?" he asked. "Or can I help you?"

"I shall have to see her later, sir." A steady gaze assessed Keith. "But I'll tell you now that I came to break it to her that Mr Corsair died yesterday. I'm sorry to be the bearer of such tragic news."

"Died," said Keith incredulously. "But he was perfectly fit and well when I saw him during the afternoon."

"He died last night, but the body was not found until this morning."

"It was an accident?"

"So it would seem." The tone was non-committal. "You say that you saw your uncle in the afternoon. What time was that?"

"After lunch—in his office on the ground floor of this building." Keith mentioned Wydspred's ownership of the block and his own connection with the firm.

"You live here then?"

"No." He explained why he was staying.

"Then you were here last night?"

"Not until late. I dined with friends and got here after midnight."

"But you were here earlier in the day."

"Not actually here. When I left the office I went to my digs to pick up some clothes. When I returned about a quarter-past six I was in rather a hurry, so I left my case in the lift downstairs."

"So you don't know what time your uncle intended to start his journey?"

"He mentioned on the telephone in the office that he'd be leaving at seven. He was going somewhere by car."

"Perhaps he planned to drive to the airport. I noticed a suitcase in the back of the Humber car by the entrance. Is that your uncle's car?"

Keith nodded. His thoughts were on the dead man. "You haven't told me how he died." As he spoke he heard the telephone ring and Minnie's quick footsteps going to the study.

The Sergeant did not reply immediately, and when he did his eyes did not leave Keith's face. "Apparently he fell out of the window of this room into a lorry that happened to be in the courtyard. The driver, who is the brother of the maid here, found the body when he went to clean out the lorry. Your uncle had broken his neck. I think I can say that death must have been instantaneous." Moving over to the window, he looked out. "I'm sorry to have to worry you with questions,

44

Mr Antrim, but I must try to establish how the accident occurred. Do you happen to know if your uncle's health was good?"

"Excellent, so far as I know. I can't remember him ever having anything worse than a cold."

"Any particular worries that you know of?"

"Just the normal business problems—but he took those in his stride."

"When you came in last night did you notice anything unusual—a rug out of place, for instance, on which he might have slipped?"

"The open window, of course, which I shut." Keith thought for a moment. "Oh, the television set had been left on. I don't think there was anything else, but I wasn't really looking. I went to bed and straight to sleep."

"Was your aunt here when you returned?"

"No. Her bedroom door was open and I glanced in. She'd gone out to the theatre. I didn't hear her come in."

"Didn't the presence of your uncle's car in the courtyard suggest to you that he had not yet left?"

"I didn't know it was there until Minnie mentioned it this morning." He explained how he had jumped over the wall and gone direct to the side-door. "She noticed it when she looked out to see the postman picking up those opera glasses." He pointed to the table.

The Sergeant examined the glasses. "Do you recognize them?"

"Yes, they're my aunt's. I've often seen them on top of the bureau over there."

"They may help us to account for your uncle's death," the Sergeant said thoughtfully. "If he was looking through them and overbalanced. . . ." He went to the window. "I noticed a cigar butt on the roof of the Humber. Did your uncle smoke cigars?"

"He smoked nothing else." Keith turned as the door opened and Netta came in, a half-smile of inquiry on her face. "This

45

is my aunt," he said, wondering how he could find the words to tell her. It was with relief and at the same a feeling that he was shirking a monstrous duty that he heard the Sergeant say, "Perhaps I could speak to Mrs Corsair alone."

"I'll be in the study when—if you need me," he said, and picking up his papers, went quickly out into the passage to find Minnie standing by the kitchen door. Her face was pallid and strained and the hand that held a balled handkerchief was shaking. "My brother Sid's just rung and told me," she whispered. "To think we was both in the lorry when he fell." She gulped harshly.

"But you couldn't know, Minnie, and you couldn't have done anything." He put a comforting arm round her shoulders and took her into the kitchen. She was drinking a cup of tea when he left her, saying, "My aunt will need you when the policeman goes. Don't tell her you were in the lorry when—"

"I won't," she promised.

Going into the study, Keith could hear the murmur of voices in the sitting-room. Putting down his papers, he waited, expecting that at any moment he would be summoned. But the voices went on quietly and without change of tone. Shortly he telephoned to explain why he could not keep his afternoon and evening engagements; then, idly picking up the letters which he had placed on the desk a short time ago, he started to separate the sealed envelopes from the printed matter, reversing a postcard with an Irish stamp so that it could be put in the correct pile. The card, from the Royalty Hotel at Killiney, confirmed the booking of a double room for the present weekend. A few seconds passed before he took in its import, and then he recalled a word that the Sergeant had spoken, which at the time he had not thought it worth while to correct. That word 'airport', the postcard, and the telephone call he had answered last night could surely have only one meaning. He ripped the postcard in half and tearing it into ever smaller pieces dropped them into a waste-paper basket. He was sitting at the desk, staring into nothing, when the Sergeant came in.

"I've told Mrs Corsair the bare facts, Mr Antrim. She has taken her loss very well and has gone to her room to lie down. The maid is with her, and I suggest that you wait until she asks for you."

Keith made a slight gesture of agreement.

"I must tell you now," the Sergeant said, "that she was here in her bedroom when your uncle fell to his death. When she went out at half-past six she thought that he was in this room—in fact, she believed that she had heard him cough a few minutes earlier. But she's a little vague about this, and she may well have heard someone elsewhere in the building and assumed it to be her husband. This was, of course, some ten minutes after he fell—and there is probably no connection between the two things. The circumstances suggest that it was an accident, and if the pathologist's report confirms that view, well and good. But meantime I'd be failing in my duty if I ignored what your aunt has said. If there was a visitor we'd like to know who it was and why he came. If I may use the telephone I'll get through to the Station." When he had made the call he turned to Keith, saying, "Detective Sergeant Cheam will be here shortly. I'll bring him in to see you, sir. Then he will wish to have a look round without disturbing you."

A few minutes after Sergeant Rollins had left the room Keith heard the doorbell chime. There came the sound of male voices, then a knock at the door.

The Detective Sergeant had the air of an up-and-coming country doctor. His complexion was fresh and his movements those of a man in the pink of physical condition. He listened to Keith's replies to his questions with his head slightly cocked, mentioned that it would probably be unnecessary at this stage to disturb Mrs Corsair, and left the study with the briskness of a man who knew exactly what he intended to do.

Keith sat down to think. Of course the police had to try

to establish what had happened. The coroner would require to know whatever facts there were. But there was one thing he would keep to himself. If only that confirming postcard had not been sent it would never have occurred to him that Halberd might have a mistress. But the suspicion, once planted, grew. Halberd had constantly been away at weekends, ostensibly on business; but he had never mentioned in the office where he had been or what business had been discussed. Dear Aunt Netta was one of the least inquisitive of people where her husband was concerned and accepted whatever she was told. Keith felt reasonably certain that it had never occurred to her that Halberd could be unfaithful. But suppose his mistress had a husband. Suppose . . . Keith got up and shook himself. Why in the world was he pursuing this idiotic line of thought? He spread his papers on the desk and endeavoured to concentrate.

Some time later Minnie came in to bring him a cup of coffee and to report that she had given Netta a sedative. "I think she's asleep now, poor thing," she said, "and it's best that she should be with all those policemen around. What are they doing, Mr Keith?"

"Trying to find out how the accident happened, Minnie."

"And what good'll that do? It won't bring him back," she said sharply, picking up the now empty cup. "If they're still messing about at one o'clock I'll bring you a bit of lunch on a tray—and I'll let you know when the mistress wakes up."

The clock in the study was chiming four when Keith decided he'd done enough work for the day. He was putting the papers into a folder when the Detective Sergeant knocked and came in. "Well, Mr Antrim," he said, accepting a cigarette and sitting down, "you would like to know that we have had the pathologist's report. There's nothing in his findings to contradict the assumption of an unfortunate accident. Nor have we found anything to indicate the presence of a visitor, authorized or unauthorized, at the time. You understand that there will have to be an inquest, but I hope it will be unnecessary for your aunt to attend. On occasions like this the coroner is usually anxious to spare the feelings of the bereaved." He tapped his cigarette over an ashtray. "You will receive a summons to attend, and you'll probably be asked a few questions about your uncle's health and so on."

Keith nodded understanding. "When will the inquest be held?" he asked.

"On Monday. You'll be informed of the time, and I suggest that you be there well beforehand." The Detective Sergeant rose and, after expressing his regrets and sympathy, departed. It was with some relief that Keith heard the front door close. The Sergeant had not noticed the torn-up postcard in the otherwise empty waste-paper basket, or had ignored it. If, however, the hotel requested payment for the unoccupied room the letter might get into the hands of the executors—perhaps into his aunt's. It would be best to write at once advising the hotel of Halberd's death and asking that any account should be sent to himself. Should an account have already been posted, he must intercept it and send a cheque. Opening a drawer, he took out a sheet of writing-paper. He was sealing the envelope when Minnie came in to say that his aunt was now awake.

Netta sat in an armchair in her bedroom. Her little round face was pale and empty of expression. He kissed her affectionately and murmured a few words of comfort, conscious as he spoke of the inadequacy of any words.

"Let's not talk about it, dear," she said with a composure that surprised and relieved him. "Would you ring up Claire and tell her? I expect she'll want to come round at once. Say I'll be glad to see her. I'll be in the sitting-room in a few minutes."

Claire and Bertie arrived within half an hour, and Bertie lost no time in recommending a glass of brandy. No persuasion was needed to encourage him to pour out a glass for himself. "Always said that windowsill was too low," he observed.

No-one appeared to think any comment necessary. In the ensuing silence Bertie sank back into his chair and inquired, "You'll be staying on here for a time, eh, Keith?"

"Yes, of course, for as long as Aunt Netta would like me to," replied Keith, to whom no other line of conduct had occurred.

"I hope you'll stay until I find another flat. I couldn't go on living here." Netta looked away from the window to which, despite herself, her eyes kept returning.

"We'll look for another one together," Claire said briskly. "It shouldn't be hard to find one you can afford—and in rather a nicer part of London. Halberd will have left you very comfortably off." With a directness that was scarcely inspired by altruism she asked, "Hadn't we better get in touch with his solicitors about the will? I expect you know who they are, Keith."

"I don't, but Miss Purslane will. In any case they'll be closed today—it's Saturday."

"Might as well find out their name," said Bertie with a business-like crispness. "The sooner Netta gets to know where she stands, the better." He gave a thoughtful "Arrhm", glanced at the cocktail cabinet, the door of which he had left open, caught his wife's eye, and subsided.

Getting up and going into the study, Keith consulted his diary and rang Miss Purslane. While he waited for her to answer he was thinking of the calmness with which Claire and Bertie had taken the news of Halberd's fatal accident. Come to think of it, he supposed that he too had accepted it without a very great sense of loss. Perhaps the fact was that Halberd had neither invited nor inspired affection. He had been first and foremost a man of business, and in that sphere his flair and judgment—perhaps, too, his ruthlessness—would be missed. But in his home, in his life with Netta. . . . He heard Miss Purslane's crisp "Hello", identified himself, and told her briefly what had happened. She, after an expression of shocked surprise, immediately became cool and practical. She would at once inform the Company Secretary and ask him to get in touch with the other members of the Board so that a meeting could be held on Monday. She gave him the name, address, and telephone number of Halberd's solicitors, adding that he had only on Wednesday asked for the copy of his will that was kept in the safe. She remembered seeing him put it into his brief-case yesterday afternoon. With a message of sympathy to Mrs Corsair she hung up, leaving Keith with a feeling not only that she would deal with the situation as competently as she had dealt with a thousand others, but that he had provided her with an occupation in an otherwise uneventful evening. Opening Halberd's brief-case, he recognized the envelope marked "Copy of Will dated March 5, 1958" which he had seen on Halberd's desk yesterday. Replacing for later consideration the other documents he had taken from the brief-case, he returned to the sitting-room. Halberd's testamentary dispositions, shorn of their legal verbiage and safeguards, were few and simple. His widow was to receive a lump sum of ten thousand pounds and a life-interest in nine-tenths of the remainder of the estate, which on her death was to be divided equally between Claire and Keith. The remaining one-tenth was to be shared by the two last-named. There were no other bequests, no reference to any of the employees who had served him for many years. It was the will of a man who had made no close friends and could see no reason to make some small gesture by which his acquaintances might remember him.

Out of the corner of his eye Keith saw a smile of satisfaction appear on Bertie's lips, to be quickly extinguished. "There's a pencil note in Uncle Halberd's writing on the front page of the will," Keith continued. "I don't know if it has anything to do with it, but it's 'E.D. £350,000' followed by a query mark."

"It must mean Estate Duty," Claire said, not disguising her interest. She had taken a small blue diary from her bag and was riffling through the early pages.

"Does that mean what the Government takes?" Netta asked in plaintive amazement.

"If the note means what Aunt Claire thinks it does."

Netta waved agitated hands. "But will there be anything left for us?"

Claire put down the pencil with which she had been scribbling. "If that's Halberd's estimate I'm sure it won't be far out. It means that when he wrote the note his estate was worth at least half a million. You won't starve, Netta, on a hundred and fifty thousand. Keith's share should be a good ten thousand." She closed the diary with a snap. "And so should mine."

"I wouldn't count your chickens before they're hatched, old girl," said Bertie comfortably, the gleam in his eye belying the warning. "We've no idea how much Halberd was worth. Pencil figure may have been put down years ago. Might be another later will." He cleared his throat. "If you'd like us to stay with you for a little, Netta, I'm sure Keith has a lot to do. There are one or two things. . . ." His gaze moved from Keith to Claire and came to rest on the decanter.

Keith, who had been feeling that discussion of any benefits accruing to them as a result of Halberd's death might well have been left to a later date, was happy to leave. He would look at the papers in the brief-case, so that any which required urgent action could be dealt with at Monday's Board meeting. It had been made crystal-clear that Bertie wished to have a private conversation with Netta, and Keith had little doubt about the subject. Poor Uncle Bertie, he thought, as he returned to the study, a floundering fish outside the Army water-tank, a good-natured bumbler always ready to produce a placatory or anodyne remark at an awkward moment. He acknowledged readily that he did not really like his Aunt Claire. Determinedly dismissing from his mind the recent scene, he sat down and opened the brief-case.

Some time later he made a final pencil notation and, deciding his return would serve to remind Claire and Bertie of the passage of time, went into the sitting-room to find it unoccupied. Voices from Halberd's bedroom informed him that Claire had taken the opportunity to examine her late brother's wardrobe. An occasional "h'm, h'm" from Bertie indicated that he approved of Halberd's taste in clothes. As Keith crossed the room to close the door of the cocktail cupboard he noticed an open cheque-book on Netta's bureau and guessed that Bertie had obtained from her the loan about which he had telephoned Halberd the previous afternoon.

Chapter Six

"FINANCIER'S DEATH FALL" ran the headline in Monday's evening paper. A statement of the known facts and the verdict of death by misadventure were followed by an account of the odd circumstances in which the body had been found, a picture of the lorry which had been the somewhat unconventional hearse, and an interview with an unwilling Sid, in which the reporter had clearly expanded a few muttered replies into the story of a man haunted by the horror of his unsuspected cargo. On the City page a reassuring statement from the Deputy Chairman of Wydspred preceded a report that shares in the Company, which were marked down when the market opened, had made a partial recovery. On page seven a picture of Halberd addressing a gathering at the Drysalters' Hall headed an account of his career from office-boy with a firm of auctioneers to "City Titan". The tone of this composition and of similar pieces in other papers was eulogistic. It is one of the minor sadnesses of death that a successful man can read his obituary notices only if they are premature.

Keith's thoughts were concerned with a very different matter as he tidied his desk, preparatory to leaving his office to which he had returned as soon as the inquest was over. Coming from the courtroom, he had hurried out of the building, swerving to avoid a knot of women who preceded him and were now almost entirely blocking the foot of the exit steps. As he came level with the group a shrill, grinding voice, redolent of malice and marital infelicity, was saying, "And, mark you, *she* was in the flat when '*e* fell out of the winder."

Her listeners nodded in venomous concert. "Makes you *think*, don't it?" came the comment, and the vulture heads nodded again. Keith's foot faltered. For an instant it was in his mind to stop and flay the mindless gossips with a few scathing phrases. Good sense prevented him. He saw the eyes swivelling towards him and knew that he had been recognized as the nephew who had given evidence at the hearing. If he were to say what was in his mind the women would sniff meaningly and deny what had been implied. What did he know about it? someone would ask. He wasn't there, was he? Shamefully conscious that silence was the best course, he walked away.

Now as he switched off the light and closed his office door he wondered whether he should not at once have reported what he'd heard to Sergeant Cheam. No, it was better to say nothing to anyone, to try to forget it. Reaching the main hall, he saw Lennie pushing a table up against the inner glass doors. "Wait a moment," he called.

Lennie turned. "Oh, it's you, sir. I saw the light in your room. Mr A.'s hard at it again, I said to myself. I'll shift this table and let you out."

"I'll give you a hand." Keith took one end of the table.

"I read about the inquest," said Lennie. "You'll be thankful it's all over and done with." He put down his end of the table. "They don't know how it happened, do they?"

"We'll never know for certain, Lennie."

"Maybe it's best that way." The night caretaker looked out into the courtyard. "The cops were at me to know if I'd seen or heard anything. I told 'em I'd let Mr Corsair in here about six on Friday to pick up some papers, and that far as I knew when I let him out he'd gone straight up to the flat. I said I'd heard the lorry go off—that was all. They asked if I'd seen you bring your bag along at a quarter-past six, and I said that would be about the time. They wanted to know how long it was before you went off again, and I told 'em I hadn't seen you go."

"They'll just have been confirming the times I gave." It hadn't occurred to Keith that the police would check what he told them, but he realized that it would have been done as a matter of routine. He moved round the table and was about to open the inner doors when Lennie said with diffidence, "Hope you don't mind me asking, sir, but I couldn't help wondering if my job here was safe?"

"As safe as mine, I'd say," Keith answered with a smile. "The Company doesn't get rid of people without a good reason. I don't think *you* need worry."

"It's just that I heard there might be changes—what with there being a new Chairman and all. But"—Lennie had not missed the emphasis that Keith had given one word—"if you say I needn't worry, I won't. Good night, sir."

Walking round to the side entrance, Keith took the lift up to the flat and came into the sitting-room to find Claire kneeling on the floor and eyeing a small suitcase. Netta, with a helpless air, was holding out a cardboard box. Bertie stood beside a sofa piled with pyjamas, socks, ties, and other clothing. As Keith entered he was saying, "No, Netta, old thing, that's not a lot of use. Can't get a quart into a pint pot. Oh, hello, Keith, you're just in time. Lend me that big suitcase of yours, will you? I'll let you have it back first thing. Nip along for it, my boy, and I'll have a drink ready by the time you get back."

Twenty minutes and two very substantial whiskies later Bertie was holding open the lift gates while Keith dumped a very heavy suitcase inside. Shortly a jovial voice floated up the shaft, "Not at all a bad bag, old girl. Had my eye on those shirts—nothing like silk for the summer. Won't need them where he's gone, poor devil."

At about the same time that Keith was talking to Lennie the postman who delivered the morning mail to Termini House was downing his fourth pint at a table in the corner of the public bar of The Hand and Flowers. As a person who had a daily if tenuous connection with the Corsair household, and particularly as the man who had actually handled the opera glasses presumed to have been used by the dead man, he was in a position of some authority among those who were discussing the day's proceedings at the Coroner's Court.

"Mind you," he was saying, "as soon as I spotted them glasses lying in the courtyard I says to myself, 'Joe, there's something queer happened here.' "

In the interval while he took a pull at his glass someone interjected, "Can't see anything queer about it myself. There's many a thing been dropped out of a window before now."

"You can't see it?" Joe looked round the group with raised eyebrows. "You mean you really can't? Well, let me tell you. If somebody drops something from a window they knows they've dropped it, don't they? And they goes down and picks it up. They don't just leave it lying, 'specially if it's worth a few quid. Now them glasses were ladies' ones, and pretty fancy at that. Came from Asprey's, they did, and you can bet your boots Asprey's didn't give them away. D'you think anyone's going to let them stay out all night? A drop of rain'd do them a bit of no good . . . and someone might have nicked them."

"But they said at the inquest that he must have been looking out of the window and the glasses must have dropped out of his hand when he fell," said a priestly-looking man who owned the next-door fishmonger's shop. "If no-one saw him fall nobody would have known nothing about the glasses."

"That's what they said." The postman's voice was heavily ironical. "Well, they had to say something to cover up what they didn't know. But you just try to look at things straight and answer me these questions. What was he looking at that he couldn't see with his own eyes?" He put down an empty tankard with a thump and caught the eye of a moustached man who had not yet made a contribution to his refreshment. Under the compelling gaze the moustache quivered and its owner, rising with assumed alacrity, went over to the bar.

"Maybe there was a judy undressing in front of a window across the street," suggested a listener.

"In one of them empty houses what's been condemned," Joe said scathingly. "You'd better think again, chum. Now here's another one for you. How come it that those glasses—ladies' glasses, mind you—were lying nice and handy for him to pick up?" He wagged a finger to quell an imaginary interruption. "You're going to tell me that his missus had put 'em out to take with her to the theatre. But she didn't take them, did she. And why not? Because they were lying down there in the courtyard."

"She couldn't know that," said the fishmonger. "Not unless she'd seen 'em fall."

Joe gave a weighty, commendatory nod as to an unexpectedly intelligent pupil.

"But she couldn't have seen 'em fall, Joe. She was in her bedroom, wasn't she?"

The postman said nothing. He was now looking up at the smoke-stained ceiling; there was an air of patient contempt on his face and in the infinitesimal shrug of a shoulder. It was apparent that he was wondering how long it would take the penny to drop. It wasn't long.

"You mean to say that she mightn't have been in the bedroom? That she got him to look through the glasses—maybe told him they weren't working right." The fishmonger passed a pale tongue across his lips and leaned forward. "You mean she could have given him a push?"

"I mean nothing of the sort, Jim Pooley," the postman said severely. "It's you what's suggesting it, not me. You want to be more careful about what you say." A stern eye cast round the assembled company compelled them into nods and ejaculations of agreement. In the ensuing silence he picked up the tankard, jerked his head at the moustached man, and drank deeply. Soon he placed the empty tankard on the table and rose. "Not that it mightn't pay someone to look in that direction," he murmured as if to himself and with a benign "Good night, all," made his way towards the 'Gents.'

Minnie met him the following morning as she crossed the courtyard to collect the empty rubbish bucket which the dustmen had as usual thrown just inside the exit way. A hand was raised to her mouth. "Morning," he greeted her. "Yawning at this time of day. Looks as if you didn't get much rest last night. Expect you'll be sleeping upstairs now that the lady's on her own."

"No, I'm staying in my own room." She took the letters from his hand.

"Ah." There was a world of significance in his tone. "There's one or two round here what's saying they wouldn't like to be alone with her at night after what happened to him."

"Her nephew's staying—" Minnie broke off as the implication hit her. She saw the sly smile on his face and anger rose in her like a tidal bore. "If you're saying what I think you're saying you'd better tell your friends to keep their mouths buttoned—and you keep your dirty mouth shut too." With a few further winged phrases she took the postman apart. It was with wrath and disquietude in her heart that she returned to the flat without the bucket and, bursting into the dining-room where Keith was finishing his breakfast, repeated what had been said.

Keith listened grimly. First those dreadful witches after the inquest, and now these whispers in the neighbourhood. How widely were the rumours spreading, and how long would it be before they came to Aunt Netta's ears? "Leave it to me, Minnie," he said levelly. "I'll see that something's done."

The man who came out of New Scotland Yard into Broadway looked to the left before crossing the road; then, as the wind from a passing car fanned his cheek, he became abruptly aware that he was now in England. This was the third time he

59

had failed to remember; it must not happen again. Joining a group at a zebra crossing, he strolled towards St James's Park.

This man's clothes were immaculate but inconspicuous. He wore no hat. His jet-black hair was brushed to a smooth polish; his cheeks seemed freshly shaven. The face was well-formed and pleasant, the chin perhaps a trifle long, the expression controlled but attractive. The eyes, observant but not seeming to observe, were an unusually dark shade of blue that was near to violet. There was nothing in his appearance, except possibly the ring he wore on his right hand, to indicate that Inspector Borges had not been born an Englishman. Nor, as Detective Chief Superintendent Mallick and other senior officers with whom he had for the past few days been in conference would testify, was there anything in his way of speech to suggest that English was not his native language. Perhaps his vocabulary was a little wider and his articulation clearer than that of most, so that one might have taken him for a barrister or teacher or Civil Service administrator. But he was none of these things. He was a policeman whose home was in Barcelona, and, at the moment, now that his official business had been completed, he was a policeman on holiday staying with an old friend.

Serendipity—that was the word that Sir Otto had mentioned last night—the faculty of making happy discoveries by accident. And London, Inspector Borges said to himself, is a city in which that aptitude need never wither. There was always something to surprise, to charm, to store in that part of the brain reserved for pleasant memories. The alleyways and covered passages leading to greenness and tranquillity, the spruce elderly men playing with boats at the Round Pond, the three-card tricksters and the 'escapologists' off Charing Cross Road. Curious, too, to find public parks treated as private bedsteads and walls crying out the liberation of smouldering inhibitions. Smiling, he paused to watch the pelicans drooping dyspeptically at the lakeside. Later, crossing

Piccadilly, he made his way to Hill Street and let himself into a house on the eastern side.

Sir Otto was pouring out sherry as he came into the study. "A drink before anything else," he said. "Now that your holiday's actually begun we can talk about what you'd like to do and see before we join my wife in the country on Saturday. I'd hoped to show you something of the City tomorrow, but I fear I shan't be able to get away from business."

"I'll be perfectly happy on my own," the Inspector assured him.

"I think you'll be happier with the alternative I'm providing." Sir Otto took a photograph from the mantelpiece and held it out. "My niece, Anthea. She's coming this evening to stay here, and she'll be free until rehearsals begin next week. She has a small part in a new comedy. I gave her a flattering portrait of you, and she'll be delighted to be your guide. She suggests taking you to the House of Commons to watch, as someone once put it, the representatives of democracy cowering under the lash of the three-line whip. I very much fear that you'll have to go. She's a determined young woman."

The Inspector looked at the face in the photograph—high cheekbones, a small, blunt nose, a mouth that seemed to promise humour, fair hair framing a wide forehead. "She can take me wherever she likes," he said.

Putting down his glass, Sir Otto said, "The son of an old friend of mine rang up half an hour ago. He's got a very worrying problem to do with his uncle's recent death and wants to talk about it. He'll be along at nine o'clock. I'll tell you what facts I know over dinner—and I'd like you to meet Keith. I think you can give him better advice than I can."

It was a quarter-past nine when Keith finished his story. "It's quite inconceivable that Aunt Netta had anything to do with my uncle's death," he said earnestly. "But if people are saying she did I don't see how we can prevent her getting to know sooner or later. As soon as Minnie told me about the postman I rang Holborn Police Station and spoke to Sergeant Cheam. He said he would do what he could, but that it was next to impossible to stop gossip and rumour."

"And you would like to stop them by establishing your aunt's innocence," said Sir Otto.

"Yes, beyond doubt and publicly."

"Do you believe that your uncle's death was an accident?" the Inspector asked.

"I suppose it must have been." Keith hesitated before saying, "But I can't really convince myself. He wasn't the kind of man who ever had an accident. He never did anything in haste, always left himself a margin of safety. He wouldn't allow a rug to be put near the window in case anyone should trip over it, and he insisted that only non-slip polish was to be used on the floor. When I came in on Friday night I was surprised to find the windows wide open. I've heard him say more than once that they mustn't be opened more than eight or nine inches. I'm sure that neither my aunt nor Minnie would have opened them to the full. Of course it was frightfully hot and sticky on Friday—and obviously someone must have opened them."

"You've spoken to your aunt about the person she heard coughing after your uncle's death?"

"Yes, I've mentioned it. She's quite sure she heard a cough, but completely vague about the direction from which it came."

"Mr Antrim," the Inspector said quietly, "there is only one way to establish your aunt's innocence and that is either to prove to the hilt accidental death or to find evidence of either suicide or homicide. You must realize that, if the case were to be reopened, your aunt and a number of other people are going to be subjected to further examination and very possibly to publicity. We have to face the fact that if any evidence of homicide should come to light your aunt cannot escape suspicion. The circumstances are not in her favour. She was in the flat when your uncle fell; she went out without exchanging the farewells that might be expected when one of a married couple is going away for the weekend. She inherits substantially under his will—though that is not necessarily a motive for disposing of him, since she may now be less well-off than when he was alive. Before you decide whether you wish the case to be reopened it would be as well to be sure that there is no other circumstance which could be construed as a motive—for instance, an extra-marital affair."

"So far as I know nothing of the kind has ever been suggested." Keith seemed surprised and spoke curtly.

The Inspector looked at him contemplatively. "Then let us return to the person who coughed, to this unknown visitor—if there was one. Who, beside your uncle and aunt, had keys to the flat?"

"Minnie and myself."

"And you were in another part of London at the time of death. So if this visitor was already in the flat when your uncle came home he must either have found the front door open or have been let in by your aunt or Minnie. It would seem more likely that he came after your uncle's return. If the door was closed he will have knocked or rung the bell. If your uncle admitted him he must either have been someone he recognized or someone whose presence he would not question, such as a meter-reader or a messenger with a reply-paid telegram. But you say that your aunt did not hear either a knock or a doorbell."

"The bell is a very quiet one, just two soft chimes, and Aunt Netta was in her bedroom with the radio on."

"But surely she would have heard something. If we are considering the possibility of homicide I find it difficult to imagine someone arriving, coming into the sitting-room, getting Corsair over to the window, and pushing him out—all without a word or a sound."

"My aunt was listening to Ravel's *Bolero*. You know how it gets louder and louder. You might hear an outside noise at the beginning, but"—Keith gave a slight smile—"you certainly wouldn't hear much else towards the end."

"You say it was established that your uncle fell at approximately eighteen minutes past six. And the *Bolero*—"

"Was then about two-thirds through. I checked the programme today. It ended at six twenty-four."

The Inspector caught Sir Otto's eye. This young man had wasted no time in finding evidence that he thought would support his aunt's story. But he had not realized that a fact may be a two-way conductor. If the music were sufficiently loud to drown other sounds it would enable someone to creep up unheard behind Corsair—and that someone could have been his wife. "How near is your aunt's bedroom to the sitting-room?" he asked. "Perhaps you would describe the flat, Mr Antrim."

"It's the top floor of an office block which my uncle had converted for his own use. The private lift is the only way of getting there. The front door opens on to a hall from which the passage leads straight ahead. On your left are the doors to the study, sitting-room, and my uncle's bedroom. Then there's a connecting bathroom between his room and my aunt's on the other side of the passage and, coming back, the dining-room, kitchen, a store-room, a spare bedroom with adjoining bathroom, and a cloakroom. It's a pretty large flat. I'd say"—he paused briefly—"that it's seven or eight yards from my aunt's bedroom door to the sitting-room door."

Looking up from his notebook, the Inspector asked, "Does the private lift serve any floor but the very top one?"

"No."

"Is there no other way of reaching the flat? What, for instance, happens if there's an electricity failure and the private lift isn't working?"

"There's a stand-by plant for the building, but I don't know if it would operate the lift. I suppose you could get into the flat from the main building by going up to the ninth floor—the top office floor—and using the Fire Emergency staircase which goes up to the roof—I mean the roof over the flat. There's a landing half-way up where the stairs turn, and a door which would bring you into the flat between the store-room and the spare bedroom. Sorry I forgot to mention it before, but it's always kept locked. I don't suppose it's ever been used."

"Have you ever been up this emergency staircase?"

"Yes, whenever there's been an office fire practice—that's every November. There's a door onto the roof, with a push-bar which can only be opened from the inside."

"Do you know who has a key to the door on the landing—the one into the flat?"

"There's a labelled key-ring on a hook on the door-jamb inside the flat, and the commissionaire keeps one in his cubicle by the main entrance. He has a glass-fronted cupboard with dozens of duplicate keys. The cupboard's kept locked, and the commissionaire hands the key over to Lennie, the night care-taker, when he goes off duty."

"So what it comes down to," said Sir Otto, "is that a visitor to the flat can only get in via the private lift and the front door."

"That's what the police say. Unless he managed to get onto the roof and enter by an open window. But he'd have to be a pretty agile cat-burglar. It's a devil of a drop to the court-yard."

It was half-past ten when Keith left, feeling rather more cheerful now that he had shared his problem with interested and sympathetic listeners. He had very much liked Sir Otto's friend—whose name, he suddenly realized, had not been mentioned. No solution had been suggested and no under-taking made, but he had no doubt that this quiet man was now considering what could be done to resolve the present perplexities. Closing the front door behind him, he walked slowly down the steps onto the pavement. So deep was he in thought that he did not notice the girl who had to jump aside to let him pass.

. In the study the Inspector accepted the proffered drink. "Keith has told us the contents of his uncle's will," he said. "It would be interesting to know what would happen to that part of the estate which was left to Mrs Corsair if she were charged with and convicted of killing her husband."

Sir Otto's heavy eyebrows rose. "A provocative point," he commented. "To the best of my knowledge a convicted murderer cannot receive benefit from the estate of his victim. After that I don't know—but I'll find out tomorrow."

Chapter Seven

PUSHING his chair back from the desk, Detective Chief Superintendent Mallick joined Inspector Borges at the window. "Well," he said, "if you'd really like to talk to the people concerned you have my blessing and the promise of any help I can give. I sent to C.2 Branch for the file after you rang this morning, and discussed the whole matter with the Assistant Commissioner. He's as anxious as anyone to put a stopper on this gossip about Mrs Corsair. I gathered that as youngsters they were friends and he still has a soft spot for her. But how the devil can one prevent people talking? Damned idle, malicious gossips!" His gesture was compound of contempt and anger. "They're responsible for more unhappiness than murderers. Because Mrs Corsair was in the flat when her husband died they jump to a totally unjustified conclusion. Unfortunately one can't *prove* an accident to which there were no witnesses any more than one can prove to a man that he's just eaten a pork sausage if he is convinced that it was made of beef."

The Inspector smiled. "One's ability to distinguish the difference is impaired if someone has put a blindfold over one's eyes, as I think may have been done in this case. If this person whom Mrs Corsair heard in the flat exists he—or she —might be able to remove the blindfold."

"If he exists—yes. She *thinks* she heard somebody cough. She thinks the cough came from somewhere in the flat. One can't help wondering whether it was some other noise which she mistook for a cough. We could find no trace whatsoever of the presence of a visitor at the relevant time. We found fingerprints, of course, but they were those of people known to have been there during the past two or three days—and all of them gave reasonably satisfactory accounts of where they were and what they were doing at the time of Corsair's fall. I've no reason to disbelieve them. Granted that all the members of the family had a financial interest in his death, but—"

"But not all rich men are murdered by their heirs," the Inspector said drily, "though a good many would be dead if wishes were lethal." After a moment he went on: "I'd like to know more about Corsair. The reason for murder often lies as much in the murderee as in the dispatcher. From what Keith Antrim has told me he doesn't appear to have been a man of sudden impulses. The evidence suggests carelessness and haste. His fingerprints were not on the opera glasses, which suggests that he snatched them up by the cord. He was still wearing his reading spectacles. I'd like to know what he'd heard that made him hurry to the window, and what he thought he might see."

"People do things that are inexplicable until one knows the explanation," the Superintendent observed. "One can only assume that what appears to have happened did happen—until it's disproved. In this case Sergeant Cheam made a very thorough investigation and came up with nothing." He sighed. "We've got a crime list in the country stretching from here to Domesday and not enough men to deal with it. I simply couldn't justify spending any more time on further investigation into a case where the only clue—if it is one—is a cough."

"And a bespectacled man looking at something through opera glasses on a dark night."

"Perhaps checking his watch against a church clock. Well, to get back to business, if any man wants to take a busman's holiday I'm not the one to stop him." Mallick looked keenly at the Inspector. "I'd have thought you could do with a rest."

The Inspector smiled. "I'm an Elephant's Child 'full of 'satiable curtiosity'," he quoted.

"And you won't rest until you've satisfied it." Mallick picked up a folder from the desk. "Here's your bus ticket— the complete dossier of the case. It'll take you through all the inquiries we've made. I can't say I hope you'll find that we've failed to spot a murderer. But if you do, we'll see that he gets what's coming to him." He glanced at his watch. "I've got to go now and see the Assistant Commissioner. If you care to run through the dossier and take any notes you want I'll be back in half an hour and we can have a final word. You'd better have some sort of warrant to put in your wallet. If you come up against any trouble or need any assistance you only have to show it to the nearest copper." As he went out he called over his shoulder, "There'll be a cup of tea along shortly."

Some twenty-five minutes later the Inspector closed the dossier and began to consider what he had read. The pathologist had reported that there were no marks or bruises on the body which were inconsistent with an accidental fall. Abrasions on the shins indicated that the dead man had pressed them against the low window-sill in an attempt to recover his balance. It was impossible to say why or where he had slipped or stumbled since any marks made by his shoes had been eliminated by the electric polisher used by the maid on Saturday morning.

The opera glasses which the postman had picked up in the courtyard had, so far as could be ascertained, been lying approximately four feet from the building. This position, according to tyre-marks left by the lorry, would mean that they lay a little below the rear overhang of the lorry. They could have bounced there or ricocheted from the wall as they fell. Fingerprints showed that they had last been handled by the maid Minnie, and previously by the postman, whose prints were superimposed on those of Mrs Corsair.

A slight burn-mark on the front of Corsair's shirt had been

caused by hot ash from a cigar. A partly-smoked cigar had been found on the roof of the Humber car beside which the lorry had been parked. Saliva tests showed that Corsair had smoked it recently.

In investigating the possibility of a third person having been in the flat, the means of access had been carefully examined. Entry was obtainable only by the front door or by the Emergency Door that opened from the flat onto a staircase coming from the office floor below. A key to the mortise lock of this door was kept in the commissionaire's cubicle, and could not have been used without his knowledge or that of the night caretaker, Lennie. A duplicate key on a labelled split-ring hung inside the flat; another key on this ring belonged to some other lock.

Leaning back in his chair, the Inspector caught sight of the cup of tea which had been brought in some time ago by a motherly woman with flat feet. "Fresh from the pot and made special for you," she had said, hovering while he took a sip of a heavily-sweetened decoction of tannin and untruthfully expressed his appreciation. Now the surface was lidded by a corpse-like skin. Going over to the window, he found that it was hermetically sealed. Of course—the building was fully air-conditioned. Baffled of this means of disposal, he returned to the desk. As he put down the cup his eye fell on a glass tray filled with sharpened pencils. Smiling to himself, he picked up one whose purple paint indicated that it was indelible and, piercing the repellent skin of milk, began to stir. He was only just in time. When the door opened and the tea-lady came to take away the cup he was able to point with embarrassment to the mauve-streaked liquid, to apologize humbly for his stupidity, and gracefully to decline a replacement. When she had gone, full of self-reproach that she had not brought him a teaspoon, he returned to his thoughts. He was putting away his notebook when the Superintendent returned.

"Well," Mallick asked jovially. "Found any pointers we've missed?"

The Inspector shook his head. "I feel like the man who arrived at the North Pole to find that some earlier explorer had erected a signpost. When he had rubbed the snow from each of its four arms he found that they all carried the same device—a question-mark."

Mallick laughed as he held out a cellophaned card. "Here's your warrant," he said. "If there's anything I can do to help at any time, give me a ring."

Shortly the Inspector made his adieux. He was walking slowly along Broadway when a voice almost at his elbow called his name. Beside him a small red car came to a halt at the kerb, and through the open window he saw Anthea's vivid face. "Hop in," she said, "and I'll give you a lift."

"D'you mean to say that you've been waiting for me?" he asked as he sat down and closed the door.

She nodded happily.

"But I asked you not to," he said in mild rebuke. "It was kind of you to bring me down here this morning, but I can't have you sitting here for two hours. There must be so many other things you could be doing. Please drop me wherever's convenient for you and let me find my own way."

She half-turned her head as she changed gear. "Uncle Otto put you in my charge," she said, and there was a smile in her voice. "I'm to take you wherever you want to go. You'd lose yourself in London on your own, and you've got a lot of people to see."

"Have I?"

"Of course you have. When you and Uncle Otto were talking last night about what that young man told you it was obvious you weren't convinced that Halberd Corsair's death was an accident. When you mentioned at breakfast that you were going to ring Superintendent Mallick it wasn't hard to guess that, even though the case was closed, you'd ask if you could try to find out something more."

"And what makes you think that Mallick said 'yes'?"

She grinned. "You underrate yourself—and me. If he'd said

71

'no' you would have asked me, 'What are we going to see today'?"

"And what are we going to see?"

"Termini House. You want to talk to Mrs Corsair first, don't you?"

He settled back in his seat. "I'm in your hands," he said submissively. "But please don't wait for me there. I may be a very long time."

She gave a little snort. "You know perfectly well that you're likely to be there all day. You've got to look round the place and talk to the maid and the night caretaker, and I expect you'll see that young man again, and probably other people as well. I'll come back at one o'clock and take you somewhere for lunch. And if you don't want to discuss the case we'll talk about other things."

"And if I do?"

"I'll listen in respectful silence." She chuckled and, turning the corner into Scott Street, drew up at the kerb.

When she had driven away with a wave of a gloved hand the Inspector entered the courtyard and, making his way to the side entrance, stood back as a couple of girls came out of the Staff Door and, with glances and expressions of busy innocence that betrayed truancy, hurried off down the alley-way past the back of the building. For a moment he stood to set the scene firmly in his mind; then, entering the lift, he paused before pressing the button that would take him to the top floor. Was Keith, he wondered, right in thinking that his aunt was ignorant of the tongues that whispered murder? If so, he must keep that knowledge to himself. To tell her would be an unthinkable cruelty; at this stage it would also be unwise. For until one has seen and talked with somebody one cannot judge whether the word "murder" will open their lips or act as an astringent to dry up the springs of memory.

Netta was at her bureau when the bell chimed. Before her lay the letters of sympathy to which she had not yet replied.

She let the bell ring again before recollecting that Minnie was out shopping. One of the shoes she had kicked off had found its way beneath the bureau, and she bent over to find it. When she opened the door she was a little breathless and there was colour in her cheeks.

The Inspector introduced himself, explaining that he was making inquiries about someone who might have been in the building on the night of her husband's death. "I'm extremely sorry to have to trouble you just now," he said, "but there have been a number of burglaries in the area recently, and I understand that you may have heard someone in your flat on Friday evening."

Within a short time they were in the sitting-room and Netta was talking. "Such a nice man and such an attentive listener," she told a friend later. "You know I had no idea that there were—well, gentlemen in the police." To the Inspector she was now saying that it couldn't have been a burglar, could it, because nothing had been stolen. "I mean," she corrected herself, "that I don't *think* anything was taken, though when I looked in my purse the next day there seemed to be less there than I'd thought. You see, I cashed a cheque on Thursday and I thought I had twenty pounds, but there were only ten there. Of course I'm so bad about money, and I *could* have spent the rest. But I must say I *did* wonder if the bank hadn't made a mistake."

Assuring her that banks seldom underpaid, he skilfully brought the conversation round to the cough she had heard. Yes, she'd taken the cough to be Halberd's because so far as she knew at the time it couldn't have been anyone else's. Though when she came to think about it later, it hadn't actually sounded as if Halberd had a *cough*. She gave the Inspector a look of helplessness. "I'm so bad at explaining things. I mean—"

"That it was the kind of cough people give if they're nervous?"

"Ye-es." She was doubtful.

73

"If they want to attract attention? An artificial cough?"

"That's it exactly." She nodded vigorously.

"If it won't distress you," he said gently, "I'd be grateful if you would go through last Friday evening until you left for the theatre."

"I'll try." She fiddled with the clasp of her handbag. "Do you mind if I light a cigarette first? Do smoke if you'd like to. It's such a relaxing habit, don't you think? I gave it up last month when I had a perfectly horrible cold, but I *had* to start again. But I do think it's unpleasant to smoke in shops, and I do agree that one shouldn't smoke in the theatre, though I really think that the actors ought to give it up too. I mean, when one sees an actor smoking on the stage, one *wants* to smoke oneself, doesn't one?"

The Inspector conveyed agreement. In due course she would come to the point. Interruption might start another train of thought; it might also serve to make her omit something of importance. She was, it occurred to him, rather like a Pekingese sleeve-dog, soft and large-eyed, delighted to have a man's undivided attention, and, so far as first impressions went, unlikely to be able either to boil an egg or to push her husband out of a window. For a moment his mind wandered.

"So I was here," she was saying, "actually in *this* chair when Halberd came in. He asked if Minnie were here, then said he'd see her after the weekend. I knew he'd had a difficult day as he sounded rather cross—and perhaps the television *was* on rather loud before I turned it down. He was saying something about taking Keith and a girl out to dinner next week when the telephone rang and he went into the study to answer it."

"And that was the last time you saw him?"

"Yes. I went into my bedroom to finish getting ready and put on the radio. They were playing Ravel's *Bolero*—such a thrilling piece. I expect you know it."

The Inspector said he did, and asked, "Did you hear the whole of the piece?"

"I missed the first two or three minutes. It ended just as I was ready to go out."

"You were dressing?"

"No, I'd dressed before Halberd came in. I was putting another coat of varnish on my nails; the same one I've got on now." She held out her hands. "Don't you think it's rather a nice colour?"

"Very nice," he agreed. "And when you'd done that did you sit listening to the music while the varnish dried?"

"Well; I didn't actually sit. You see, there was that lovely music getting more and more thrilling, so I—I moved round the room in time to it. I slipped off my shoes," she confessed. "Barefoot dancing is so good for the feet, you know."

"Then I think you came in here for a moment before leaving?"

"I expect I was here for three or four minutes. You see, I couldn't put on my gloves until the varnish was quite dry, so I turned up the television to hear what they were saying—but not enough to disturb Halberd." She looked up wide-eyed. "You see, I hadn't any idea that the poor lamb wasn't in the flat. I mean I'd seen him—and there was this cough as well."

"Have you any idea at all from which direction it came?"

"I wasn't really listening, if you see what I mean," Netta said vaguely. "It sounded quite near."

"The windows in this room were open. Could it have come from one of the offices below?"

"I suppose it could. But I wouldn't have thought it was in the flat if it wasn't, would I? I mean, if I thought it was Halberd. . . ."

He smiled reassuringly. "Then, as soon as your nails were dry, you went out. Had you intended to take your opera glasses with you?"

"I'd meant to, and I was sure I'd put them down somewhere in the room. While I was looking for them I saw it was nearly half-past six, and I had to meet my friends at a quarter to seven. So I picked up my bag and gloves and just rushed."

"Leaving the television set on?"

The Pekingese brow wrinkled. "I suppose I must have. I was terribly late, and I *tore* into the lift and dashed off to find a taxi."

"What time did you return from the theatre?"

"It was after midnight, perhaps half-past twelve. You see, we had supper after the show, and you *know* how it is when you get talking."

"Did you see your husband's car in the courtyard?"

"I wasn't actually looking. The driver brought me right up to the side-door, and I was trying to find the right money in my purse."

"Did your husband mention where he was going for the weekend?"

"He said something about Manchester—or was it that he wasn't going there?" She waved a helpless hand. "I don't know."

"Was he travelling by himself?" The violet eyes watched her face.

"Oh, yes. He always went alone. He said he couldn't *think* if anybody was chattering." After a moment she said, "He didn't ever talk very much." Her eye caught the clock on the mantelpiece. "Inspector, do stay and have some coffee. I'm sure Minnie won't be long."

"It's very kind of you," he said. "If I had time I should be delighted. I think I heard Minnie come in a minute ago. May I have your permission to speak to her and to look round the flat before I go?"

"Yes, of course." She sounded a little disappointed.

Minnie was unpacking a shopping-basket when he reached the kitchen. He introduced himself. It seemed to her quite natural that he should perch himself on one end of the table and talk while she prepared the luncheon vegetables. Listening to his warm voice, she soon shed her metaphorical cap and apron. If he wanted to do what he could to clear the mistress's name she was ready to help. Soon she was telling him how her brother Sid had turned up unexpectedly last Friday. "I'd got the kettle on for Lennie and myself, so I sat him down and gave him a cup of tea and a slice of the cake he'd brought. We were having a good old natter when he saw it was coming up to ten-past six. He said he'd have to be off and he'd drop me where I could catch a bus to Finchley. So I did a quick tidy, and off we went. Of course as soon as we got to the lorry I had to go back for some knitting. I wasn't more than a couple of minutes away. Sid started off—and then there was this thump." She drew her breath in sharply at the recollection. "Sid said it was just a clutch or something slipping, but I've often told myself since that we ought to have got out and looked."

"It's no good thinking about it," he told her kindly. "You'll feel better if we go on talking. Tell me, when you left your flat did you notice whether the lift was up or down?"

"I think it was down, but I wasn't really looking."

"Did you close the side-door, the one into the courtyard?"

"No, I don't shut it till I go to bed. That was Mr Corsair's orders."

"Then it was open when you came home at eleven?"

Minnie thought for a moment. "No, it was shut. I had to use the key."

"Did you notice Mr Corsair's car as you came in?"

"I didn't come by the front, but by the alley from Mohun Street—that's at the back. It saves quite a few steps if you're walking from that side."

"And when you came in?"

"I went straight into bed."

"You didn't come up here—to the flat?"

"I'd no cause to. I'd turned the beds down before I left, and if the mistress or Mr Keith was in I didn't want to disturb them."

"And the next morning?"

"I was up early to give the place a thorough clean before getting the breakfasts."

"Looking back, was there anything to suggest to you that Mr Corsair hadn't gone away for the weekend?"

"I can't call anything to mind. I'd packed his case with clean things and his spare razor and put it in the car." Minnie peeled a potato while she thought. "His brief-case was on the table in the passage, and I took it into the study. There was one thing that made me say to myself, 'He must have been in a hurry'. When I went to shut the cocktail cabinet there was a glass with something in it and a siphon alongside. I asked Mr Keith if it was his and he said 'no' and took a sniff at it. 'It's neat whisky', he said. 'Better put it back in the decanter.' So I did."

"Did you mention this to Sergeant Cheam?"

"It didn't come to my mind until now," she confessed. "It's not important, is it?"

"Probably not," he said. "When you're ready I'd like to see the rest of the flat."

"Now's as good as later." She dried her hands. In the passage she pointed out the table where the brief-case had been. Beside the table was a closed door. On the left-hand upright and some two and a half feet above a light-switch, a pair of keys on a split-ring hung from a brass hook. A round white plastic tag on the ring bore in clear red capital letters, FIRE—EMERGENCY EXIT.

"Is this door always kept locked?" he asked.

"Always. Mr Corsair said no-one was to use it unless there was a fire." Minnie hesitated. "Matter of fact, I did open it a week or two back so's to sweep up the dust just under the door. But that's all I did. It's the office cleaners' job to keep the stairs and landing clean."

"Are you sure you locked the door again?"

"Sure as I'm here. I wouldn't have dared to let Mr Corsair know I'd opened it."

"Was he so fierce then?" the Inspector asked with a smile.

"He was all right with me, but I've heard . . . well, he wasn't always." She looked away.

Going down the passage to the front door, he opened it,

examined the latch, and closed it again. "Have you ever had difficulty in closing this door, Minnie?"

"Not from this side. It needs a firm pull when you're going out."

"But not everybody gives it a firm pull," he suggested.

"I've sometimes had to latch it after the mistress."

"Can you tell me who, apart from Mrs Corsair, Mr Antrim, and yourself, has been in the flat since Mr Corsair died?"

"Only the Colonel and Mrs Summersby and Miss Purslane that I've seen. And there was a lawyer after the funeral service —and, of course, all those policemen."

"Has anyone come to the door whom you haven't let in?"

"Just the laundry, and Harrods delivery, and a man selling brushes."

"And the newspaper-boy?"

"No. The papers and the post and the milk are left down-stairs."

"D'you know of any spare keys other than those you gave to Mr Antrim?"

"There's just the four sets that I know of."

She took him into Netta's bedroom, where he paused for a moment to look at the dressing-table, and then showed him the rest of the flat. When she returned to the kitchen he took down the split-ring from its hook. The second key opened the Emergency Door, and he came onto a landing from which flights of stairs led up and down. Before his feet lay a narrow line of dust which had collected under the door since Minnie had swept there. It looked, he thought, as if someone had put a foot down and pivoted slightly, perhaps to reach the light-switch in the passage. But when the footmark had been made and by whom it would be impossible to tell from such tenuous evidence. He straightened himself, and taking the upward flight, came to a door secured by a heavy bar-lift fastening. This he raised and, stepping onto the roof, confirmed that there was no means of opening the door from the outside. For a little while he stood gazing at the city spread before him, enjoying a breeze that blew softly from the south. Then, returning, he closed and barred the door and went down the stairs to the top floor of the offices. From the foot of the staircase the corridor ran each way. A faint smell of food hung in the air before a door labelled "Directors' Luncheon Room". From the adjoining door the sound of a running tap and the clink of crockery indicated the kitchen. Behind the other closed doors there was silence. From the lift shaft came the click of closing gates and the whine of one of the two lifts in motion. Slowly he went back to the flat and, letting himself out, went down in the private lift. In the courtyard he stopped to look at the dark-green Humber, which had apparently not been moved since its owner's death. The polished coachwork and the spotless windscreen showed that whichever member of the Company's staff had been charged with the job of keeping the car clean still continued to carry out his duty.

Standing directly below the window of the sitting-room ten floors above, he stared upward. Where he now stood the lorry must have been parked, that unlikely hearse which, by receiving Corsair, had delayed the discovery of the body and the subsequent inquiries. Surely its presence in that place and at that time was fortuitous.

Unconscious of idly curious faces at office windows, the Inspector paced to and fro, hands clasped before his chest. It had seemed to him while talking to her that Netta's hearing was very slightly subnormal. With her door closed, the radio playing loudly, and the partly muted television in the sitting-room, it was reasonable to conclude that she would have heard only the most piercing of noises. If her story were true she had returned to the sitting-room at about twenty-five past six, by which time Halberd's body was well on its way to North London, and a visitor, if there had been one, would have had ample time to leave or to conceal himself. The fact that a whisky had been poured out supported the possibility that Halberd had been disturbed in the act of mixing a drink—perhaps by someone ringing the doorbell. But, the Inspector gave himself a mental slap on the wrist, it is tempting to fit facts into a theory. Proof might well not exist in tangible form. It might, however, still be found in someone's memory; for, though one may shut the door on memory and double-lock it, the key can never be destroyed this side of the Styx.

Chapter Eight

CLUTCHING a bunch of papers, Keith hurried along the passage and put his head in at the door of his secretary's room. Miss Bohun looked up from her typewriter. "There's a police inspector to see you," she said. "I've put him in your office with *The Times*."

"Did he say what he wanted to see me about?"

"He gave me the impression that he'd dropped in for a chat. He didn't seem to have any handcuffs on him." Her charmingly asymmetrical face broke into a smile. "He's rather nice. I think he'll let you off with a caution."

Keith shook his head. "I'm afraid they've found the missing Rembrandt under the bath. I should have chosen a better place," he said lightly, as he gave her a sheaf of handwritten notes. "Type these up, will you, and let me have them after lunch if I haven't gone to gaol." Opening the communicating door, he went into his room to find the man he had met last night at Sir Otto's house standing by the window. "Oh," he exclaimed in surprise. "My secretary said you were a policeman. She must have misunderstood you."

"I'm afraid she didn't." The Inspector's tone was gently apologetic as he explained his position. "I'm sorry we could not tell you last night, but you will understand that I did not wish to offer any help without first asking the permission of your police."

"Then you're going to find out what actually happened and put an end to those poisonous rumours about Aunt Netta."

"I would like to try," the Inspector said with a smile.

"Do you really think there could have been someone in the flat when my uncle died—I mean someone as well as my aunt?"

"I think it's possible." He moved towards a chair. "But, before you accept my help, you must understand that I shall be acting as a policeman as well as a friend. If I should come to the conclusion that your uncle was murdered I must try to find the murderer, and that means that I must consider all those who could in any way benefit from his death."

"You mean I'm on your list," said Keith cheerfully. "Yes, of course I must be—and Aunt Claire and Uncle Bertie."

"And your Aunt Netta, too."

"But you can't suspect her." The young face tautened.

"I have talked to her this morning, Mr Antrim. I do not suspect her. The word is yours, not mine. I have no reason to suspect anyone yet—except perhaps this unknown visitor who coughed but whom no-one saw."

Keith smiled faintly. "Well, you know where I was at the time."

"I know what is in the police report, and you have already given me a general outline. I would like you to tell me in detail."

Keith gave a meticulous account of his day up to the time when he put the suitcase in the lift and went off to the Tube station.

"Why didn't you take it up to the flat?"

"There was just time to get to Warwick Gardens by Tube and so save a taxi-fare of ten bob. I knew if I went up and saw my aunt I shouldn't be able to get away for ten minutes."

The Inspector smiled understanding. "And what time did you reach your friends' house?"

"A little after seven. There was a breakdown of some kind and the train was stuck between stations for a quarter of an hour." He glanced at the Inspector's impassive face. "I expect the Sergeant can confirm that—I got the impression that he was going to check. In any case there was a paragraph about the breakdown in the *Daily Telegraph* next morning."

"Was there anyone you knew on the train?"

"Not anyone I actually knew. I shared a strap with a man I'd seen once or twice before in the train going home. We exchanged grins and he said 'Bloody awful crush', and I agreed."

"When you returned to the flat after midnight was the side-door closed?"

"Yes, I'm quite sure it was."

"And was the lift up or down?"

"Down."

"Was your suitcase where you left it?"

"It was in the flat. Minnie must have taken it in. I was picking it up when I saw a light in the sitting-room and thought my aunt must have returned. But there was no-one there, and, when I'd closed the window and switched off the TV, I was—well, I went to bed."

"But not immediately." The momentary hesitation had not escaped the Inspector.

"Almost at once." Seconds passed during which he was clearly endeavouring to make up his mind. "The 'phone rang. Someone asked for my uncle, and I said he'd gone away for the weekend."

"Did the caller give a name?"

"No."

"Or leave any message?"

"None."

The Inspector smiled. "You're not very forthcoming, Mr Antrim. Was it a woman who rang?"

"Yes, but I've no idea who she was."

"I think you have. You didn't mention this call to Sergeant Cheam, did you?"

"It had nothing to do with my uncle's death, so there was no need to tell him."

"Not when it was thought that your uncle died by accident," the Inspector agreed. "But now that we're looking into other possibilities you must tell me everything. Last night you evaded a question I asked you. Was it because you did not wish to say you had found out that your uncle had a mistress?"

Keith nodded, then said, "I didn't actually know for certain."

"But you were fairly sure—and, if your aunt didn't already know, you wanted her to remain in ignorance."

"I'm sure she knows nothing at the moment."

"But you had some knowledge which this telephone call confirmed?"

"I knew my uncle had booked a double room at an hotel for the weekend. There was a card in the post on Saturday confirming it. I tore it up before anyone else could see it." Keith waited for comment. "You may think I was jumping to conclusions."

"Had you ever previously suspected that he had a mistress?"

"It just hadn't occurred to me."

"Have you any idea who it might be?"

"None at all. I didn't recognize the voice."

"Would you know it if you heard it again?"

"I think I might. But surely it can't matter who she is? She couldn't have had anything to do with his death. She didn't know he was dead."

"Can you be sure of that? Suppose the purpose of her call was to establish in your mind ignorance of his death. Suppose she had been in the flat earlier in the evening—and that it was she whom your aunt heard coughing. We must talk to this lady." The soft violet eyes were on Keith's face. "You must help me by finding her."

"But how can I possibly find someone about whom we know nothing at all?" Keith was taken aback by the sudden assignment.

"We know that the woman who telephoned exists. If you are right in thinking that she was your uncle's mistress, then

85

she can be found. He may have taken every possible precaution against discovery—but even the Invisible Man could not help leaving footprints." The Inspector rose. "Perhaps when I see you next you will be able to give me the answer to this question—and to others." He gestured goodbye and was gone. Crossing the main hall, he was thinking of the casually made statement by which Keith had destroyed his own alibi. He was going down the steps when the sound of running feet caught up with him and Keith drew level. "I've remembered something to tell you," he said, "and I've never thanked you for giving up your holiday to help my aunt and me. Please will you have lunch with me?"

"I should have been delighted. . . ." The Inspector was about to say that he had a previous engagement when he saw the small red car turn into the courtyard. "But I fear my chauffeur has turned up."

"He can have lunch in the staff canteen, if—" Keith stopped short as Anthea waved a gay hand. "I mean wouldn't she—perhaps like to join us?"

"Let us ask her," the Inspector proposed.

"I'd love to," was Anthea's reply, "if I may leave the car here." She indicated the "Management Cars Only" sign painted on the concrete.

Modestly Keith said that he thought he might be regarded as junior management. "It's something I haven't really considered before," he confessed. "I haven't got a car." He was wondering why such an attractive girl should have chosen to become a police driver. The Inspector interpreted his expression. "She is my host's niece, Mr Antrim, and she's helping me with the inquiry. You may speak as frankly to her as to me."

While they ordered and ate their lunch he sat back and listened to them as they chatted, discovering mutual friends and acquaintances. It was some time later that he reminded Keith of the point he had mentioned.

"It was when I brought along my suitcase and rang to bring

the lift down," Keith told them. "I remember thinking that someone must only just have taken it up as the cables were still vibrating."

"Mightn't passing traffic start a vibration, or could it have been a draught from the side entrance?" Anthea asked.

"I suppose so. I just thought I ought to mention it." He looked at the Inspector, who nodded, then asked if Keith was quite sure he had put his suitcase under the seat.

"Yes, it wouldn't be in anyone's way there, and it just fitted nicely into the space."

"Is the case identifiable as yours?"

"There's a label on the handle with my name and address. At least it was there when I lent the case to Uncle Bertie last Monday. He said he needed a large suitcase to take away some clothes and asked if he could borrow mine. He promised to let me have it back quickly, but I think he's forgotten about it."

Waiting until the others were eating the pudding which he had declined, the Inspector said, "You must forgive me if I leave you in a minute or so." He offered no explanation, but it was clear to Anthea that he wished to leave them alone. Was it, she wondered, because they were getting on so well together, or because he thought that she might learn something that Keith had not told him? "Don't you want me to drive you somewhere?" she asked.

"Not at present, thank you. I shall be in this neighbourhood for most of the afternoon."

"Then I'll be outside the office at five," said Anthea, "and if you've gone on somewhere you can leave a message with the commissionaire, and I'll come and pick you up."

"Let's have some coffee and talk about something else," Keith suggested when they were alone.

"Black or white?" asked the waitress, who, her other customers having departed, had been hovering near their table.

"Black," they both answered.

Despite his intention Keith found himself talking about the assignment he had been given. "If my uncle had a mistress I'm quite sure Aunt Netta didn't know—and I hope she never will. I don't really want to find this woman, and, even if I did, I haven't the slightest idea where to start."

"We must find her. Even if she herself can't tell us anything she could be a reason for someone else to want your uncle out of the way. Look, Keith"—she leaned across the table, unaware that the waitress had returned, and unthinkingly put a hand on his wrist—"you can't have a mistress without somebody knowing. I can see that you don't want your aunt to find out, but—"

"If he's not the marrying sort," said the waitress, putting the coffee cups on the table, "I'd give him up, dear. A girl with your looks won't have no difficulty in finding Mr Right. You don't mind me giving you a bit of advice, do you, seeing as I'm old enough to be your mum?" She turned a cold eye on a now fiercely blushing Keith and went off with an expressive shrug of her plump shoulders.

The lunch-time crowds were thinning as the Inspector walked back to Termini House. From restaurant and café basements came the sounds of crockery and cutlery being washed and stacked. From swinging pub doors men stepped into the street exchanging well-worn witticisms, their voices louder and more confident than they had been an hour earlier. Along Euston Road the traffic proceeded jerk by jerk, emitting the malodorous fumes of part-burnt oil and petrol. At request stops queues lengthened while bus-drivers sailed past with averted gaze.

Reaching Termini House, the Inspector took a diagonal path across the courtyard to the side entrance and entered the main building by the Staff Door. On his left a row of closed doors carried the names of those whose seniority entitled them to a private office or to a share in one. On his right stood a solitary unoccupied desk. Past the desk a vast space, open to the passageway, housed the typing pool. Heads blonde, brunette, and greying bent over keyboards. Unnoticed, the Inspector came into the main hall and, turning right, passed Keith's office and knocked on the adjoining door.

Miss Purslane's room looked as if she had been searching for something and finally acknowledged defeat. The drawers of the stack of filing cabinets were all partly open and the three chairs piled with papers and folders. She turned inquiringly as the Inspector knocked and came in, smoothing her hair with dusty fingers.

"You seem to have unleashed Niagara," he said with a smile, introducing himself.

"Mr Wolfe's moving into the Managing Director's room tomorrow," she told him, "and his secretary's coming in here with me. I'm getting everything into apple-pie order so that she can take over as easily as possible."

He looked at the neat-featured face, the neat short-nailed fingers, the neat blouse and skirt, and knew that he would get direct answers to his questions.

"Mr Antrim mentioned that you might be coming to see me," she said on a note of query. "I suppose it's something to do with Mr Corsair's death."

"There are one or two points to be cleared up, and I think you may be able to help me." He took a piece of paper from his pocket. "But, first, would you do me a favour? Could you find a messenger who would buy something for me at the chemist's?"

"Certainly." She looked at the paper, then picked up the telephone. While she spoke he put some money on the desk. Soon the messenger had come and gone, and the Inspector was helping her to clear two chairs. "I really am sorry to have to trouble you with questions," he apologized. "This must be a trying time for you. I understand that you were very happy working with Mr Corsair." The warmth of his voice, more than the words, conveyed his sympathy.

"I was. He was an easy man to work for—if you didn't make stupid mistakes. He was tidy and careful and never wasted time, his own or others'. He worked to a timetable and hated interruptions. I wouldn't call him a very considerate man—but he never asked for the impossible."

"Did you ever do small personal services for him—answering private letters or paying accounts?"

"An occasional letter, yes, but never any accounts unless they were chargeable to the Company."

"Did he seem much as usual last Friday?"

"He was perfectly normal. There was a great deal of work to be got through before he went off for the weekend, and he had to finish it by a quarter-past four to attend a City meeting."

"Would you go through his day so far as you know it—appointments, the people who came to see him, anything else you can remember."

She opened a desk diary. "This is better than my memory. He came in as usual on the dot of nine, read through the letters I'd put on his desk, dictated replies, and asked me to obtain birth certificates for his wife and himself. He intended to discuss life assurance on Monday. When Mr Antrim came in he was talking on the telephone to his solicitor. Mr. Antrim stayed a few minutes. Then Mr Corsair read various reports and dictated the rest of his letters before going out to lunch."

"Do you know what he spoke about to his solicitor?"

"I heard him mention adding a codicil to his will. He'd asked me two days before to let him have the copy that was kept in his private safe."

"Do you know if he took it out of the office?"

"He put it in his brief-case on Wednesday. I saw it on his desk on Friday morning and again during the afternoon, when he returned it to the case with some other papers."

"Did he take the brief-case with him to the City meeting?"

"Yes." She referred to the desk diary. "He was back from lunch a little later than usual. Mr Antrim had been waiting in his office for about ten minutes. We were both with him when Colonel Summersby rang. Then he saw a Mr Livings who had an appointment." Meticulously she went through the rest of the afternoon until Corsair's departure at four-fifteen. "That," she continued evenly, "was the last time I saw him. I remember hoping that he wasn't going to work too hard over the weekend on the papers he'd taken, as I knew he was tired."

"Do you mean he'd mentioned being tired?"

"No, but he'd shown it in small ways. There was a moment when he snapped at Mr Antrim, and just before that he'd been rather impatient with Colonel Summersby."

"Do you know what Colonel Summersby telephoned him about?"

"It was a personal matter." The neat features tightened.

"Miss Purslane," the Inspector said gently, "death is a personal matter, and an investigation concerned with death cannot but invade privacy. If you don't wish to tell me I shall have to ask Colonel Summersby. But before you reply I would like to ask you another question. Has anyone hinted, either to you or to your knowledge, that Mr Corsair's death may not have been an accident?"

For a time she was silent, then she said, "Yes, there has been some office gossip, but I am not going to mention any names."

He nodded. "You know then why I am making these inquiries. If a rumour has no basis in fact it must be scotched. What Colonel Summersby said to Mr Corsair is probably unimportant; but so long as I do not know what it was I cannot dismiss it. Anything said or done that day might help to explain Mr Corsair's actions when he returned home. Was he looking out of the window because he expected someone? Was he watching somebody going away? Had he some problem on his mind that made him careless?" He noted the shadow of indecision on her face. "Did Colonel Summersby wish Mr Corsair to do something illegal or discreditable?"

"No, of course not." She relaxed. "I think he was asking for a loan—I'm sure he was."

"And what did Mr Corsair say?"

"That he'd let him have it."

"At once?"

"He asked him to look in on Monday evening."

"When Mr Corsair left on Friday afternoon, were you here until the office closed?"

"Yes, until five or a little later."

"Did anyone come in the hope of seeing him?"

"No-one."

"Or telephone?"

"No-one asked to speak to him. Mr Killigrew rang shortly before five about a report that he wished him to read over the weekend. I told him that although Mr Corsair had left the office he would not be leaving home until seven o'clock, and I suggested that he send it up to the flat before that time."

"Did Mr Killigrew say why it was so urgent that Mr Corsair had this report before Monday?"

"No." Miss Purslane hesitated almost imperceptibly before her instinct for the truth prevailed. "He didn't have to." Somewhat shamefacedly she told of the information she had passed on to Miss Brind and her reason for doing so. She had just completed her confession when the messenger-boy returned with a small packet and some change, which she passed over to the Inspector.

Thanking her, he went on: "When Mr Corsair went away on his weekend trips, did you usually make an hotel booking for him?"

"Until about two years ago. Since then I think he stayed with whomever he was going to discuss business. His expense slips were only for car mileage and the cost of entertainment."

"Then you had no idea of where he'd been?"

"Sometimes I knew from the bill-heads. I can't remember

him actually telling me where he'd been. He seldom spoke of anything but the business in hand."

"Have you ever been to his flat upstairs?"

"Once some years ago when he was in bed with a cold and I took up some letters for signature."

"Is that the only time?"

"Yes."

"Have you not been there this week?"

"Oh, I thought you meant while he was alive. I went on Monday to see Mrs Corsair and express sympathy—and to ask if she would like any help in replying to the letters of condolence."

Apologizing again for taking up her time, the Inspector rose. At the doorway he turned. She was looking out of the window at the metal sculpture in the patio. In a day or two, he thought as he went out and closed the door quietly, another neat and competent woman will be sitting at that desk, guarding her employer against interruption and petty anxieties. Miss Purslane must be worried about her future. When a managing director dies his secretary's chair is pulled from under her. A lesser job may be offered which pride urges her to decline. But pride is a luxury which a working woman approaching her fiftieth year cannot afford.

Julian lay back in his chair, gazing at the office ceiling, idly wondering when one of the office cleaners would notice and remove the cobweb which had been hanging in the corner for at least three months. Now that the uncertainty of the days following Corsair's death had been resolved he felt at peace with the world. Half an hour ago he had been summoned to the Managing Director's room.

"I've read the report you wrote last week," Wolfe had said. "You made a good case for your paper." His hand moved towards a sheet of typed figures. "Did you know that Caddis had put in a memorandum to Mr Corsair at the same time?"

Steadily Julian looked into the assessing grey eyes. He had met Wolfe only once some six months ago and knew little about him except that he was a shrewd businessman. If he had not been he would not have been Corsair's deputy. But, on coming into the room, Julian had noticed among the financial journals neatly laid out on a side-table copies of the *Spectator* and the *Times Literary Supplement*. These suggested that Wolfe, unlike Corsair, was not a literary barbarian. He made up his mind to be frank. "I heard about it," he said, "and wrote my report at once. It would have been stupid to let my case go by default."

"You were afraid that Corsair would decide to close down the *Bookman's Weekly*?"

"I feared he might. But I think now that I allowed myself to be panicked unnecessarily."

"Perhaps." Wolfe smiled. "Well, I won't keep you on the rack any longer. I like the way you run your paper. It's the only weekly of its kind now left, and it would be more than a pity if it were to die. The days of private patronage are over, but if this Company can afford to subsidize art forms of that sort"—he pointed with a grimace to the metal rhomboid outside the window—"it can certainly afford a small gesture in defence of literature. I've had a word with our advertisement department, and I think you'll find they'll be putting something your way that'll help to balance your books." He picked up the sheet of paper, tore it across, and dropped the pieces into a waste-paper basket. "Any questions?"

"None, sir." Julian did not attempt to conceal his relief. "Just thank you."

"That's all, then." Wolfe rose. "You'll be putting a short obituary of Corsair in the next issue."

"Yes, of course," said Julian, to whom the idea had not previously occurred.

"Miss Purslane can give you all the facts. And you'd better check with Mrs Corsair. She may give you some personal details that will help to fill it out." He held out his hand. "If you've got any problems, come and talk about them. Otherwise I shan't interfere."

On the way into his office Julian stopped to give Miss Brind the news. A little later he heard through the closed doors her prattling delight as she relayed the information to Miss Purslane over the telephone. "If Mr Corsair were alive," she was saying, "I'm sure he'd have closed down the paper. You might say his death was a blessing in disguise." That Miss Purslane did not entirely share her feelings about the workings of Providence became evident a moment later. "Of course I know how you've suffered, dear," Miss Brind said quickly. "But, as I always say, there's two sides to every penny, aren't there?" An offended gasp suggested that Miss Purslane had hung up her receiver. Julian's lips twitched as he returned to contemplation of the cover for the coming Christmas issue.

The design submitted by the artist was in traditional style. It was certain to give no offence to the paper's older readers, who, Julian readily allowed, were in the majority. But most of those readers would continue to buy the paper until they or it departed this life. It was essential to attract new buyers, and the younger they were the better. A good cover should not be lost among the bright, brash pictures of the dozens of pop and teenage magazines. It should have what an advertising accounts man had described to Julian as "psychedelic appeal". When Julian asked the meaning of the adjective he raised his eyebrows and said that he thought everyone knew it meant "consciousness expanding". Did, Julian wondered silently, all those violently coloured dress materials and paper bags really increase one's consciousness—and, if so, was that sort of consciousness in need of expansion? He was idly considering the impact of a multi-coloured Albert Hall when Miss Brind knocked and came in, her face alight with excitement. She had been waiting for this moment ever since learning on her gossip network that a police inspector was in the building. It had been a considerable disappointment to her that, instead of asking any of the questions to which she had prepared exhaustive replies, he had politely inquired if Mr Killigrew were in his office. She sat at her typing desk, her open mouth indicating a considerable degree of deflation.

"I'm sure there are a great many things you could tell me, Miss Brind," he said with a smile that charmed her, "and I shall rely on your help when I need it. Perhaps you will ask Mr Killigrew if he can see me now."

The papers on Julian's desk fluttered at her entry. "That policeman wants to see you," she said in a quivering whisper.

"Then show him in, Miss Brind. I don't suppose he's after either of us. You haven't been planting any bombs in Embassies, have you?"

"Oh, Mr Killigrew, of course I haven't." She gave a giggle, hovered as if there were something she thought of saying, then went out.

Julian was standing when the Inspector came in. He shook his hand firmly and asked him to sit down. "I've been expecting you to look in—and so," he said with a smile, "has my secretary. How can I help you?"

"I don't know that you can, but I hope so. You were actually here in your office, I understand, when Mr Corsair fell."

"Yes, I was, but I didn't know about it until the next day. An unpleasant accident, but a mercifully quick death." He waited for the other man to speak, then said on a note of question, "I'm afraid I can't add to what you already know."

"Perhaps you wouldn't mind running through the facts again." The Inspector sketched apology. "It sometimes helps one to recall something one may have forgotten."

"There isn't much to remember. I was writing a report which I wanted to get to Corsair before he went off for the weekend." Succinctly he gave the details which the Inspector had already been given by Miss Purslane. "I packed Miss Brind off home at five. I don't think she'll ever forgive me for depriving her of the opportunity of being—how shall I put

96

it?—in at the death. It must have been nearly six when I finished redrafting the report for the Xth time, read it through, decided I couldn't make any improvement, and began to type it up with a couple of carbons. By the time I'd finished and made out an envelope it wasn't far off six-thirty, and I was getting a bit nervous about missing Corsair. I packed up quickly and dashed down to the hall to find that Lennie had a table up against the inner doors with some boxes on it. I asked him to let me out smartly as I wanted to catch Corsair. He said I needn't worry as Corsair hadn't left. I gave him a hand with the table, and he saw me out. Then I went round to the side entrance, found the door open, and propped the report on the letter-box by the lift where Corsair couldn't fail to see it when he came down." Julian picked up a cigarette packet and put it down as the Inspector made a declining gesture. "Well, that was a weight off my mind. I had a drink at a pub on the way home, washed, changed, and went out to have supper with some friends. I think that's the lot—unless you have any questions."

"There are always questions." The Inspector's tone held regret. "The first one in my mind is, if Corsair's death was not accidental—though it may well have been—was there something in the man himself that invited a violent end? If so, what was it? I've been able to form some sort of picture from what other people have told me. I'd be grateful for anything you can add."

Julian gave his swivel chair a quarter-turn and stretched out his long legs parallel to the desk. "Practically nothing, I'm afraid. I know it sounds unlikely, but I've really only spoken to him once." He described with wry humour the interview at which Corsair had given the paper a year's grace. "I suppose since then we've passed each other in the building some six or seven times, and we shook hands at the office party. Each time he acknowledged my winning smile by a distant nod as if my face was unfamiliar and not particularly prepossessing. From that one interview, and from what I've been told here and there, I judged him to be a pretty cold fish unlikely to bring a note of gaiety to any gathering. But for reasons why anybody might wish to kill him you'll have to ask those who knew him a great deal better than I did."

"Then let us return to last Friday." The Inspector walked over to the open window. Below him and a little to the left the coachwork of the Humber shone richly in the October sunlight. "Corsair must have fallen past this window," he said abruptly.

"Yes. If I hadn't been sitting here with my back to the window I suppose I should have seen him falling. But even if I had it would have been too late to save his life, though perhaps I could have saved him that undignified ride in a dirty farm lorry." Julian made a gesture of distaste. "I don't remember hearing the lorry go off, but one becomes deaf to traffic noises in London." He passed a hand over his head. "You know, I've thought several times since then that if I'd finished that report a little earlier and taken it up to the flat I might have prevented whatever happened from happening."

"Then you had considered delivering it personally?"

"Yes, but I decided against it. I felt he couldn't fail to put two and two together if I turned up hotfoot and pressed the report into his hand. Then poor Miss Purslane would have been in trouble. Again, Corsair was going off within the next half-hour—and when a man's on the wing and checking that he's got his toothbrush, enough money, a change of socks and so forth, he doesn't welcome a last-minute interruption. But when he goes out and sees a letter on his post-box he's going to look at it and, if it's for him, shove it in his pocket."

"And not put two and two together when he finds what it contains?" the Inspector queried.

"Not, I think, when he reads that I'd consulted the Chief Accountant a week earlier about the relevant figures. A slight anticipation of the truth, but"—Julian shrugged—"a pardonable protective measure."

The Inspector agreed. "Do you think it is possible that

there was someone else in the office part of the building as well as yourself and Lennie?" he asked.

"I suppose it's possible." Julian was dubious. "I didn't hear anyone and, when I left, I didn't notice any lights except those on the ground floor."

"Have you ever been up to the top floor, Mr Killigrew—I mean the one immediately above this?"

"I don't think I have. I know the directors' luncheon-room is up there, but no-one has ever asked me to join them for lunch. I'm pretty low down in the pecking order here. I don't rate a carpet; just lino and a second-hand rug."

"Perhaps you were away when the last office fire practice was held?"

"No, I was here. I remember it was damned windy up on the roof. Yes"—he smiled—"you've caught me out in a misstatement there. We trooped up, a dozen at a time, to the floor above and took a staircase up to the roof. It all seemed a bit pointless because no-one told us how we were to get down to terra firma—or, if they did, I was too cold to take it in. The others had had the sense to put coats on. I, like an idiot, hadn't thought of doing so." Momentarily Julian hesitated. "I don't want to pry unduly, but am I right in thinking that you've an idea that someone could have got into Corsair's flat from the staircase? H'm, it's an interesting thought. I suppose I realized without actually knowing it that the door on the half-way landing could lead nowhere except into the flat. Come to think of it, I suppose it's their emergency exit on to the roof. I assume it's kept locked; but someone might have got hold of a key or even picked the lock with the traditional piece of bent wire." He laughed. "You know, I've often thought of trying out that wire trick. Is it really feasible?"

"I imagine it needs practice," the Inspector said drily.

"Quite a lot, I should say. But to get back to the subject, if you're investigating the possibility that someone helped Corsair out of the window I'd think there's quite a large field of folk who didn't much care for him. He had enormous business ability, but his methods were sometimes rather unconventional—or so I'm told. Mind you, that's true of other tycoons, but it means that you wouldn't have to look far to find one or two men with some sort of grudge against him. You might find something in his private life, but I can't help you there. I believe he dodged the column during the War and made a small fortune. I don't know in what—I was out of the country."

"You were in the Army? I should have said you were too young, Mr Killigrew."

"That's because I use Y's face cream twice a day." Julian's eyes twinkled. "Yes, I was in the War—doing a bit of this and that. I had a licence to kill if that's what's in your mind. I shed blood because I had to, and I learned one thing—that a man with blood on his hands can't afford to hesitate at the prospect of having to make them bloodier. I lost some too—and had a pint or two pumped into me. I remember a nurse saying when I got a bit fresh with her that, if blood could tell, mine would tell me a thing or two." He smiled at some memory. "But you didn't come here to listen to the reminiscences of an old sweat. Let's get on with the inquisition."

"I've no more questions at the moment," the Inspector said.

"If you think of any I'm usually here. If I'm not here Miss Brind will know where I am, what time I'll be back—and probably what I'm doing at that actual moment." Half-way to the door Julian added, "She's a reliable secretary, but there are times when I could put her over my knee and smack her."

The Inspector walked thoughtfully along the passage. While he waited for the lift he felt a growing conviction that Julian had been concealing something behind an arras of words.

His next step was to repair what seemed to him a discourtesy by a visit to the new Managing Director. To him he apologized for taking up the time of members of the staff.

"There's no need to apologize for doing your job, Inspector," Wolfe said friendlily. "You've got the run of the building, and if I can give you any help it's yours, though I'm very sorry to learn that there are any doubts about Corsair's death. To prevent you wasting time by looking in the wrong direction, let me assure you that the affairs of this Company are in perfect order. Corsair was in his own way a man of genius. At times he played rough—a little too rough for my taste. Outside business we had little in common. My personal interests are music and literature; his principal interest, his only one so far as I know, was commerce."

"I understand that he was often away on business at weekends. I assume he will have discussed these visits with you beforehand and afterwards."

Wolfe chuckled. "You don't really assume it—and you're perfectly right not to. I haven't the slightest idea where he went or why. Certainly I've sometimes wondered, but I never raised the subject with Corsair. One puts one's own interpretation on matters of that kind—and very possibly your interpretation is the same as mine. But I'm not saying I'm right. All the psychologists in the world cannot assess a man with absolute certainty that they have assessed him completely, because to each of them he will have shown a different set of facets. You have probably arrived at some opinion of Corsair's character, and I have given you mine—or rather mine in part. For he had a side of which very few people know. He was a generous supporter of Boys' Clubs, both financially and with his own time. Several members of the staff here and at the factories are boys he met at these clubs. If they prove to be lazy they go; but if they're prepared to work hard they can get to the top."

When, some time later, the Inspector rose to go he had learned a little more about the dead man, though nothing, he felt, that would help him to solve the problem of how he had died. He had nearly reached the hall when a girl carrying a folded hand-towel ran past and disappeared into a cloakroom. Almost at once a woman, similarly armed, emerged from the same door. A glance at his watch disclosed that it was nearing five o'clock. Going through the hall, he came into the courtyard to see the small red car parked beside the Humber. Propped against a spoke of the steering-wheel was a piece of paper on which Anthea had scribbled, "Have gone up to flat. Please wait for me."

Chapter Nine

FOR a short time the Inspector stood at the back of the hall watching the homeward exodus. Girls, laughing and chattering, clattered down the stairs and emerged from the lifts. Some turned left to use the Staff Door and go through the side entrance down the alleyway to the next street. Others swept across the hall to the main doors. A few waited to be joined by smiling young men who tucked arm into arm and bore the beloved of the moment out for whatever entertainment could be afforded on a Wednesday night. A little later came the older staff: the brief-cased men preparing to face the rush-hour chaos, to buy an evening paper, to snatch, if they were lucky, a seat in bus or train; the women to family kitchens or—the Inspector took in the overbright faces and the lines of disappointment—to the friendless silence of bed-sitters or one-room flatlets.

At the main doorway the commissionaire stood in an attitude of relaxed attention. His expression, perfected over the years, combined parade-ground severity with watchfulness for the passage of the more important members of the Company's staff. Every now and then the gloved hand rose and the waxed moustaches quivered as he responded to a "Goodnight, Sergeant". As the minute hand of the clock jerked to ten past the hour stillness fell on the building. Stiffly the commissionaire strode to his glass-sided cubicle, drew off his gloves, and, removing his cap, passed a podgy hand along the red line which the pressure of the leather lining-band had left on his forehead. He was taking keys from a trouser pocket when he heard footsteps and turned.

"Has Mr Antrim left?" the Inspector asked.

"Yes, sir. He came into the hall about ten to five and went to speak to somebody outside. He didn't come in again that I saw."

"Have you a few minutes to spare?"

"Certainly, sir. I shan't be leaving yet awhile. I have to see that everything's in order before I hand over the keys to Lennie—that's the night caretaker."

"What keys are those?"

"The main doors, the Staff Door, and this cupboard." He pointed to a glass-fronted cupboard in which rows of labelled keys hung on brass hooks. "There's a duplicate key there for every lock in the building—except, of course, the flat on top."

"You have a key to the Emergency Door in the flat, I believe."

"Yes, sir, the one on the left of the bottom row. That's to comply with regulations. Mr Corsair took charge of the rest of the keys when he moved into the flat."

"Is this cupboard always kept locked?"

"Always, as I told the Sergeant. I doubt if it's opened more than once or twice a year—that's when someone's lost a key or left it at home. If a key's been lost I send to the bank down at the corner for the other set of duplicates that's kept in their strong-room and have a new key cut."

"How many keys are there to this cupboard?"

"Just the two. One in the bank and the other—this one"—he held out a hand—"which I hand over to Lennie when I go off duty."

"When you leave, what is the routine for ensuring that the building is secured?"

"I set the locks on the main doors and the inner ones. It'll be simplest, sir, if I show you." Leading the way, he pulled forward one of the outer doors and, turning a knob at the side of the lock, released the door, which swung shut with a metallic clang. "Now you can open only from the inside unless you have a key." At the inner doors he went through the same actions. "It's the same with these doors."

"Can anyone working late let themselves out of the building?"

"They could do—but Lennie's here to open and close the inner doors. Whoever's going out can't open the main doors until the inner ones have shut and closed a circuit. It's as safe as the Bank of England, maybe safer."

"Provided the Staff Door is closed," the Inspector observed casually.

"I lock that sharp at five-fifteen, and then I'm off home." He looked up at the clock. "I'd better do it now, sir, if you don't mind coming along with me." A moment later, as he closed the metal door and turned the key, he said, "This stays shut till seven in the morning, when Lennie opens it to let the cleaners in. The main doors aren't opened till I get along at a quarter to nine. That goes for Monday to Friday. Weekends Lennie's here on his own. He's got a place downstairs where he can have a kip, and the canteen people leave grub that he can hot up when he wants." As they returned to the main hall he commented, "Must be a lonely sort of job, not one I'd fancy for meself. But it suits Lennie. He likes his own company and he can get on with his hobby."

"Does no-one ever come into the office on Saturday morning?" the Inspector inquired.

"Not these days. It's a five-day week for everyone, and Mr Corsair wouldn't have any overtime. They could take work home if they wanted to, but he wasn't going to pay 'em for it."

"He was a hard task-master, then?"

"I've heard some say he was, sir." The commissionaire was not going to be drawn. "If he was paying a man for a job he expected it to be done. He didn't stand no nonsense. I reckon we could do with a few more of his kind today." He stayed briefly silent. "Funny thing. He said to me only last week when one of the staff got knocked about in a car crash, he said, 'You know, Sergeant, most accidents are the result of not thinking ahead. I've never had one.' He had a good conceit of himself, Mr Corsair had, but I reckon he wasn't far wrong there." He cocked a red-veined eye at the Inspector. "When I heard he'd let himself fall out of a window I couldn't believe it."

"And what did you believe, Sergeant?"

The veined eyes assumed blankness. "Well, I had to believe what happened, didn't I?" Baffled in an attempt to elicit the reason for a renewal of inquiries into his late employer's death, the commissionaire retired behind his uniform. "If you don't want me any more, sir, I'll be off in a minute. Here's Lennie. I expect you'll want a word with him."

The elderly man who had just come up the stairs by the lift-shaft carried a stout cardboard carton and a dimpled whisky bottle. He did not immediately notice the grey-suited stranger who was largely hidden by the commissionaire's substantial bulk and, putting the things on a table, came over with outstretched hand. "I'll take the keys, Wilf, and you can be off home." Then, observing the Inspector, he came to a halt.

"Gent here wants a word with you." The commissionaire took a step forward and dropped the keys into Lennie's hand. "Rozzer," he mouthed, then aloud, "I'll just get my coat and you can let me out." He turned to the Inspector. "If there's anything else you want to ask, sir, I'll be here in the morning." In a minute's time the glass doors closed with a double clang behind him and he was marching across the courtyard. There was purpose in his stride, the purpose of a man to whom a couple of pints of beer were a necessary emollient after a wearing day.

Lennie looked sourly at the Inspector. "Thought we'd seen the last of you lot round here," he said. "If it's about Mr Corsair falling out of the window I've told all I know—and that's nothing."

"You saw him shortly before he died," the Inspector said evenly.

"So what?"

"Did he seem worried or unwell or anything outside the normal?"

"He looked all right to me." Lennie said shortly. His voice rose a tone. "It's no use you asking questions. I don't know nothing what happened."

He may know nothing about Corsair's death, the Inspector said to himself, but there's something he doesn't wish me to know. He's heard the rumours that are going round, and he's afraid. "You were probably the last person to speak to him before he went up to the flat."

"Maybe I was." Lennie's tone was belligerent. "Maybe I wasn't. I don't suppose I was the only one around the place."

"You mean he could have met someone after he left you?"

"Well, he could, couldn't he? He came in to pick up some papers. Maybe he was going to pass them on to someone else."

"What did he actually say to you?"

"Not much. He wasn't one to waste words. I saw him crossing the yard, and he signed that he wanted to come in by the Staff Door. Of course it was against the rules to let anyone in after hours, but you can't say no to the boss. He didn't even say a thank-you—just marched into his office. When he came back he was putting some papers into his brief-case. I let him out the way he came in, and that's the last I saw of him."

"How long was he in his office?"

"Not much more than a couple of minutes."

"And when he'd gone you returned here—to the hall?"

"I went to the lav first, then back here. You want me to tell you everything I did for the rest of the night?"

The Inspector ignored the sarcasm in Lennie's voice. "It may save my having to ask you later," he said pleasantly.

"Well, I got on with my work until Mr Killigrew came tearing down. He wanted to get something to Mr Corsair before he left. 'What's the exact time?' he asked, and I told him it was just short of six-thirty by the clock and he needn't get all het up because Mr Corsair hadn't gone off."

"You meant that you hadn't seen him go?"

"I knew he hadn't as his car was still outside."

"Then you knew he was taking the car?"

"I'd seen Minnie earlier on and she'd said so."

"Was Mr Killigrew the only person working late that night?"

"There was someone went off while I was in the lav after Mr Corsair'd left. I heard the doors shut themselves."

"Could anyone have left later without your knowledge?"

"No." Lennie shook his head with slow certainty. "I'd have known even if I was somewhere else in the building. I put my work-table up against the inner doors soon as I got back here. I always have it there. The light's good, and I can see if there's anything going on outside. If anyone went out they'd have to shift the table and they wouldn't be able to put it back in the same place as the doors open inwards. Give me a hand and I'll show you."

Together they placed the table against the inner glass doors. No further proof was needed to show that Lennie's statement was unassailable. Seeing the Inspector glance at the whisky bottle, Lennie grinned. "It's empty," he said.

"But it would not be here unless you had a purpose for it." The Inspector waited, then smiled. "You're not going to tell me what the purpose is?"

"Give you a couple of guesses. A copper shouldn't need more."

"Perhaps not." A glance at the carton, at Lennie's hands, at the threaded needle in the lapel of his jacket. "Am I right in thinking that you're making a model ship to put in the bottle?"

"Well, I'm jiggered." Astonishment puckered the

weathered face and a roughened hand went out to the carton. In a moment he was carefully taking out a miniature sailing vessel. The graceful hull was perfect to the last detail, the masts lay flush with the deck, sails neatly furled. From various points of masts and rigging double threads passed over the stern, the loose ends being secured in a neat knot. The Inspector examined it with patent admiration. "A gaff schooner, I think," he said.

"Fancy you knowing that." Lennie was surprised and pleased. Setting the model down, he began gently to pull on the threads. The masts rose, the sails began to unfurl. "That's what it'll be when it's in the bottle. I've got to make a bit of sea—plaster of paris and a touch of the paint-brush—and then the job's done."

"You make these for your own pleasure?" the Inspector asked.

"I sell 'em. I've got orders that'll keep me going for a year and more."

"I see. I. . . ." The Inspector left his thoughts unsaid. "Were you working on this ship last Friday?"

"I was rigging it. Bit of a fiddling job. Takes time and patience."

"So you couldn't pay much attention to whatever was happening outside?"

"Not after Mr Killigrew left. Mrs Corsair went out of the yard while we were talking. Then he went off and I got down to work. There was one or two went by later—there's always someone using the alley to the next street. I heard 'em go by but I didn't see any of 'em."

"Would you know from the sound if they were men or women?"

"Some of each. There was a chap with a walking-stick after Mr Killigrew went and a woman running at maybe eight o'clock. I reckon it was the same woman as came back two or three minutes after. There was a copper, too. You can always tell a copper. Flat feet and two miles an hour." Lennie chuckled and pulled a chair forward. "Like to sit down if you're not going straight off?"

The Inspector took the proffered chair. "How long have you worked here?" he asked.

"Coming up for five years now."

"Then you knew Mr Corsair quite well?"

"Didn't hardly know him at all. He wasn't one to take notice of the likes of me. Maybe he'd say good night if I was in the hall when he left. Maybe he wouldn't. Toffee-nosed he was and a proper stickler for the rules. Gave the sergeant a ticking-off one night for having too many lights in the hall after the staff had gone. I thought he was going to pick on me too, so I made myself scarce."

"Do you make a round of the building during the night?" the Inspector asked.

"No, I'm supposed to stay on this floor—and I do except for when I go downstairs to get my grub."

"You must get some sleep, surely?"

"Not at night I don't. Weekdays I get down as soon as I get home—I've got a room near by. Weekends I have a kip in the mornings down below. I don't need more than four or five hours."

"And if someone wants to get into the building while you're asleep?"

"They haven't yet, and they wouldn't get in if I was by myself—except it was the boss," Lennie remembered to add.

"Have you ever had to take a key from the cupboard in the commissionaire's cubicle?"

"No-one's ever asked me to, and I've had no call to want one." Lennie put an elbow on the table and looked hard at the Inspector. "I'm not so blind I can't see what you're driving at," he said, with a slight return of his earlier sourness. "Maybe it's just the tittle-tattle that's been going round, but seems to me that something's come along to make you think Corsair was knocked off, and you've got a notion that someone could have got himself into the flat by this Emergency

Door. Well, they could if they had the key, but they'd have to nick it and get it back without Wilf or me knowing. Mind you, I'm not saying that there wasn't no-one else in the building on Friday except me and Mr Killigrew. A bloke could lie up in one of the offices without me being any the wiser. But he couldn't get out of the place without shifting my table."

"Unless he stayed until Monday and just walked out."

Lennie grinned. "Brought his razor and grub for a couple of days?"

"If he'd planned it, yes. Alternatively he could have left the flat by the front door when the coast was clear."

"If you ask me that's the way he'd have gone in too," Lennie said positively. "What's put you on to this Emergency Door?"

"You think I needn't consider it?"

"I'd forget it if I were you. I doubt there's many that know about it, and most of them won't know there's a key down here. I'd forgotten myself until you put the thought into my head. Don't think I've been up those stairs more than once since I got this job."

The Inspector made no comment. "I believe you saw Mr Antrim that evening?"

"Not to speak to. He was crossing the yard to the side-door. Had a biggish bag and was striding out like he had no time to lose."

"What time was that?"

"Just short of six-fifteen."

"And you didn't see him come back later."

A negative gesture. "I wasn't watching for him."

The Inspector stood up and helped Lennie to move the table away from the inner doors. With a final look at the model schooner he said good night. Lennie watched him go down the steps and passed a hand reflectively round his chin.

Approaching the little red car, the Inspector saw that it was empty. Anthea's message was still propped up on the steering-wheel. He opened the door and sat down to think.

Lennie had jumped with suspicious rapidity—or was it un-suspected intelligence?—to the possibility that the flat had been entered by the Emergency Door and had been at pains to assert that he had forgotten the existence of the key in the cupboard. A caretaker left alone in charge of a building, not only at night but every weekend, would surely have fami-liarized himself with it. He would know where to find the key to any locked door and would have in his mind the lay-out of each of the nine office floors. It was beyond question that he could have let himself into Corsair's flat and could probably have done so unseen and unheard.

Taking out his cigarette case, the Inspector felt in a pocket for his lighter. His fingers met the small packet which the messenger had brought to Miss Purslane's room. Removing the wrapping and folding it neatly, he put it in his pocket and examined the bottle in his hand. In gold letters on a heart-shaped label were the words "Maison Petronelle—Nail Lacquer—Rose Huître". Twisting the plastic cap, he brought out an attached brush laden with nacreous pink paint and experimentally dabbed it against the thumb that held the bottle, achieving a thick blob. Well, he said to himself, now I've started I'd better complete the job. Putting the bottle on top of the dashboard and checking the time on his watch, he began to spread the lacquer as thinly and evenly as he could. It was a more difficult process than he had anticipated. Intent on his workmanship, oblivious of all else, he finished painting the nails on his left hand and replaced the brush. Time passed. He examined his nails for the sixth time and tested the varnish. It had now dried. Ten minutes from start to finish. Allow for painting both hands and also for Netta's greater expertness in applying the varnish—say, twelve minutes altogether. Suddenly conscious that someone was standing by the car, he turned his head. Anthea stared at his hand in astonishment.

"Painting your nails?" she asked incredulously.

"An experiment," he replied. "Not unsuccessful, I think."

"Not bad for a first attempt," she said. "But why the experiment?"

"To test the probability of a statement."

"If you're not going to tell me about it you can wait while I tell you something." She opened the door and sat down, her face alight with happy excitement. "I think I know how we can find Halberd's mistress."

"While you're telling me, will you drive me to Colonel Summersby's house?" He gave her the address.

"Are you going to talk to him?"

"Yes, if he's in."

"With your nails like that!"

"*Dios mio!* I'd forgotten about them."

"We'll stop at a chemist and get some remover." She started the engine and drove out into the street. "Now I'll tell you what I've been doing. After you left us at lunch Keith told me about this mistress, and while I was doing some shopping late· on I was thinking about how to find her. Then I thought, well, of course he'll have given her presents, things like flowers and scent. He'll have paid cash for small things, but if he gave her anything expensive like jewellery he's almost sure to have paid by cheque. So I waited outside the office for Keith, and we went up to his uncle's study and looked for his cheque stubs. We didn't find them, but we did find his bank statements at last and, as he banked at Coutts, they gave the payees' names. He's made out three cheques this year for quite decent sums to Symington's, the jewellers. I wrote down the details and Keith was just going to show me out when Aunt Netta heard us and called. We pretended Keith had just brought me in, and he took me into the sitting-room and introduced me. Then I couldn't get away. She insisted on giving me a glass of sherry—and I expect you know how she talks. That's why I was so long—and I'm sorry. But I did find out something useful from Netta. Halberd gave her a piece of jewellery every year on her birthday in November. He hasn't given her anything this year. So the chances are that what he bought at Symington's was for his mistress. We'll go there tomorrow morning and find out. Oh, good, there's a chemist open." She drew into the kerb and was out of the car onto the pavement before the Inspector could make any protest.

The young Police Constable who was strolling on the other side of the street caught sight of the stationary car and, crossing the road, approached it, fingering the flap of his breast pocket. Anthea, leaving the chemist's shop, saw him take out a notebook and hurried over. "I'm just going," she said. "I had to get something at the chemist's."

"Didn't you see the double line, miss?"

"Yes, I did," she acknowledged. "But I was only going to be a second."

The constable looked at the charming upraised face. Momentarily he felt his heart soften; then he pulled himself together. "Sorry, miss, but I've got to do my duty. May I see your driving licence, please?"

"It was entirely my fault, constable." A deep voice came from the car. The policeman bent to see a man leaning over from the passenger's seat. A glimpse of neatly brushed black hair, a tanned skin—then a broad male hand whose fingers ended in nails thickly painted with shining pink varnish. Blimey, he said to himself and, ignoring the passenger, turned to the girl. "Your licence, please, miss," he said sternly.

The man in the car smiled and, pulling out his wallet, extracted the cellophaned card which Superintendent Mallick had given him. "This lady is assisting me. She stopped here on my instructions," he said. "I take full responsibility."

"The young lady is in charge of the vehicle," the constable said, glancing at the card held out to him. "She—" He stopped speaking, looked again at the card, then once more at the lacquered nails. He was still staring dumbstruck when Anthea got into the car and with a sweet smile and a "Thank you, officer," drove off, stifling laughter.

"You left the poor man wondering if he could believe what

he saw," she said a minute or two later as she drew up in Sycamore Terrace. "It wasn't fair not to explain to him."

The Inspector smiled. "It would have been much more unfair to deprive him of the story he's going to tell." He held out his left hand. "You'll be better at this job than me. Please remove the evidence of a rash experiment."

The pungent smell of acetone was still in his nose as he rang the bell of the end house.

Chapter Ten

BERTIE had been enjoying a rest when the bell rang, and he went to open the door. The newspaper in his hand was folded open at the sports page and there was more than a trace of whisky on his breath. A potato peeling lodged in the turn-up of his trousers provided evidence of an earlier occupation. He stiffened slightly when the Inspector introduced himself, but his voice was casual as he said, "Better come inside. 'Fraid the place is in a bit of a mess." He stood back with an expansive gesture. The Inspector squeezed by a crowded hall-stand and a tall cylinder of beaten brass containing a rolled umbrella, a shooting-stick, two walking-sticks, and what appeared to be the top joint of a chimney-sweep's brush, and came into the sitting-room. Bertie, following, picked up a copy of *Horse and Hound* from one of the two armchairs, waved the Inspector towards it, and sat down heavily. "Well, what's the matter this time?" he inquired. "Thought I'd seen the last of you chaps at the inquest. Nasty business that, very nasty. Don't suppose we shall ever know how the poor devil came to fall."

"Perhaps not." The Inspector paused. "I'm afraid I've come with rather unpleasant news, Colonel Summersby. It has been suggested that your brother-in-law's death may not have been an accident."

"Not an accident?" Bertie sat up. "But the inquest. . . ."

"The verdict was on the known facts. In the light of fresh information I regret I have to make further inquiries."

"But, my dear fellow." Bertie was startled into forgetfulness of the fact that he was speaking to a policeman. "If it wasn't an accident and suicide's been ruled out, that leaves—" He gagged on the word and shook his head slowly. "No, I can't believe that."

"No-one believes in murder until it has taken place," the Inspector said. "No-one except the murderer knows why and how." The soft eyes rested on his listener's face. "He will be found if the evidence is brought to light. It is my duty to find it if it is there. But I do not wish to alarm you. We do not yet know for certain that it was not an accident—and, of course, I have not mentioned any other possibility to Mrs Corsair."

"I should think not. Poor little thing. Can't have her worried more than she is." His voice tailed away as if his thoughts were on another matter. Frowning, he said, "But if someone pushed Halberd out of the window—take it that's what's in your mind—he must have got into the flat and out without Netta knowing." He cleared his throat. "Suppose that's possible. Remember reading t'other day about some burglars cleaning out a place while the family were playing some game or other. See what you're after. Chap's snooping about the flat. Halberd catches him at it and gets chucked out before he knows what's happening. Looks like an accident until you come across something that makes you think again. Suppose you can't tell me what you've found?"

"Not just now. All I can say is that there may have been a visitor to the flat last Friday who was not a stranger to Mr Corsair. And that is where I need your assistance, Colonel Summersby."

"My assistance?" Bertie appeared taken aback. "Don't see how I can help. I was here all afternoon and evening, as I told your Sergeant."

"Perhaps you would be good enough to tell me what you remember telling him."

Bertie looked up with sudden sharpness. "Y'know, Inspector, I might take offence at that." He gave a snort that indicated strained patience. "But suppose you've got your duty to do. Take a few minutes, though—so if you'd care to join me in a drink? Sure you won't? Got to stick to the rules, eh?" Going over to a bookcase in an alcove, he picked up a decanter from a tray and poured generously, adding a splash of soda. Sitting down again, he sipped at the glass and, with a word of thanks, accepted a cigarette from the proffered case. "Well, now for the facts. Fellow next door moved last week —gave me some books and said I could have that bookcase over there. Pretty scruffy-looking thing it was then, all scratched varnish, but solid enough as you can see. Take off the varnish, give it a coat of good paint, and it'd be just what we wanted. " He sipped appreciatively. "My wife went out on Friday after lunch to play bridge—suppose she left about two-thirty—and I got down to work. Sandpapering the varnish off took a devil of a time, but if a job's worth doing it's worth doing well, what? Then I gave it a coat of paint— good stuff—one coat's enough and it dries quickly. I'd just finished and was doing one or two other things when my wife returned."

"Do you remember what time that was?"

"I'd say," Bertie paused judicially, "a minute or two after seven-thirty. Sandpapering must have taken me up to six. Then I made myself a cup of tea and turned on the television. Bit of a lucky chance I did or I'd have missed seeing an old friend of mine. Came on just after six-forty-five. Hadn't seen him for years, but there he was, looking much the same, talking to some long-haired chap about a head, Roman, I think it was, that had been dug up on his land. Distinguished bloke. Expect you've heard of him—Field-Marshal Craddock. Dropped him a line next day. Thought we might meet and have a chat." Bertie drained his glass and looked at it speculatively. "Well, that's what I was doing. Alone all the time and fully occupied."

The Inspector glanced at the bookcase and, crossing the room, looked at it with interest. He had guessed aright. Battles, horses, and derring-do covered Bertie's literary tastes.

They were, he thought, the tastes of a simple and not very strong-minded man who found in them a reflection of the man he would like to have been: a synthesis of Cary Grant, Monty, and Don Bradman, with a liberal but not too exuberant leavening of Casanova.

"A lot of good reading there." Bertie was at his elbow, replenishing his glass. "Say the word if you've changed your mind, Inspector. No? Well, never press a man." He gave a little cough. "Anything more I can tell you?"

"I believe you spoke to Mr Corsair on the telephone after lunch on Friday." The Inspector returned to his chair. "I gather you wished to see him."

"Yes, I rang about a purely family matter. Nothing urgent. He said he was pretty busy and wanted to get off early on some business trip. Suggested we had a chat on Monday. Suited me all right, so I said so and rang off."

"It might be helpful if you could tell me something about your late brother-in-law—about his friends, his habits, his plans, and so on."

"Friends—never met any of them." There was the faintest implication that Halberd's friends were unlikely to have been Bertie's type. "Habits—smoked cigars, moderate drinker, methodical chap—kept a thermometer in the bathroom to test the heat of the water. Plans—don't know anything about his business—not my line of country. Talked of going off to Bermuda for a holiday in the New Year."

"Do you know if he was unfaithful to his wife?"

Seconds passed while Bertie took in and rejected the question. "Don't think it's any business of yours, Inspector."

"It might be a reason for someone to dislike him."

"Hm. See what you're driving at. Jealous husband and so forth." Bertie moved to the fireplace and leaned against the cluttered mantelpiece. "Heard some gossip the other day. Nothing definite, mind you. Must say I've sometimes wondered about those business weekends. Leaving li'l Netta alone." His head wagged at the thought of such iniquity.

"I expect she has plenty of friends." The Inspector's tone invited information.

"Heard her mention one or two." Bertie blinked rapidly. "All women, though. Pretty li'l thing, Netta, but not interested in men s'far as I know. Though Claire's not so sure. Said she was there t'other day, must have been Thursday, when some chap rang to find out if the coast was clear—fellow called Bobbie. Shouldn't think myself there was anything in it, but women are usually pretty sharp about that sort of thing."

"What are women usually sharp about?" Claire stood in the doorway. The Inspector had heard the sound of a latchkey in the door and was on his feet. Bertie hastily put down his glass, lumbered forward, and muttered an introduction. "Just having a li'l chat, old girl." Though the Inspector could only see the back of his head, he had no doubt that some signal had passed from husband to wife. "Police seem to think that Halberd's death wasn't an accident."

"I said that the possibility had to be considered, Mrs Summersby."

"I see." Claire raised her eyebrows. "It comes to much the same thing, doesn't it?" She put her handbag on the table and began to take off her gloves. "I don't understand, Inspector. I thought it was made clear at the inquest that it could only have been an accident, since there was no-one else in the flat but my sister-in-law." Her voice was frigid as she went on, "It seems to me that you're implying that she—"

"I'm implying nothing, Mrs Summersby. If Mrs Corsair was in her bedroom at the time she could be completely unaware that someone had come to see her husband. If we can eliminate those who could not have been there our inquiries will be simplified. Your husband has been good enough to amplify the account he gave to Sergeant Cheam of what he was doing last Friday. Perhaps you would do so too."

"I can only repeat what I've already said." Claire was coldly disdainful.

"Why not tell him again, old girl?" Bertie said pacifically. "It won't take a minute."

"Very well." Her manner as she sat down made it clear that she intended the Inspector to remain standing. "I went out after lunch to play bridge with friends in Chelsea. We finished the final rubber at about a quarter to six, and I left a few minutes later. I had a splitting headache and needed fresh air, so I walked along the Embankment. The headache had gone by the time I reached Dolphin Square, and I called on a cousin, but she was out. I was coming away from her flat when I found I hadn't got my cigarette lighter, so I went into a call-box and rang my friends to ask if I'd left it there. I had, and they said they would put it in the post to me. I rang my husband from the same call-box—it was then about twenty-past six—to tell him I would pick up a bottle of wine on the way home and to ask if we had enough potatoes for dinner. He said we had and that he'd peel them as soon as he'd finished painting the bookcase."

"I think you omitted this from your account, Colonel Summersby," the Inspector observed.

"'Fraid I did. Thought you only wanted the main facts."

"I'm sure the Inspector wants to know everything, even the domestic details," Claire said acidly. "When I left the call-box I caught a bus to Victoria and came on by train. On the way from the station I went into an off-licence and bought a bottle of claret. I was home at half-past seven. Perhaps I should add," she went on ironically, "that when I came in my husband was cooking the potatoes—in fact, he had over-cooked them."

"Made 'em easy to mash," Bertie said. "Never could get the hang of these electric cookers. Fact is, can't cook for toffee." He chuckled. "Can't make toffee either."

Claire's glance was a command to silence. "I'm sure we're keeping you, Inspector. You must have a great many other people to see. Frankly I find it impossible to believe that there could have been another person in the flat without Netta

121

knowing, and I certainly can't see Halberd letting himself be killed without a struggle."

"It's because no-one apparently did see that I am trying to find out what happened," the Inspector said mildly. "Please do not think that I have been wasting your time—or mine. What you have told me has been most interesting." He moved towards the door. "When I have made further inquiries it is quite possible that you may be able to help me again."

"Perhaps you would telephone beforehand so that I can tell you when it would be convenient for you to call," Claire said icily.

"If it is possible, I will do so." The soft violet eyes met hers. "I am never intentionally discourteous."

There was silence in the room when he went. With him, as he closed the door, he carried the sound of Claire's indrawn breath and the shuffle of Bertie's feet.

"I put the question you asked me last night to a barrister friend," said Sir Otto, setting down his after-dinner coffee-cup. "He says that if Mrs Corsair were convicted of killing her husband there would be an intestacy of that part of his estate which had been willed to her. That part would then be shared equally by the two nearest of kin—his sister and his deceased sister's only son."

"That's Keith and Claire Summersby." Anthea's brow wrinkled as she turned to the Inspector. "But why did you want to know this? You don't think Netta killed her husband, do you?"

"I think it's unlikely. If she was varnishing her nails—and I can't see her inventing that part of her story—she would scarcely have finished the job when he died. My own somewhat ill-timed experiment confirmed that the lacquer could not possibly have dried by then." He smiled at the memory. "I doubt if any woman of Netta's sort would think about pushing a man out of a window while her nails were still tacky. Apart from the likelihood that she'd smear the lacquer on him or on his clothes, she'd almost certainly have to repair some damage to her own nails."

"She'd take the spoiled varnish off before she repainted her nails," Anthea put in. "And she wouldn't have time to do all this before she went out at half-past six."

"So the suggestion is," Sir Otto said, "that someone intended Netta to be suspected; that when, to their disappointment, a verdict of accidental death was brought in, they contrived to start a rumour of murder and to bring to your notice a motive—that Corsair was unfaithful to her."

The Inspector assented. "Another motive has now been suggested—that she herself had a lover. We don't yet know whether either motive has a basis in fact, but it is a coincidence that both motives were suggested by the people who would benefit substantially if Netta were convicted of her husband's murder."

There was a moment of silence; then Anthea said unbelievingly, "Do you mean that because Keith told you about the postcard and the telephone call he must be trying to throw suspicion on his aunt? You know perfectly well that he wouldn't have said anything if you hadn't forced it out of him."

"I did not compel him to tell me." He saw the heightened colour on her cheeks and went on gently, "You mustn't misunderstand me, Anthea. Keith destroyed his own alibi by saying that he read about the Tube breakdown in the following morning's paper. So without having himself been involved in that breakdown he could use it to account for an otherwise unexplained quarter of an hour. For that reason I cannot say, 'This young man is completely free from suspicion'. But it does not necessarily follow that I suspect him of having anything to do with Corsair's death. Similarly, I cannot dismiss Colonel and Mrs Summersby. I do not believe that she telephoned him at twenty-past six. I doubt whether she rang him at all. But disbelief is not enough. If I can prove that one of them has lied I shall perhaps be able to make them tell me the truth. At the moment I am not convinced that one of them was not in the flat last Friday night—possibly both of them."

"Then you think that he lied about seeing this Field-Marshal friend on television," said Sir Otto, "and that she did not ring to ask her bridge hostess about her lighter."

The Inspector shook his head. "Those may be the only points on which they both told the truth."

Chapter Eleven

THE Inspector picked up his shaving-brush and began to
lather his face. There was something conducive to productive
thought in the leisurely movement of the hand, the soothing
touch of a badger-hair brush, the visible growth of foam. The
off-white beard, too, gave an air of sagacity which must
surely be reflected in the working of the mind. There was
really a great deal to be said for the tools which had served
one's forefathers well. The man who had been seduced by the
insidious pen of the advertising copy-writer into buying an
electric razor could never again enjoy a meditative shave. The
irritable buzz of the motor imprisoned in its plastic carapace
destroyed connected thought—in fact, made thought of any
kind almost impossible. Only a man incapable of thought—
an idiot, perhaps—would dream of buying one of those expensive playthings. Mentholated lather stung his tongue as
he smiled. He must really get rid of those two costly and dis-
ruptive toys in the top drawer of his bedroom chest at home.
Only a fool. . . . He dipped the brush in the hand-basin and
resolutely set his mind to more immediate matters.

It required, as Sir Otto had mildly suggested last night, a
considerable stretch of the imagination to conceive the
kind of person who would kill with the intention of obtain-
ing a fortune by so incriminating the murdered man's widow
that she would be convicted of the crime. It also presupposed
a knowledge of Corsair's will. That Corsair had disclosed its
provisions to the beneficiaries was possible but, given the
type of man he had been, improbable. But what of the copy

that had been kept in his private safe and which Miss Purslane had seen on his desk last Friday? Could Keith have read it while he was alone in the office before Corsair returned from lunch? Keith had also been in the room when Corsair spoke to his solicitor about a codicil to the will—and Corsair had died before he could add that codicil, but not necessarily before someone knew or guessed at its terms.

While it was impossible to ignore the evidence which had so far come to light, Keith had, so far as the Inspector knew, not lied to him on any point, though he might well have withheld compromising information. Lennie, on the other hand, had undoubtedly lied about the Emergency Door. But what motive could Lennie have had to dispose of his employer?

The Inspector laid down the brush and, picking up his safety-razor, felt the milled end to make certain it was screwed up tightly.

Bertie and Claire had offered alibis which leaked at every joint—though for that very reason they might be genuine. Claire's account of her movements after leaving the bridge party lacked any corroboration, except possibly for the telephone call and for the purchase of the bottle of claret—if indeed she had bought it that evening. As for Bertie's story, who could say how long it would take an unskilled man to sandpaper the old varnish from a bookcase? Bertie claimed to have spent over three hours in making a thorough job of it, and to have painted the bookcase after a break for a cup of tea during which he had watched a television programme. But supposing he had lied about times, could he not have been the man with a walking-stick whom Lennie had heard crossing the courtyard shortly after Netta had left the flat? Comparatively few men who lived in cities carried a walking-stick nowadays. Bertie had two, the handles of which were well polished by use.

The Inspector put down the razor and looked reproachfully at his image in the mirror. You must stop trying to build up a theory on suppositions, he admonished himself. One might as well practise psephomancy. He dried his face, finished dressing, and went down to breakfast. Bertie, he said to himself, had neither the intelligence nor the purpose to plan and commit a murder. But the plan and the purpose might well be Claire's.

At ten minutes to nine he folded his napkin and made a final protest. "I can't have you driving me around today," he said to a laughing and determined Anthea. "I may be a long time at some of the places I'm going to."

"I've got nothing else to do until lunch-time, and you can't get rid of me," she told him firmly. "I promised to go and see a friend in a nursing home this afternoon, but I'll come to Termini House at five to pick up you or a message from you."

He looked across the table at his host for help, but Sir Otto offered none, saying, "You'd better give in. If you don't she'll turn detective herself—and heaven only knows what she'll get up to."

The Inspector accepted defeat with good grace. Shortly after nine o'clock they reached Golden Square, where he got out of the car and she circled round the square in the hope that in due course a parking space would be vouchsafed. Following her directions, he came into Regent Street and turned right. Soon he reached Symingtons. Behind the grilled window of the shop a single piece of jewellery, a platinum collar with brilliants, lay on a bed of black velvet. This and the name in cursive script were the sole intimations of identity and occupation which the firm chose to offer to the public. For two centuries, ending with the First World War, their clientèle had embraced the aristocracy and most of the crowned heads of Europe. Now that the majority of crowns had been melted down and the few remaining royal heads were covered, if at all, by the products of some commercial hatter, Symingtons still maintained their dignity and old-fashioned courtesy. Whoever the customer might be, pro-perty millionaire, Neanderthal crooner, kept quean, or shy young man seeking an engagement ring within the limits of a slender purse, he left the tranquil shop like a dog whose ears have been massaged by an expert and understanding hand.

"If you wouldn't mind waiting a minute," said the immaculately suited young man to whom the Inspector briefly explained his purpose, "the senior partner will be free."

The man into whose office he was shortly shown listened without interruption. "Well," he said, "I'm not going to ask you why you require this information. If I did I should expect to be snubbed," he smiled, "though with the utmost courtesy. Yes, Mr Corsair was a customer of ours for many years. This ledger confirms purchases that tally with the cheques you mention. The purchases were a gold link-bracelet, a cat's-eye pendant, and a very charming Georgian locket. Mr Corsair took them all away himself, so I have no —no certain knowledge for whom they were intended as gifts."

"But you can hazard a guess." The Inspector had not missed the almost inappreciable pause.

"Perhaps a little more than a guess." A glance at the ledger. "The locket was brought in by a lady three weeks ago for the chain to be slightly shortened. We sent it back to her the following day by hand. The name of the lady is Mrs Ducayne, and this is her address." He pushed a card across the desk.

"Do you know at what time of day she came in?"

"Just before eleven o'clock."

"Can you tell me anything about her?"

"Very little. The assistant who saw her says that she is about thirty-five and charming. She had a boy of about ten with her." With regret he added, "I'm afraid that isn't very helpful."

A few minutes later the Inspector was back in Golden Square. It was, he agreed with Anthea, too early in the morning to call on Mrs Ducayne. The fact that she had come into

Symingtons in the middle of the morning with a child who was presumably hers suggested that she was not a working woman. Certainly a telephone call would establish if she were at home, but he did not wish to anticipate his visit. Meanwhile there were others to whom he must talk.

Minnie, opening the front door, bid the Inspector a friendly good-morning. "Mrs Corsair's dressing," she said. "I'll tell her you're here."

"It's you I came to see, Minnie." He waited until she had closed the door and was facing him. "You remember telling me yesterday that when your brother came last Friday you had the kettle on for yourself and Lennie. Were you going to give him a cup of tea?"

"Yes, I was. But what with Sid coming unexpected and us talking away, it slipped my mind and I didn't think of it until just on six. So I popped out with a cup, knocked on the Staff Door, and called out, 'Tea's up'."

"And he came to get it?"

"He called back 'Coming.' So, as I wanted to get back to Sid, I put it down by the door."

"Have you been giving him a cup of tea every day?"

"Just that week, while the electric kettle he has in the basement was being mended. I like a cup myself about that time, so it wasn't any trouble to give him one. He'd put the cup outside the door as soon as he'd drunk it so's I could wash it up with my own things."

"And last Friday you picked it up before you went out?"

"I clean forgot about it, what with having Sid and me going up to Finchley."

"Then it was there when you returned that night?"

"No. Lennie'd broken it. He popped out to tell me Saturday morning when the police were in the place and it was all right for him to leave it in their charge."

The Inspector nodded. Was it really so urgent to tell Minnie of the breakage that Lennie had left his post? It was more likely that, confined behind locked doors while the police went to and fro and told him nothing, he had come out to learn from Minnie as much as she could tell him. If so, was it just the natural curiosity of a lonely man? Or could it be that Lennie wanted to assure himself that the police had neither asked nor been told about something he did not wish them to know? And, if so, was there some connection with the question that Halberd had asked Netta during their last reported conversation? "When did you last see Mr Corsair?" he asked.

"When I gave him his breakfast."

"Did he say anything to you—apart from good-morning?"

"He reminded me to pack his denture-cleaning powder. I'd forgotten to put it in the last time he was away and he was a bit shirty about it when he got back."

"Did he remind you pleasantly?"

"He said it casual-like without looking up from his paper."

"Have you ever seen or heard of a friend of either of them called Bobbie?"

"Not that I mind of. They didn't have many people here." Minnie thought for a few moments. "There's a Mr Roderick who comes about the television. His shop in Bute Street's called 'Roddie', and that's what everyone calls him."

"Has he been here recently?"

"I haven't seen him since July. But he comes every three months, so he may have been when I wasn't in."

"What sort of man is he?"

"The kind that gets fresh if you give him half a chance." Minnie smiled reminiscently. "I had to give him a clip the first time I saw him."

The Inspector looked at her well-covered arm. "I imagine he didn't try again," he said drily.

The window under the sign "Roddie's Electrics" would have won no prize for artistic arrangement; it did, however, appear to contain a specimen of every kind of electrical apparatus used by the housewife or the handyman. In the forefront, between chromed statuettes of nubile and unclothed nymphs whose hair-do's included brass lamp sockets, a black-lettered card extended an invitation to the passing public. "If it's not in the window," it read, "try inside. If it's not in the shop, we'll get it." A youth whose London-pale countenance was a battleground between acne and blackheads, looked up as a buzzer heralded the Inspector's entry. An expression of eager willingness lit the cratered face, disclosing a set of teeth that were a credit to his mother and the free supply of milk to school-children. "Can I help you, sir?" he inquired.

"I'd like to speak to Mr Roderick," the Inspector said.

"Purchases, accounts, contracts, servicing or complaints?" The young man's fingertips pressed against the counter as he leaned forward. "If it's a complaint it'll be the first this year and you'll have to speak to Mr Roderick personal. If it's anything else, yours truly will deal with it."

"It's purely a private matter."

"Private." He scrutinized the pleasant, uninformative face. "You're not a debt-collector, 'cos we ain't got no debts. Traveller?" He shook his head. "You're not the chap who's taking over the shop next door? No, didn't think you were. Today's Thursday, so you can't be from the Pools to say he's won a ticket to Park Lane. 'Tisn't often I can't spot a man's trade." He turned, took three paces, and, opening a door, shouted, "Gent to see you. Won't say anything 'cept that it's private."

"Send him through, Bert," came a somewhat indistinct reply.

Angle-iron shelving lined three sides of the room behind the shop. Every shelf bore neat piles of boxed and labelled accessories. By the empty case of a television set a fair-haired man of about thirty was sitting on an upturned wooden crate. On top of the case were a mug and the remains of a currant bun.

"Just finishing my elevenses." Bright eyes flicked over the visitor. "Care for a cup?" A jerk of the head indicated a bottle of coffee essence and a steaming electric kettle. "Sure you won't? Take a pew then." He put the remains of the bun in his mouth, picked up the mug, and flicked a few crumbs off the case.

"I take it that you're Mr Roderick?" The Inspector sat down.

"That's my moniker. Not that anyone calls me anything but Roddie unless they're trying to sell me something." He cocked a querying eye.

The Inspector regarded him mildly. "Do you know Termini House?" he asked.

"Yes—got a television out on rental there—couple called Corsair. Poor bastard copped it last week—fell out of a window."

"I believe you were in his flat shortly before he fell?"

"You believe—" Roddie gave a snort of amused disgust. "So you're a cop. Well, I'd never have guessed it." He bent to put the empty mug on the floor. "So it wasn't an accident?" He straightened up and the blue eyes narrowed.

"If you can help us to prove that it was I shan't have to make any further inquiries."

"Me help you? Come off it, chum. Whatever happened happened after I'd gone."

"Then you know what time he fell?"

"I don't know a thing about it, chummie, 'cept what I read in the papers, and they said he landed in the lorry as it was going to move off. When I drove out the lorry was standing there and there weren't no-one in the cab. It couldn't drive itself, could it? So it stands to reason he was still up top where I'd seen him."

"You saw him in the flat?"

"Outside it—on the landing. He came out of the lift and I got in. Looked proper narked he did, had a rolled-up newspaper in his hand and was smacking it into the other hand. Just grunted when I said good night." Roddie sniffed. "As I said, I've got a rented set there, and I pop along about every

"Surely you realized it was your duty to tell the police that you had seen him only a few minutes earlier?"

"Come off it, chummie." Roddie was ironically tolerant. "If I'd gone along to say I'd seen him go into the flat, all the thanks I'd get would have been for some smart bloke to say 'How too kind of you to let us know, Mr Roderick! You mean to say you actually saw him enter? Most interestin'. I know we're a shower of soft-headed b.f.'s here, but one or two of us had a kind of feeling that since he fell out of one of the windows of the flat he must have been inside it at the time.'" Roddie resumed his natural voice. "I'd have been asking for it, wouldn't I? That's not to say that if I'd seen or heard anything queer I wouldn't have told 'em. I would."

"Just as you've now told me."

Roddie grinned. "If I've told you anything you didn't know before," he said, "you're welcome to it."

"Do you think Roddie's told you the truth?" asked Anthea as she drove westward.

"He hasn't told me anything that I recognize as a lie."

"Isn't it a bit odd that Mrs Corsair didn't tell you he'd been in the flat that afternoon?"

"I didn't specifically ask her what she was doing before her husband came home. Even if I had I doubt whether she would have mentioned that an electrician had made a service call."

"You don't think she's having an affair with Roddie?"

The Inspector shook his head.

"Nor do I." Anthea was smiling as she added, "Women whose spiritual home is Harrods don't have affairs in their own homes with the lower classes. That would be non-U."

"You mean it's all right for them to let themselves go when they're away from home."

"When they're abroad, yes. That's what abroad's for. Liberty, equality—"

"And fraternization," the Inspector suggested.

135

Anthea chuckled as she turned into a short street of Victorian houses. Beside almost every door a row of bell-pushes, each flanked by a card in a brass frame, indicated that the houses had been converted into flats or flatlets. The street had the air, so prevalent in London districts near the Royal Parks and so often misinformative, of being inhabited solely by senior civil servants, solicitors, and the relicts of suffragan bishops. An acid-green door stood out among its jet-black neighbours like a four-letter word on a page of Hansard.

The Inspector rang one of the three bells of Number 12. A moment later he was surprised to hear a pleasant voice almost in his ear. "Push the door, it's open. And please come up. It's the first floor."

In an open doorway at the top of the stairs stood a fair-haired woman in a short-sleeved white overall. "I hope you weren't startled by my voice coming out of the wall," she said.

"Just a little," he acknowledged. "Walls have ears but seldom voices. I take it that this is a two-way telephone—that you could have asked me who I was and heard my reply."

"Yes, it's two-way. If someone comes with a parcel I don't have to run down and take it in. I can tell him to leave it in the hall and to close the door when he goes."

"And if someone comes whom you don't know you can find out what he wants before you press the button that opens the front door. But you didn't ask me who I was."

"I saw you arrive. I'd come out of the kitchen into the sitting-room to smoke a cigarette, and I saw you get out of a red car and talk for a few moments with a very pretty girl. You were both such obviously nice people that when you rang I asked you to come up." She stepped back, and amusement showed in her eyes. "Hadn't you better come in and introduce yourself?"

She took him into a small sitting-room and, asking him to sit down, herself sat on a sofa that faced the window, so that the midday light fell full on her face. Her nose is too short, he said to himself, her cheekbones too high, her mouth too full. Yet the sum of her faults is a pleasure to the eye.

"You are Mrs Ducayne?" he asked.

"Yes, Pamela Ducayne."

He told her who he was, and she nodded with polite incuriosity, as if to say that a visit by a police officer would explain itself in due course.

"I'm making inquiries in connection with the death last Friday of Mr Corsair. I understand that you knew him."

"Very well," she said simply. "But why are you making inquiries? I thought—" She hesitated. "It was an accident, wasn't it?"

"Have you any reason to think it might not have been?"

"None." She shook her head. "Except that Halberd wasn't the kind of person to whom accidents happen. He was too careful, too anticipatory. When I read in the papers how he had died I wanted to know what had happened—what had made him careless and why."

"You were expecting to see him last weekend?"

"We had arranged to meet on Friday evening."

"And you rang his home after midnight to find out what had delayed him?"

"I rang up a number of times and got no reply until some young man told me that Halberd had gone away for the weekend. I wondered whether it was the nephew he had told me about."

"It was." He looked at the hands that lay folded on her lap, and then at the eyes that met his candidly. "Mrs Ducayne, are you prepared to answer some personal questions?"

"I think so." She considered him. "Yes, I am."

"Had Mr Corsair arranged to come to this flat last Friday?"

"Yes. I expected him shortly after seven."

"Were you and he then flying to Ireland for the weekend?"

She smiled a little. "You seem to know something of my private life. If I tell you the rest it will be easier—for both of us. I was introduced to Halberd nearly three years ago at a dinner to which a friend had taken me. I thought him pompous and autocratic. I didn't think I'd ever see him again—and I didn't particularly want to. In any case I was happily married. A month later my husband was killed in a smash-up at Brands Hatch. I was left with a son of seven, very little money, and no qualifications except that I was a good cook. In the past I'd made one or two short recordings for the B.B.C. about old country recipes. I went to see a producer whom I knew, and he gave me a trial run. Now I give a twice-weekly cookery talk and write for a couple of magazines. I make enough for my son and myself to live on." She looked at her watch. "You'll have to excuse me for a few minutes. I'm trying out a recipe which a listener sent in, and if I don't follow her instructions exactly I'm not giving it a fair trial." She was out of the door as she finished speaking.

Left alone, the Inspector went over to the window. Anthea had taken her car to the other side of the road, on which the sun was shining. Her face was out of his line of vision, but he could see that she had a notebook on her crossed knee and was writing. Somewhere near by a man was talking on the radio in a precise, academic voice about the connection between fashions in clothes and morality. He dwelt with appreciation on cleavages and cod-pieces. The Inspector left the window to examine the contents of a bookcase by the fireplace. A dozen or so volumes about vintage cars and racing drivers attested to the late Mr Ducayne's interests. A shelf of poetry, another of plays, and a variety of books by writers who had stood the test of time reflected a taste which must surely be that of their present owner. He was replacing a copy of *Texts and Pretexts* when Mrs Ducayne returned. With her there came a warm, rich scent of baking pastry.

"All's well," she said. "There won't be any more interruptions." She waited until the Inspector had resumed his seat. "About a year later I was coming out of Hamley's with my son Mark and ran into Halberd. It was shortly before Christmas. He insisted on taking us back into the shop and buying something for Mark. I was certain he would buy some ostentatiously expensive toy—that was the kind of man I thought he was. But I was wrong. He said to Mark, 'Now we've got ten shillings to spend. What do you want to look at first?' and they spent half an hour examining various toys and discussing their merits and demerits. He talked to him as an equal, and when he left us Mark said, 'Isn't he a nice man, Mummy? Shall I see him again?' A few days later he rang up to ask if Mark and I would come for a drive in the country on Sunday. We had a lovely day. By the time we had been on several outings I had told him all about myself, and he had told me a great deal.

"He said he was married, but that he and his wife led entirely separate lives. It was probably his fault, because business had been his chief interest. When he mentioned that they had no children I realized from his abrupt manner that he had wanted them very much and that this was one reason for the unsuccessful marriage. After a few months he asked if I had any plans for Mark's education. I said I would have liked him to go to a private school, but this was out of the question. He told me that he had already provided for his only nephew and would like to finance Mark's education through some insurance scheme. 'I want to be completely truthful about this,' he said. 'You and I both want the boy to have the best possible education, but I have a secondary motive. If he goes to a boarding school you will have most of your weekends free during term-time. I would like us to spend them together. You don't have to give me a decision now. Think it over for a week or two. But I want you to know that your saying "no" will not affect my offer to provide for Mark's education.' I said I'd give him an answer the following weekend. I didn't really need any time to think it over. I knew what my reply was. Asking for time for consideration was really nothing more than a concession to the remnants of a puritan heritage."

The Inspector did not break the ensuing silence. Interruption would only destroy her mood, her readiness to confide in a receptive stranger. In the last few minutes she had given him a picture of Halberd Corsair so different from that which others—with the exception of Wolfe—had painted that it was hard to reconcile them. To her Halberd had shown himself kind, unselfish, and unwilling to accept what was not freely given. That this attitude was a pose adopted for the occasion the Inspector did not believe. Mrs Ducayne would have detected a false note. She was an intelligent person and, he judged, honest with herself. She was also an exceedingly charming woman with a serenity of expression and voice that could not have failed to attract other men than Halberd. Why then. . . ?

"I could have married again," she said as if she had been following his thoughts, "but I knew that to neither of the men who had asked me would Mark have been anything but an unwanted extra attached to the main package. To Halberd I felt that he was the son he would have liked to have had. I wasn't in love with Halberd, nor he with me—we didn't try to deceive ourselves or each other—but there was an affection between us that I felt would last. We were fonder—that's an inadequate word, but I think you will know what I mean— fonder of one another when he died than ever before. If you're wondering why he didn't get a divorce it was because we both wanted to test the genuineness and strength of our relationship before considering marriage. For me the testing time was over. I was ready to marry Halberd." She pressed one hand on the other that lay on her knee. "I think he would have proposed last weekend. He rang up earlier in the week, and from the careful way he spoke I knew he was in his office. 'Until I have a new document prepared by my solicitors,' he said, 'I propose to add a rider to the present one. Have you any Christian names besides the one I know?' I gave him my middle name, and he rang off. I guessed then that he was going to add a codicil to his will and that the new document he mentioned was the will he would have to make after our marriage." Her eyes seemed focused on some mental image behind the Inspector. "No, I was wrong to say I guessed. I knew as surely as if he had told me that we would be married as soon as his divorce was through."

"He was certain that his wife would give him a divorce?" the Inspector asked.

"As certain as one can ever be about another person. He felt sure that she would agree rather than see him leave to set up home with me. To have your husband living openly with another woman because you refuse divorce is a confession of self-righteousness and obstinate stupidity if you're not a Catholic. Netta was generous-minded."

"You have met her then?"

"That was Halberd's opinion. I've never seen her, or if I have I didn't know it was her. I know where they live, of course, but I've never been to—never been inside the flat. Halberd always came here to pick me up. He never stayed for the night. We used to spend weekends at small hotels in the country and never saw anyone we knew. Last weekend he wanted to look at some factory near Dublin and asked me if I'd like to come. Of course I said 'Yes'. He was going to collect me on the way to London Airport. There we'd separate and travel singly. At Dublin there'd be a hired car waiting. Everything was planned—it always was with him. I was packed and ready by six—and then it was half-past seven and he hadn't come." With the last few words her voice, which had been even and matter-of-fact, faltered.

The Inspector rose and went to the window so that she could unleash her feelings unwatched. Very soon he heard her blow her nose. "It's all right," she said, and her voice was again under control. "Is there anything else I can tell you?"

"You said you telephoned several times," he prompted.

"Yes, at least ten times before his nephew answered. I'd thought at first that perhaps business had delayed him and

141

that he might even be on his way while I was on the telephone. As time went on all sorts of other possibilities came into my mind. Had he been taken suddenly ill? Had I somehow misunderstood the arrangements? Had he been unable to start the car? Could he have taken a taxi to the Air Terminal and be waiting there, unable to let me know because I was using the telephone? Or could he have gone to the Airport? I rang both places several times, to learn at last that he was not on the 'plane when it left. At some time after one I went to bed—but not to sleep. I stayed indoors all Saturday waiting for him or for some message. And then the papers came on Sunday morning, and I read what had happened. I sat down and told myself 'It's not true. It's not true.' But I knew it was—and what made it so much worse was that there was no-one to whom I could go for comfort, because no-one knew about Halberd and me. It had been our secret—and now it was mine alone for ever and ever."

The Inspector turned from the window. Nothing that he could think of to say seemed adequate. How could it be? He made a gesture which he hoped would convey understanding and sympathy.

Her voice was once more steady as she continued, "I pulled myself together during the afternoon and began to think of a future without Halberd. Mark's education was assured. What my mother had left me covered the rent of the flat. The radio talks and cookery articles brought in enough for me to live on and to buy Mark's clothes and look after him during the holidays. If an emergency occurred I had some family jewellery and three or four pieces that Halberd gave me. Oh, yes, I was all right." Her voice was suddenly bitter. "I'd lost nothing by knowing Halberd, and I was accustoming myself to the knowledge that I'd never see him again. Since no-one knew of our friendship I should never hear his name mentioned—or so I thought until you came. Tell me, please, how you found out about me."

There is no reason why she should not know, the Inspector

thought, no reason in the world why I should not assure her that only Anthea and myself know and will keep that knowledge to ourselves. "We traced you through cheques that Mr Corsair paid to a firm of jewellers."

"You traced me," she said thoughtfully. "But why was it necessary to find me? No, you needn't answer. If Halberd did not die by accident, then someone killed him. Could it be his mistress? You see me and I tell you about the codicil he is going to add to his will. But suppose I have lied to you and that I knew that the codicil had been added. What better motive could I have had for killing him before he changed his mind?"

"How could you know that the codicil had been added?"

"I don't, but I do know that when Halberd made a decision he acted at once."

"Suppose I were to tell you that I know the provisions of the will?"

"I don't deal in suppositions, Inspector. Tell me the truth, please."

"There is no codicil."

"And no mention of my name in the will?"

"None."

"Thank you," she said simply. "I'm glad, very glad."

When a little later the Inspector left the house he was asking himself why Mrs Ducayne should be thankful that her name was not mentioned in Halberd's will. She had spoken with a sincerity that he found impossible to doubt. She had been frank, with the candour of a child who has nothing to hide and nothing of which to be ashamed. Nevertheless there had been a moment of quick self-correction which, while it might indicate nothing more than an unusual partiality for verbal exactitude, might also suggest that she had something to conceal.

"If you'd been five minutes longer I was going to come and rescue you," Anthea said as the Inspector reached the car.

"Did she receive you in a négligée and have a toy poodle which she clasped to her bosom when she wasn't feeding it marrons glacés?"

"She wasn't anything like what either of us expected. She's a gentle and attractive young widow with a son of ten, and she was wearing an overall and cooking something which smelled delicious. I think she would have made Halberd a very good wife."

"You mean he was going to marry her."

"So she said."

"And you believed her?"

"She believed it, and I believed her belief."

"But what about Netta?"

"Apparently Halberd was certain she would give him a divorce."

"He couldn't be certain until he'd asked her."

The Inspector said nothing; it was as if he were waiting for her train of thought to catch up with his. She drew her breath in sharply. "Perhaps he did ask Netta. And if he did, she's going to keep it to herself. No-one else need ever know that if he'd lived he would have left her." Her face creased in query. "But you think it's unlikely she had anything to do with his death, don't you?"

"Yes, if she was painting her nails at the time."

Anthea nodded agreement. "And where was Mrs Ducayne?"

"Waiting at home for Halberd." He gave a quick résumé of her story.

"Do you think she told you the truth?"

"There's something she hasn't told me. It may be personal and irrelevant to the case, but, like everyone else, including you"—he smiled—"she's withholding something."

"Including me?" Anthea was puzzled.

"You told me you had a luncheon engagement, but you omitted to tell me with whom." He looked at his watch. "I'm afraid you'll be a little late, and it's my fault. Will you please

144

drop me at the nearest Tube station—and give Keith my apologies for detaining you?"

"How did you know?" Anthea pulled out to pass a bus. "No, of course you didn't. You were guessing."

"I should prefer to call it an intelligent deduction from observed facts. But why didn't you tell me? Were you afraid I'd say that I thought it unwise?"

"I didn't want to risk your asking me not to."

"You're quite sure of his innocence, aren't you?"

"Of course I'm sure. If I weren't I wouldn't have accepted his invitation. He wouldn't have been so stupid as to destroy his own alibi if he'd needed one," she said with partisan illogicality. "But you don't have to worry. We're lunching at his club." Laughter bubbled in her voice as she went on: "I don't think anyone's been murdered there yet, but I'll ask the hall porter if you like." She braked and drew into the side of the road. "South Kensington station's just across the road. Are you sure you don't mind being left here?"

"Quite sure." He watched the car out of sight and was about to cross when his eye was caught by a man standing outside the station. A brief-case was in his left hand, and in the other he held a tightly rolled umbrella which he was impatiently tapping against his thigh. "Had a rolled-up newspaper in his hand and was smacking it into the other hand," Roddie had said.

A rumble in his stomach turned his thoughts to a more personal matter, and he remembered what a much-travelled friend had said years ago: "If you want a good meal in France, follow a priest; in England, nothing less than a bishop." Hopefully he scanned the crowded street, but it was empty of gaiters.

Chapter Twelve

COFFEE slopped from the cup into the saucer as the waitress slapped them down. At the adjoining table a young man with a blond beard that badly needed a dose of fertilizer combed his shoulder-length hair, while his companion, mirror propped against a salt-cellar, applied orange-coloured lipstick to her mouth. Why, the Inspector wondered as he tried with his tongue to dislodge from his back teeth what felt like a scrap of flannel, why was it considered ill manners in England to use a toothpick in public? Picking up the cup, he poured back into it the contents of the saucer, tasted it, added a spoonful of sugar, and directed his thoughts to less controversial matters.

Life was so full of coincidences that one was apt to overlook or disregard them. Was it solely by chance that Keith had come to stay in his uncle's flat on the day the latter died? That a lorry had been standing directly under the window to receive the body and so to delay its discovery? That the driver of the lorry was Minnie's brother? That two floors below the window from which Corsair fell Julian Killigrew had been working late on a report which he wished the dead man to read? The facts had been acknowledged readily by the people concerned, either because they wished to tell the truth or because witnesses made it impossible to deny them. But what of the statements to which there were no witnesses? Many of them, the Inspector had no doubt, were untrue. But why should anyone lie unless he feared that the truth would necessitate explanations which could not be given without involving himself or someone else in suspicion?

There was the matter of Keith's suitcase, which he claimed to have left in the lift and to have found in the flat on his return. Minnie said she had not gone up to the flat. Netta had rushed out at six-thirty intent on finding a taxi, and she had returned home some time after Keith. Halberd could not have known about the suitcase unless he had gone out to the lift only some three minutes before his death. One explanation was that Keith had himself taken it up. Lennie had seen him with the case at about a quarter-past six, but, though Keith claimed to have left immediately, no-one had seen him go.

It was difficult to visualize Keith as a murderer; it was, for that matter, difficult to imagine any intelligent, well-educated person of one's acquaintance in that rôle. But, though education and intelligence might discourage people from killing, they did not prevent them. The Borgias' victims would have kept a hard-working sexton on permanent overtime. Armstrong, Crippen, Landru, Haigh—the roll-call of death-dealers stretched to Hell and back again. In Keith's case one could adduce motive and means of entry. Was it not possible that the opportunity had been deliberately created? Was it. . . ? Heads looked round startled by the crash of a fist on a table. Keith claimed that the ceiling of his room had fallen down— but had it? The Sergeant had not checked his story. Why should he do so if he were satisfied that Halberd had died by accident? The Inspector opened the map of London that Sir Otto had given him. Shortly he rose and paid his bill.

Outside 10 Pearson Place a builder's hand-cart was drawn up against the pavement. Boards nailed to either side bore the words "Geo. Farthing and Son, Builders and Decorators", followed by an address and a telephone number. In the cart on a pile of empty paper sacks a ginger cat with battle-scarred ears lay asleep. A trail of plaster led across the pavement and up two steps to a closed door. At the windows of the ground floor and the basement white nylon-net curtains protècted passers-by from the risk of seeing whatever might be happening in the house. Strolling past, the Inspector considered his approach to Mrs Biddle, Keith's landlady. To disclose himself as a policeman making inquiries about Keith might well prejudice her against her lodger; it might equally well serve to fetter her memory. A slight subterfuge was both justifiable and desirable. He climbed the steps and rang a well-polished bell. The door was opened by a stout middle-aged lady in a print apron. She wore felt slippers, and her hair was tied up in a bright purple scarf. In one hand she had a yellow duster. Behind her a narrow hall led to a flight of stairs. The floor of the hall and as much as could be seen of the stairs were covered with sheets of newspaper.

"You'll have to excuse the mess," she said with a helpless gesture. "I've got the builders in, and there's plaster all over the place. If you've come about a flat I shan't have one free till the end of the month. One of my gents is getting married then and moving out to Ealing." She looked her visitor up and down with a landlady's tried eye and nodded to herself as if she were completely satisfied. "I expect you'll be the friend Mr Amberly said was coming along. If you're a pal of his I won't want no other references."

"I'm afraid I don't know Mr Amberly," the Inspector said apologetically. "I live not far away, and I'm looking for a reliable builder to make some alterations. I noticed you were having some work done and wondered if you could recommend your builder. I'm sorry to disturb you when you're so busy."

"Busy or not, I've always time for anyone who asks polite." Mrs Biddle put the duster into an apron pocket and composed herself for conversation. "Yes, you'll be all right with Mr Farthing. Nothing fancy about his work or his prices. Takes after his dad, who passed away at Christmas. Just finished his dinner and was pouring out the port. Dropped right out of his hand the bottle did and was all over the carpet before Joe—that's his boy what's got the business now—could get to it." An expulsion of air paid tribute to the double loss. "Well, I mustn't keep you standing. Talk never bought the baby a pair of boots, as they say. You'd best come in and see for yourself what sort of a job Joe's doing. He's off home to dinner, or he'd have showed you himself." She turned, beckoning the Inspector to follow. "Mind the paper on the stairs in case it slips. It's the first floor front where the ceiling fell last week—Friday it must have been because Mr Amberly had cod for his supper. Missed Mr Antrim but made a proper mess of things. If I'd had a room empty he could have had it, but there wasn't nothing free but the boxroom, so I was glad when he said he'd be staying with his auntie." Reaching the landing, she paused for breath before ushering her visitor into the room.

Dust-sheets covered the furniture stacked in the centre of the room, which smelled not unpleasantly of paint and distemper. The Inspector gazed with what he hoped was professional intensity at the ceiling and the rest of the new decoration. Some comment seemed to be called for. "Excellent work, excellent," he observed judicially, and nearly laughed to hear himself unconsciously burlesquing Bertie.

Mrs Biddle agreed. "Joe'll be off today as soon as he's cleaned up. Never leaves the place dirty like some I could name. Yes, the room looks nice enough now, but you ought to have seen it last week. Plaster everywhere, and Mr Antrim in his dressing-gown saying it must be his fault. There'd been a crack in the ceiling for months past and he thought it was getting bigger so he gets on a chair and gives it a poke. Before he knew what was happening there was half a ton of plaster on the floor. I was bringing up his breakfast and thought the house was coming down. When I opened the door he was poking at another piece which he thought would fall at any minute. He had his breakfast in the bathroom and was dressed and off to work before Joe came, though he was along by nine. Joe reckoned it was them aeroplane bangs that brought it down. Better tell the gentleman, he said, not to go poking at it any more or he might do himself a mischief. So when Mr Antrim came to fetch his things I told him, and he said he'd done enough as it was and wanted to pay. But I couldn't let him, could I? I mean to say, you can't expect things to last for ever." She stooped as a piercing whistle came from the basement. "That's the kettle for my tea. It won't come to no harm for a minute or two. If you'd like a cuppa, now—"

Courteously the Inspector declined. Behind a curtain of thanks and apologies he regained the street. Male frogs, he was thinking as he turned a corner, may not lead the most exciting of lives, but the good God has seen to it that most female frogs are born dumb. Some twenty minutes later he left King's Cross Tube station. Within ten minutes he acknowledged that Anthea had been right. Without a guide he was using time that could not be spared. Unfolding his map, he was peering at the infinitesimal type when a friendly and amused voice said, "A policeman lost in London? Surely not?"

He looked up to see Julian Killigrew. Smiling, he quoted, "Laugh'd and shouted, 'Lost! lost! lost!' I was, in fact, on my way to your office."

"Then we are well met since you wouldn't have found me there. I was about to keep an appointment with a publisher when I found I'd left at home some papers I needed. It's only a few doors up the street. If you'd care to come with me we'll have ten minutes before I must rush off." He brought him to an arched entrance on whose keystone the name of Rossetti Mansions had been incised in an almost illegible Gothic lettering. A board in the hall gave the names of the sixteen tenants. Striding ahead, long-legged, along an uncarpeted passage, he was turning a key in the mortise lock of his front door as the Inspector arrived.

"Just let me find my papers first," he requested as they entered a sitting-room. "If I don't I'm sure to forget something."

The Inspector looked round the room. It was clearly the

home of a man who lived alone and cared little for his surroundings. The carpet should have been sent to the cleaners some time ago. The curtains were faded, and at least two curtain-hooks were broken. The glass of the sash windows was grimy and a window-catch was missing. The bowl of an electric-light fitting held dust and a few dead flies.

"Do sit down," Julian said, "or look at the books if you wish. If you're like me—well, it's the first thing I do when I go into anyone's home for the first time. They say you can judge a man by his books. As a policeman, what do you think?" While he talked he was riffling through a pile of papers on the desk.

"Not in your case." The Inspector looked at the shelves that filled two of the walls. "You live and work among books. You have a great many sent to you for review. Some you will never look at again, but you put them on your shelves for the time being. Then every so often when there's no room for any more you weed out the unwanted. I think I might learn more about you from what you discard than from what you keep."

"Then I must confess that I get rid of all autobiographies by soldiers, politicians, and self-made men." Julian stuffed papers into a bulging brief-case. "Does that tell you anything?"

"That you dislike self-justification and are exasperated by indifferent English."

"But those are feelings common to all reasonable people. Doesn't it tell you anything about my character?"

"Perhaps. When as a child you were told to do something and asked 'why?' did your parents reply 'Because I say so'?"

"They did, and I resented it. Arbitrariness always puts my back up." Julian closed the flap of the brief-case and snapped the lock. "But let's stop talking about me. Have you established how Corsair came to fall?"

"I've made a little progress—and I've thought of one or two things I should have asked you yesterday."

"Well, ask me now," Julian said readily, "and let's sit down for a moment." He perched himself on the desk.

"You said that as far as you knew at the time Lennie and you were alone in the building on Friday night."

"Yes. I didn't know until Miss Brind told me that Corsair had come in to pick up some papers. She's my unfailing source of office news. I suppose he used the Staff Door."

"You mean you would have heard if he'd come in or left by the main entrance?"

"I'm pretty sure I should. I've been in my room two or three times after working hours, and on each occasion I've heard the main doors close after someone's departure. They make a loud and distinctive sound which one couldn't mistake for anything else."

"And you didn't hear them close on Friday night?"

"Yes, I did, but not long after everyone had gone home, perhaps a quarter or twenty past five. The commissionaire leaves about that time and, if I thought about it at all, I suppose I assumed it was him going out. If anyone left later I didn't hear them. I wouldn't if I was typing flat out. But Lennie would have been in the hall all the time. He could tell you whether anyone left and who it was."

"Lennie heard someone leave while he was in the lavatory, and at about the same time another witness saw a man on the steps outside the main doors."

"Was this before or after Corsair's death—or rather his fall?" Julian asked.

"Shortly before."

"Then either of these people—or it may have been the same man—may have been near at hand and seen what happened." Julian rubbed his chin thoughtfully. "Can your witness identify the man who was on the steps?" He glanced interrogatively at the Inspector. "No? But surely it shouldn't be hard to find out who left the office at that time? Couldn't you get the departmental or section heads to ask their staff?"

"If whoever it was has not yet come forward, don't you think he has some good reason for not doing so?"

"I suppose so." Julian seemed disappointed that his suggestion had fallen flat; then he laughed. "Of course you're right. I shouldn't be much good as a detective. I'd go hurtling up the first blind alley. I haven't got any of the necessary qualities for detecting."

The Inspector smiled. "And what are those qualities?"

"Oh, patience and persistence—a sympathetic personality—a poker face—an ability to sift the wheat from the chaff, to spot the lie and the half-lie—and the half-truth." From his perch on the desk Julian looked down quizzically. "Do you recognize yourself?"

"I recognize the flattery." Amusement flickered in the violet eyes. "But we've wandered away from the subject. When you left your office last Friday Lennie told you that Corsair had not yet gone off for the weekend. Did he say how he knew this?"

"He said there were lights in the flat and pointed out that Corsair's car was still outside. He'd started to say something more when a woman came from the side of the building across the courtyard. She seemed to be in rather a hurry. I must have made some comment because Lennie said she was Mrs Corsair and not a bad looker for her age. Then we exchanged a word about the weather and I went off to the side entrance."

"Can you remember what time you reached it?"

"At two minutes after half-past six, give or take a few seconds." Julian held up his left wrist. "I don't think this watch has varied more than that since I bought it five years ago."

"When you left your report on the letter-box, did you notice if the lift was up or down?"

Julian thought for a moment. "Up, I think."

"You're not sure?"

"Pretty sure."

"But Mrs Corsair must have brought it down a minute or so earlier."

"Yes, of course." Julian frowned. "Then someone may have been waiting to take it up. If he'd come by the alley that runs to the back. . . . Heavens, how stupid can I be? It could have been someone pressing the button outside the flat to bring the lift up, someone who had waited in concealment until Mrs Corsair left and he was able to come down unseen. To think that if I'd been a little later I'd have met him coming out of the lift—not that it would have for a moment occurred to me that he might be a murderer."

"Nevertheless it would have been an interesting meeting," the Inspector said drily. "Your description of this person would have been invaluable, assuming that he existed."

"You mean that I'm allowing my imagination to run away with me," Julian said a little sadly. "Perhaps I am. Life would be pretty dull if one didn't overcolour it occasionally. I'm afraid I must run if I'm going to keep my appointment—or, if you wish, I could ring and ask if I may defer it for half an hour."

The Inspector made a gesture of refusal. "No, you must keep your appointment. I think we've covered all the points I had in mind."

"Then I'll look forward to seeing you again. It's really rather satisfying to learn at first hand something about a case in which one is, however slightly, involved, instead of having to rely on Miss Brind's vivid if inaccurate gossip." As he bent to pick up the brief-case he was seized by a fit of coughing that brought a clenched hand to his diaphragm. "Damn doctor told me to cut down smoking," he gasped. "I told him I was down to thirty-nine a day instead of forty. He took me to the window and pointed somewhere up north. 'The crematorium's over there,' he said. 'You see that smoke pouring from the chimney. It's cigarette smoke'." Julian straightened up and taking from the desk a small, flat tin opened it and popped a lozenge into his mouth. "I'll walk to the corner with you and put you on the right road." Slipping the tin into a pocket, he picked up brief-case and umbrella and ushered the Inspector into the passage. At the end of the street he stopped. "When you've crossed the main road turn left, take the first right, then first left, and you'll be in Scott Street. Oh, by the way, I'm putting a short obituary of Corsair in the next issue of the paper. If you find out how he died let me know, and I can add a paragraph." With a wave of the hand he went off in the opposite direction to that which the Inspector now took.

The Inspector reached the main road as the traffic lights released a rush of impatient drivers. Behind him as he stood on the edge of the pavement a knot of pedestrians grew. In front, buses, vans, cars, and lorries rushed past to catch the next green light. A blast of diesel-oil fumes from some un-cared-for engine sickened his lungs. As he bent forward a sudden pressure against his lower spine pushed him off balance. A step forward might have enabled him to regain equilibrium, but something touching his shoe held one foot against the other so that neither could be moved. He felt himself totter. He saw the enormous tyres and rust-streaked radiator of a lorry and, through a dusty windscreen, an aghast face. A blue-clad arm glanced off his chin to his throat and stayed rigid, seeming to flatten his windpipe as it brought him back on his heels. Somewhere up the street traffic lights changed and the roadway was suddenly clear. The waiting pedestrians hurried across. Either they had noticed nothing unusual or they wanted no part of it. As the blue-overalled arm fell and a hand gripped his shoulder, the Inspector sucked in air.

"Not safe to let you out by yourself," said a voice he had heard that morning. "What's the matter, chummie? Come on all over faint, did you? No, you can't answer till you get your breath back. Just you hold on till you're better. I bet you thought you were a goner. If I hadn't stopped you they'd be mopping you up off the road and you'd be queuing up for your harp."

The Inspector managed a pale smile. He felt cold to the marrow in his bones. The wings of Death had never brushed him more closely. He looked at the handsome face bent over him in concern. Beads of sweat testified to the exertion that Roddie had made. The Inspector strove to express his gratitude and produced half-strangled thanks.

"Nothing to it, chummie," said Roddie. "If I hadn't been there it'd have been someone else. But me saving a copper— that's a rich 'un. I reckon they should give me the George Medal. Feeling better? That's the stuff. If you want a bit of a sit-down there's a caff just up the road."

"No, I'm all right now. I must have slipped on something." Colour was returning to the Inspector's face.

"Slipped?" Roddie's eyebrows rose. After a moment he said, "Well, you know best, chummie. Say the word when you're ready, and I'll see you across the road if you still want to go there." He let a length of copper piping slide through his left hand until one end rested on the pavement.

"Yes, I'm on my way to Termini House."

"Still on that Corsair lark, are you? I suppose the big brass has handed you the baby and you can't say 'no'. Seems to me though that if someone helped him out of the window and you find who it was it ain't going to do anyone a bit of good. I look on it this way. Corsair's up there trying out his wings, and the bloke what sent him there's satisfied. He's not going to pussyfoot round snuffing off a lot of others—not unless he's off his nut. If he is and you put the cuffs on him they'll shove him into some looney-bin and let him out again when they get tired of seeing his face. If he isn't and he gets a lifer he'll be out again when his time's up, hating everybody's guts and ready to do someone else in."

"You mean," the Inspector spoke more easily, "it's useless catching a murderer if he's not going to be hanged."

"That's it, chummie. Them chaps what wrote the Bible had it right. If you dish out to a bloke what he's done to someone else he's not going to do it again. It'd make a copper's life a bit easier too." Roddie grinned. "If you think you can make it across I'll be getting back to the shop."

"I can make it—but first I'd like to ask you something."

"Ask away."

"When you met Corsair as he left the lift, was he carrying anything except a newspaper?"

"Just the paper, like what I told you."

"Could he have been holding something under his arm?"

"He could—but he wasn't. Come on, we can get across now if we're nippy." Putting a hand on the Inspector's arm, he hurried him over to the other side. "Sure you're O.K. now? Right, I'll be off then." He gave the Inspector's shoulder a friendly punch. "Look after yourself, chummie."

Left to himself, the Inspector stood still for a short time. The shock of his narrow escape was passing, but not the thoughts it had engendered. He was making his way towards the turning for Scott Street when in the distance he saw a man walking away from him. It was too far for recognition, but the tall, well-held figure, the military step, and the briskly swinging walking-stick were parts of a picture to which a name might—perhaps too readily—be given.

Miss Purslane looked as if Time's scythe had lopped ten years from her age. Behind the neat and efficient secretarial façade happiness glowed. "I didn't expect to be here myself," she said, looking with an air of proprietorship round the office which when the Inspector last saw it had been awash with files. "But Mr Wolfe's secretary had to leave suddenly. Her fiancé's been posted abroad, and they're getting married so that she can go with him."

"I'm delighted to hear it, for both you and her." The deep voice communicated genuine pleasure. "But you must be even busier than before. I could return—"

"You're very considerate. But Mr Wolfe's at a meeting, and I'm well up with my work." She gave the typewriter a dismissive pat. "You want to ask me something?"

"Yes—but first let me say that I hope you'll be happy with your new employer."

"Miss Minton—that's his old secretary—says he's a joy to work with. Not that Mr Corsair wasn't," she added hastily.

"I gather he wasn't in a very good mood when he reached home last Friday. You mentioned he had been at a City meeting. Do you happen to know what the result of that meeting was?"

"It was with Pan-Finance and, from the letter they sent, everything seems to have been agreed satisfactorily. Mr Wolfe could tell you all about it if you could come back in half an hour."

"No, you've told me what I wanted to know. Had you any idea that Mr Corsair was going to Dublin last weekend?"

"Not until Monday, when the travel agents rang to ask where they should send the account for the unused ticket. Then I remembered that he'd asked a few days before for the file of correspondence with a firm in Dublin and hadn't given it back to me."

"Is it here now?"

"Yes, it was among the papers that Mr Antrim found in the brief-case and gave me for Mr Wolfe to see. It's on his desk now if you'd like to see it."

"Please."

When she returned he saw that clipped to the outside of the file was a sheet of paper torn from a memo pad. A neatly written note read: "Meet Kelly Shelbourne Hotel 10.30 a.m. Saturday. Quick decision re financing extension required. ? Debenture." Underneath in a large firm hand was a note: "Kelly rang Monday. Discuss with Antrim view him flying Dublin next week."

"The first note is Mr Corsair's and the second Mr Wolfe's," Miss Purslane said. "Mr Kelly is the managing director of the Irish firm."

The Inspector glanced through the half-dozen letters in the file and handed it back to Miss Purslane. Shortly he thanked her and went out. If she had not known that Corsair was flying to Dublin it seemed unlikely that anyone else had known. And yet. . . . Thoughtfully the Inspector entered the hall.

"Good afternoon, sir." The commissionaire was at his elbow. "A Miss Merrow telephoned to ask if you were here. When I said you were she asked me to tell you that she'd be here with the car about five o'clock."

The Inspector looked at the clock. It was twenty to five. "What time does Lennie arrive?" he inquired.

"He's here already—downstairs. Shall I have him fetched?"

"No, thank you. I'll go down." Following directions, the Inspector went down the stairs by the lift-shaft and turned left. The air in the passage was warm. It smelled—he sniffed analytically—of stored paper and toasted cheese. Arriving at an open doorway, he saw Lennie sitting at a table cutting up the remains of a Welsh rarebit. Before him an evening paper was propped against a teapot. Beside the table an electric fire tilted dangerously forward and, held in position by a string attached to a table-leg, had apparently been in use as a toaster. Although the fire was now switched off, the little room was intolerably hot.

Lennie looked up as a shadow thrown by the lights in the passage fell across the table. "Oh, it's you," he said. He sounded neither surprised nor unwelcoming. "Can't let a chap have his tea in peace, can you?" He waved towards a neatly made bed. "Make yourself at home. If you'd like a cuppa there's one in the pot. You won't. Well, maybe you're best off without. It's been standing for a bit."

Sitting down on the narrow bed and leaning against the wall, the Inspector looked round the room. Apart from the table, chair, and bed the only piece of furniture was a large cupboard to one side of which two brass hooks had been screwed. On them hung a jacket, a cap, and an old mackintosh. The floor was covered with carefully assembled offcuts from the linoleum he had seen in the offices above. Pictures of sailing-ships were pasted to the distempered walls. A check tablecloth, a rectangle of green stair-carpet before the bed and a yellow shade on the single hanging lamp-bulb completed the furnishing. It was the room of a man who had no home and few personal possessions, and who had made a nest in his place of work.

Lennie swallowed the last mouthful of rarebit, emptied his cup, pushed the used crockery to one side, folded the newspaper, and sat back. "Better get down to it," he said. "I got to be upstairs in fifteen minutes. What was it you wanted to ask me?"

"About a brief-case."

"What brief-case?" Lennie inquired without interest.

"Mr Corsair's. The one he was carrying when you saw him last Friday night."

"Black one, wasn't it, with his initials in gold?"

"It was. Do you remember seeing it in his hand when he left?"

"Can't say I do." Lennie looked vaguely into space. "Not lost, is it?"

"No. What time was it when Minnie brought you a cup of tea?"

The sudden change of subject seemed to startle Lennie. "After six," he said at last.

"Did she give it to you or leave it outside the Staff Door?"

"She banged on the door and called out, and I came along to pick it up."

"What did you do with the empty cup?"

"It slipped out of my hand and broke."

"And the saucer?"

"Gave it back to her Mon—no, must have been Saturday."

"When you let Mr Killigrew out of the building you were able to assure him that Mr Corsair hadn't gone off for the weekend since there were lights in the flat and his car was in the courtyard."

"That's right. He could see the car for himself."

"How did you know that there were lights in the flat?"

"How did I know?" For a moment Lennie sat motionless. "Well, it stood to reason that if Mr Corsair was there he wouldn't be sitting in the dark."

"For all you knew he might have been on his way down."

"Leaving his missus without a light?" Lennie asked scornfully.

"How could you know she was at home?"

" 'Cause I saw her going off later while I was talking with Mr Killigrew."

"But you'd already told Mr Killigrew about the lights in the flat," the Inspector said mildly.

"Says who?" asked Lennie in a belligerent tone.

"You told me so yesterday."

"You must have got me wrong."

"Mr Killigrew confirms it."

Lennie stared fixedly at the table. "Calling me a bloody liar?" he asked.

"I think you're trying to keep someone else as well as yourself out of trouble."

"Who else?"

"Minnie." He watched Lennie nervously rub forefinger against thumb. "Do you want to tell me about it?"

"I wasn't born yesterday. Suppose you tell me."

"Very well." The Inspector appeared to have expected the reply. "When Mr Corsair went up to the flat after leaving you he was out of temper. He asked if Minnie were in and when he found she was downstairs said he would speak to her on Monday. It was clear that she had either failed to do something or had done something wrong. She had carried out his instructions about packing his case and putting it in his car. She had brought the car keys up to the flat. Could he have objected to the lorry being parked in the courtyard? Possibly —but he could not have known whose lorry it was. Nor, had he known, could he have been angry with Minnie for giving her brother a cup of tea. He was angry with her for giving you one, but much more angry with you because you had broken the security regulations. He sacked you, didn't he?"

"I'm not saying." Lennie's voice was a harsh whisper. "I'm not saying a word."

The Inspector nodded regretfully and rose to his feet. "Is that because you're afraid I'll think that you killed Corsair?"

"I never set eyes on him after he went up." Lennie looked desperately round the room. "But what's the use of telling you? You won't believe me."

"Why shouldn't I believe you if you tell the truth?" The Inspector's tone was friendly and the touch of his hand on Lennie's shoulder reassuring. "Let's start with the cup of tea that Minnie left outside the door. Had you time to drink it before Mr Corsair came along?"

"I was drinking it in the doorway when he came in. 'Buxton,' he snapped, 'what the devil are you doing?' Gave me such a start that the cup slipped off the saucer. 'Get inside so's I can talk to you,' he said, and followed me in and shut the door. Then he jawed me like you said about breaking regulations, said I was leaving the place open to thieves and encouraging Minnie to think that rules weren't meant to be kept. He went on and wouldn't listen to me saying I wouldn't do it again. 'You won't have the chance,' he said. 'You'll get your cards Monday.' Then he was out of the door, and that's the last I saw of him. And I stood there cursing myself and him. Jobs aren't so easy to find for someone like me."

"You were wounded in the last war?" the Inspector asked.

"Went down with a destroyer—but I was one of the ones that came up again." His hand went to his face. "Lost a bit of my stomach and spoiled some of my beauty—not that I was ever much of an oil-painting." He gave a lop-sided grin.

The Inspector held out his cigarette case. In a moment Lennie went on: "It wasn't until I'd wrapped up the bits of cup that I saw he'd left his brief-case behind. I was in two minds what to do about it—to let it lie and pretend I hadn't seen it or to let him know. Well, I got on the blower and told him, and he said he wanted it but I wasn't to leave the offices. I said of course not, but I could come up in one of the office lifts and put it through the Emergency Door on the stairs. By half-past six he said and hung up without a thank-you. Then, when I'd been to the lav and shifted the table across the doors, I got the key from the cupboard and went up. I could hear him moving about in the flat—at least I thought it was him—and I gave a sort of cough to let him know I'd come with the brief-case. Then someone must have turned up the telly, and I knew he wouldn't hear me over that, so I left it on a table in the passage and went off down. I'd just put the key back in the cupboard when Mr Killigrew came down in a hurry and asked to be let out." He met the Inspector's eyes. "That's the truth. Honest it is. I didn't tell you before because I didn't want Minnie and me to lose our jobs."

"Does anyone else know that Mr Corsair was going to dismiss you?"

"I told Minnie about it. Said she wasn't to say anything to anyone about bringing me the tea as she'd get into trouble —and now I've gone and told you the lot. I s'pose you'll have to tell Mr Wolfe that I was given the sack—but you won't split on Minnie, will you?"

"I won't have to split on anyone, Lennie, if what I've learned has nothing to do with Mr Corsair's death."

"You mean you'll keep to yourself all I've told you?"

"That's what I mean." The Inspector held out his hand. Lennie stood up and grasped it. Whatever he may have intended to say remained unsaid, but for the next fifteen minutes the Inspector's fingers felt the intensity of his gratitude.

Chapter Thirteen

BERTIE closed his battered copy of *The Experiences of an Irish R.M.* and brushed tobacco ash from his waistcoat. By jove, those two women could write. Made you chuckle. Wonderful lives people lived in those days—not so long ago either. Hunting, hacking, fishing, rough shooting. Servants too. Whisky—spelt it with an 'e' in Ireland for some queer reason—at less than the price of a poor cigar. On five hundred a year you could live like a king. He sighed. Still, with what old Halberd had left to Claire they could now afford a bottle or two. That frog-faced solicitor had been a bit unwilling to cough up an advance, but when Bertie'd told him he'd sit there until he did—well, he knew he was beaten. Odd sort of feeling not to have any outstanding debts. He glanced up at the mantelpiece. Not a single unpaid bill behind the clock. Great Jehosaphat and a gunboat—half-past four already. Better get the luncheon things washed up before Claire came home. Get some potatoes peeled too—no, why not dine out? He rose decisively. Put the book back, then she won't be able to complain. Damn that hole in the carpet. Bertie stumbled forward, bringing a foot heavily against the bookcase. A thumb-sized chip of paint fell from the pedestal. Give it a touch-up next time I have the paint out, he promised himself as he replaced the book between *Jorrocks's Jaunts* and a morocco-bound copy of *With Gun and Rod around the World* by someone who modestly concealed his authorship behind the letters QQ. No, better touch it up now before Claire saw it. He ambled off to the broom-cupboard to collect the necessary equipment. Ten minutes later he finished cleaning the paint-brush and put it back on the shelf in the cupboard.

After a moment of indecision he briskly placed a footstool over the hole in the carpet and was about to take off his jacket in the kitchen when the front-doorbell rang. The girl to whom he opened the door smiled with a trace of shyness. "Colonel Summersby?" she inquired.

By jove, what a stunner! Bertie said to himself. Reminds me of whatsername in *The Glass* something. "Yes, I'm Colonel Summersby."

"Is your wife in?" she asked.

"Not at the moment. Shouldn't be long, though. Is there anything I can do?" Bertie took a step backward. "Perhaps you'd like to come in."

"Oh, thank you," she said gratefully. "I was going to ask if I could." She slipped past him.

"Don't think we've met before, have we?" Bertie closed the front door and followed her into the sitting-room.

She shook her head. "I don't think so. I'm sure I should have remembered if we had. My name is Sidebotham—Cynthia Sidebotham." Her smile was still shy. "I called here last Friday, but couldn't get any answer. Perhaps you were both out for the afternoon."

"Friday." Bertie scanned the charming face. No, it was ridiculous to imagine that her question was anything but innocent. Stupid to be jumpy. "Let me see. My wife was out playing bridge, but I was here all afternoon. Matter of fact, I was painting that bookcase over there."

She glanced at the bookcase, then looked at it more closely. "It looks very nice." She thought for a moment. "It was after six when I rang. Perhaps you'd gone out to buy an evening paper."

"Didn't go out at all." Why couldn't the girl accept a plain statement? "Can't understand how I didn't hear the bell. But there it is—I didn't. Sorry you had to make a second journey

165

—though I'm very glad you did, ha! Now what was it you wanted to see my wife about?"

"Actually I was going to ask if I could see her kitchen."

"The kitchen," Bertie repeated in surprise. "But what on earth. . . ?"

"Well, I'm supposed to see it. I mean I've got to tear off the labels as proof." She laughed suddenly and so delightfully that Bertie found himself laughing too. "Oh, I *am* stupid. I should have told you that I'm a research assistant. I'm working on a survey of domestic—"

"Well, I'm jiggered," Bertie interrupted. "I've been doing the same—"

"Let me finish, please," she begged. "It's a survey of household cleaners, and there's a ten-pound award if you have packets of the right kind in the kitchen. Do you use 'Glister for Grime' or 'Scrimp the Cleanser that *Really* Saves'?"

"Might do. Can't remember the names." Bertie looked thoughtful. "A tenner you said. We'll have a look together in a minute. Extraordinary thing our both doing this market research. Wonder if we're working for the same firm. Might find ourselves in the same team, what?"

"I don't think so," the girl said regretfully. "The firm I'm with is American and it's just opened an office here. I expect yours is one of the well-established firms."

"Pretty well established," Bertie said judicially. "I've been working for them for over six months now. Had some rum inquiries to make. Shan't ever forget one for some sausage-makers. People didn't realize that they'd been eating plastic sausage skins for years. There was a woman in Baron's Court —Oh, must you go? Still a few calls to make, eh? Yes, do look in again." Bertie closed the front door and, removing his jacket, went into the kitchen. He was about to turn on the taps above the sink when the rattle of a latchkey announced Claire's return.

"Who was that girl who's just left?" she asked as Bertie turned to greet her.

"Just someone doing market research. Wanted to know what kind of cleaning stuff we had in the house."

"Was that all she wanted?"

"That's all. Said she'd called last Friday evening and couldn't get any answer. I just said I'd been here all the time."

"Are you sure that's all you said?"

"Didn't have time to say any more. She was in and out of the place in a couple of minutes." Bertie turned on both taps. If Claire wanted to cross-examine him she'd have to shout. She did.

"Turn those bloody taps off!" Claire waited, then said levelly, "That girl drove off in a red Mini as I came up the street. I'm sure it was the same car that was parked on the other side of the road when I came in last night and found that detective here."

"Oh, come, old girl. London's chock-a-block with red Minis —and in any case policemen don't go about in them. You're letting your imagination run away with you." Bertie patted her shoulder with a damp hand. "You'll feel better when you've had a drink."

"Yes, I think I will." Claire went into the sitting-room, peeling off a glove with automatic fingers.

Turning on the taps, Bertie squirted liquid detergent into the basin. As he sloshed the mop round in the growing lather he was thinking that the girl had gone off without making any further reference to that ten-pound note. She hadn't even looked in the kitchen.

It was five-past five when the Inspector came into the main hall. Brief-cased, umbrella'd, and in a few cases hatted, the last of the senior staff were sedately departing. "Looks a bit gusty," a pot-bellied man in a blue pin-stripe was saying to a grizzled man in a Gannex coat. "Flying up North tonight, aren't you?"

Gannex nodded. "Hope I can find a taxi to take me to the Air Terminal."

"Got my car round the corner," said Pin-stripe. "I'll give you a lift; it's on my way. You can charge a taxi up to expenses and treat yourself to a couple of drinks on the 'plane."

"A thoroughly immoral suggestion," Gannex commented. "And you a churchwarden and a pillar of the. . . ." The rest of the sentence was lost as he passed out of hearing range.

The Inspector came to an abrupt halt, then turned apologetically to a man who had been unable to avoid bumping into him. How could he have missed the point when he was talking to her this morning? he asked himself. Across the now nearly empty hall he caught sight of the clock and, comparing it with his watch, registered that if the clock were correct his watch was a minute slow. Was he being infected by the English passion for time-keeping? It was only in England that people asked one for "the exact time", as if they expected one to produce a chronometer. Even Lennie had used the phrase—or was it Lennie?

"The young lady's waiting for you outside," came the commissionaire's voice in his ear. "And, begging your pardon, but have you finished with Lennie as it's getting near locking-up time?" The veined eyes were bright with the hopeful curiosity of someone whose colleague has attracted the attention of the police.

"Yes, I have. I don't think I shall have to trouble either of you again."

"You mean you're packing up the case, sir?" The tone betrayed the speaker's wish to be first with whatever news there might be.

"I'm still sorting out the contents," the Inspector replied as he moved towards the doors.

Behind him the commissionaire raised a puzzled hand to the back of his head. That was a queer answer to a straightforward question. The Inspector must have misheard him.

"You really mustn't do that sort of thing again," the Inspector said with unaccustomed severity.

"But you said you didn't believe Bertie's alibi"—Anthea looked up with innocent eyes—"or that Claire had telephoned him when she said she did. I thought he was much more likely to tell the truth to a casual caller than to a policeman. So, when I had half an hour to spare after leaving the nursing home, I thought up a good story and went to see him. And I did spot the lie about the bookcase, didn't I?"

"You did indeed," the Inspector said warmly. "And it should help me to get the truth out of him. But how in the world did you come to know such a thing?"

"Because in my first rep company I was a sort of general dogsbody. I was props and painted scenery and furniture, did box-office and programmes, posted bills, played small parts—oh, everything. Now I'm supposed to be a 'promising young actress', and Bertie really fell for my performance. He's not very bright, is he?"

"Not so far as I can judge. But put yourself in his place. Just suppose he's killed a man accidentally or on purpose, suppose he's mentally unbalanced, abnormal, and a girl comes along and questions him about last Friday evening, what's going to be in his mind? He's as likely as not to think that she knows something and must be got rid of."

"But he hasn't the slightest idea who I am."

"How do you know he hasn't?"

"I told him I was Cynthia Sidebotham."

"Sidebotham," the Inspector repeated witheringly. "No-one who looks like you could possibly be called Sidebotham—or if they were they'd find some other name."

"But I had to think up some name, and that was the first one that came into my head." She accelerated to pass a bus and then asked with unconvincing casualness, "Is Keith still on your list of suspects?" When he did not answer at once she added, "You let me lunch with him."

"In a public place, yes." Before she could say anything he went on, "If a personal liking and a private judgment were reliable tests of innocence neither of us would have any doubt

169

of Keith's. But if I were to say to you at this point, 'I'm giving up the inquiry because I shall never find the answer', wouldn't it be unfair to him? Would you ever be able completely to forget the evidence that points to him and remains unexplained?"

"But why should I have gone to Termini House?" asked Mrs Ducayne. "And what makes you imagine that I did?"

"You told me so this morning," the Inspector said gently. "You were expecting Mr Corsair to pick you up here in the car. It wouldn't have occurred to you that he had forgotten this arrangement and taken a taxi to the Air Terminal unless you had seen that his car was still outside the building. You also stopped yourself from saying that you had never been to the flat and corrected the 'to' to 'inside'."

Her head was lowered and she stayed silent.

"It was about eight o'clock, wasn't it?" he asked.

Into the quietness came abruptly a metallic rattling, then the sound of some liquid sizzling on a hot surface. He looked at the bent head and, rising, went out of the room. In the kitchen a pan of water boiled furiously on an electric cooker. Turning the switch to "OFF" he found a cloth beside the sink and, mopping up the water that had bubbled over onto the hot-plate, squeezed out the cloth. Then he returned to the sitting-room. The fair head was raised and a smile lit her face. "Thank you," she murmured, and then, "I went to find him —to find out what had happened."

"Yes," he said, and there was in his voice a note of sympathetic encouragement such as one uses to a child when one is trying to find out how some small injury or misadventure occurred.

"He was always so prompt. If he was going to be late he always rang so that I shouldn't worry. I remember saying to him that I'd never thought any man could be so considerate. He answered, 'I'm not like that except with you.' Perhaps he wasn't—but that was the Halberd I knew." She shook her head as if to break the strands of remembrance. "When half-past seven came and he hadn't arrived or telephoned I began to get anxious, as I told you. When I couldn't bear it any longer I put on a coat and took a taxi to the corner of Scott Street. There were lights on the top floor and his car was in the courtyard, so I thought he hadn't left. I went to the side entrance and rang the bell—and I kept my finger on it until I knew that no-one was going to answer it and I went away."

"And came back here?"

"What else could I do? I continued to ring the flat—until half-past twelve. And then somebody answered—and I thought it must be Halberd until he spoke and told me that Halberd had gone away." She put a hand to her forehead. "That's all. Would you get me something to drink, please? There's whisky in the sideboard. Please drink with me."

He poured out two fingers for her and a token measure for himself and, adding soda, brought the glasses over. "Why did you not tell me this before?"

"It wasn't relevant. According to the inquest he'd been dead for nearly two hours when I went there."

"Were you at the inquest?"

"No. I had no evidence to give."

"Did you attend the funeral?"

"No."

"Or send flowers?"

"Yes, anonymously." She turned the glass in her fingers. "Do you have to ask me these questions?"

"I ask them because you said this morning that you were glad there was no mention of you in the will."

"I was glad," she said simply. "I still am."

"Would you tell me why?"

"No. It's a purely personal reason."

"Will you allow me to tell you?"

"If you wish to."

"You kept silent for Mrs Corsair's sake," he said and, watching her face, saw her surprise. "You told yourself that

171

for her to have lost a husband whom she thought faithful was sufficiently hard and painful, but for it to become publicly known that he had had a mistress and intended divorce and remarriage was an indignity and a humiliation that she need not suffer." If she accepts this picture of herself, he thought, then I shall know that she had not told me the truth. "Am I right?" he asked.

Unexpectedly she laughed. "Of course you're not—and you know it perfectly well. I'm not a plaster saint. I'm an adulteress—and I was a very happy one. How could I have cared an atom about a woman I'd never seen? I kept silent for the sake of my menfolk and myself. For Halberd's sake because I loved him and didn't wish to see his name in the gutter Press. For Mark's sake—and the reasons there need no explanation. And for my own sake because branded women are often barred by self-righteous institutions like the B.B.C., and because most men think that a woman who has been loved by a married man is an easy tumble." She drew a sighing breath. "Perhaps it would have been better if I had been."

The Inspector stayed silent, but there was question in his face and attitude.

"Because if I'd been that kind of woman I shouldn't have loved Halberd, and I'd only have to nod to replace him. Because it's lonely without him and I can't any longer say to myself 'I'll be with him on Saturday or Sunday.' Because no woman likes to spend her nights uncomforted." Her nose wrinkled in irony. "Chastity's a cold bedfellow and bedsocks are no substitute for affection—even if one's man snores as Halberd did."

It was those last few words which were in the Inspector's mind as he left her. Could any woman say them of a man whom she had not long sent to his death?

The doorbell rang as Claire came into the sitting-room. "I'll answer it," she said to Bertie. Her face froze when she opened the front door to find the Inspector waiting. "I thought I asked you to telephone if you wished to see either of us," she told him icily. "We shall be having supper in a few minutes."

"I hoped to find you both in at this time," the Inspector said blandly. "If you had told me the truth on my previous visit I should not have had to disturb you again."

Claire drew breath sharply. "You'd better come in and explain what you mean." She stood aside to let him pass and, closing the door, followed him into the room, where Bertie was levering himself up to stand in uncertain silence as if he were waiting for the prompter's voice.

"Does either of you wish to revise your accounts of last Friday evening?" His eyes rested momentarily on their faces, then turned to the bookcase. "Then we must reconstruct them. But first let me ask you a question, Colonel Summersby. There is a small patch of new paint on the pedestal of the bookcase. Is it still wet?"

"I expect so." Bertie was perplexed. "I touched it up less than an hour ago."

"Then please accept my apologies. I fear you will have to touch it up again." While he was speaking he took a piece of paper from his pocket and went over to the bookcase. A brisk rub uncovered the underlying dark varnish. Rising, he dropped the paper into a wastepaper basket. "Ordinary paint won't hold on varnish, I'm afraid." There was the faintest tinge of admonishment in his voice. "You need a special paint or a special undercoat. I expect your local shop will supply it."

"Well, really, Inspector." Claire's tone would have quelled a sergeant-major. "Is this—this exhibition a part of your inquiry?"

"It shows us that your husband was not telling the truth when he said he spent until six o'clock sandpapering the bookcase so as to remove every trace of varnish before he painted it."

Claire gave an exclamation of contempt. "It only shows he was boasting about his workmanship. He always does."

173

"Why should he wish to boast to me?" the Inspector inquired. "No, Mrs Summersby, it seems to me more likely that he was trying to account for time during which he was doing something else. But let us return to that point later." He turned to Bertie. "I believe you borrowed Mr Antrim's suitcase on Monday?"

Bertie blinked at the sudden change of subject, and his face bore the expression of one choosing his words before he committed himself to an answer. "Had to have something to pack some of Corsair's clothes in."

"Was there no other suitcase in the flat which you could have taken?"

"One or two, but they were all small."

"You needed a large suitcase?"

"Easier to carry than a lot of little ones," Bertie said readily.

"How did you know that Mr Antrim had brought a large suitcase with him?"

"Saw it—I mean must have seen it somewhere. Can't remember where." Bertie passed a hand over his chin and looked at Claire as if she might be able to supply the information.

"How can the size of a suitcase possibly have anything to do with Halberd's death?" Claire asked acidly, "You come here, Inspector, play a silly game with paint, accuse us of lying, and ask a number of footling questions. My husband has told you all he can. He may have slightly exaggerated the work he had put in on the bookcase. But if he wasn't here, how could he have seen the television programme in which his old friend appeared?" With a triumphant smile she picked up a letter from the mantelpiece. "This is from his friend saying that he had no idea that he was going to stand up and jaw about the Roman head. The archaeologist who dug it up was taken ill at the last moment, and my husband's friend was asked to say a few words in his place. If you think my husband could have known about this in advance perhaps you'd care to read the letter."

"There is no need for me to read it," the Inspector said. "I am not questioning whether Colonel Summersby saw the programme. What I am questioning is that he saw it here."

"Where else could he have seen it?" Claire rapped out.

"In the Corsairs' sitting-room. As you will recall, Colonel Summersby, the television set had not been switched off."

The silence was broken by Bertie's expulsion of pent-up breath. Claire, who had involuntarily drawn back half a pace, recovered herself sufficiently to snap, "You're letting your imagination run away with you, Inspector."

"I'm using my imagination. If I am wrong Colonel Summersby will tell me. If I am right I hope he will say so." He turned to Bertie. "You will have to tell the truth sooner or later," he said reasonably. "Someone will have seen you leave the house last Friday. Someone will have seen you return."

Bertie's eyes wavered between his wife and the Inspector. "Better tell him, old girl," he muttered at last.

"Tell him yourself," Claire said coldly. "I don't know why I've wasted my time trying to protect you."

"Don't you?" asked Bertie without any expression, taking a handkerchief from his sleeve and passing it over his forehead. "Better sit down, Inspector." He indicated an armchair. "Don't mind if I stand, do you? Easier to confess that I've been a bit of an ass. Should have told the police at once, but got cold feet when I heard that Halberd had taken the count, poor chap. Not that I'd seen him that night. I hadn't, but people mightn't believe me." He cleared his throat. "Better start right at the beginning, though I expect you know all about it."

The Inspector made an encouraging sound.

"I rang Halberd on Friday after lunch," Bertie began. "Had a bad run on the horses and needed a loan. Bookmaker was cutting up rough. Said if I didn't pay up on Saturday he'd have me put on the black list, and then nobody'd take a bet from me. Said something about letting the boys know. Sounded like a threat to me, though he said it wasn't. Any rate, I got through to Halberd and asked him for a loan. He wasn't too pleased, but he said I could have it on Monday. I tried to tell him I must have it at once, but he rang off. Well, my wife went off to play bridge and I started to clean up the bookcase. But by the time an hour had gone by I knew I'd never finish the job. Thought if I slapped the paint on thick enough the varnish wouldn't show. So that's what I did, and I was tidying up when the 'phone rang. It was the bookie. He just said, "See I get the money tomorrow," and didn't give me time to say a word. It wasn't so much the reminder as the way he spoke that made his meaning clear. Put the wind up me, I can tell you."

"You haven't told the Inspector how much you owed the bookie," Claire interposed coldly.

"Twenty pounds," said Bertie after a moment of hesitation.

"There was also the final rates demand and about twenty-five pounds' worth of overdue bills," Claire continued remorselessly. "I'm sure the Inspector wants to have the whole sordid truth."

The Inspector stayed silent. Why was Claire so determined to strip Bertie of the remnants of his dignity? Was this her normal practice or had she some ulterior motive?

"Well, I had to have the money," Bertie continued, "and there was no one but Halberd who could let me have it. He'd said on the telephone that he was leaving at seven and, as it was now about six, he ought to be at home. Only thing was to go round and see him. So I did. Found I'd got just three-pence on me, so had to walk. Got there at twenty-five to seven. Saw Halberd's car outside and lights in the flat, so I was sure I hadn't missed him. Side-door was open and lift there, so I didn't have to wait."

"And when you were in the lift you noticed a suitcase under the seat. You looked at the label, saw it belonged to Keith, and took it with you into the flat."

Bertie nodded. He did not appear to be surprised at the Inspector's knowledge. "Seemed the decent thing to do. Netta'd told my wife he was staying there. Probably quite safe where it was—but might have been taken." He paused. "To tell the truth, I thought the fact that I was bringing it in might help to get over the awkward moment when Halberd came along. So it was in my hand when I rang the bell. No-one came, so I rang again. Thought I heard it chime but wasn't certain, so I knocked and the door swung back a couple of inches. Latch must have stuck, I suppose. Any rate, I went in, put the case down, and called out. There was a light in the sitting-room and someone talking, so I went along. Television was on and the window wide open, but no-one there. I had a look round the flat and sat down to wait for Halberd. Thought he'd be along any minute. Watched the television—and that's when I saw old Craddock with this head. The programme he was on finished at seven. I waited another fifteen minutes or so, then gave up and came home."

"If you needed the money, why didn't you wait a little longer?"

"Because he wanted to be home before I returned between half-past seven and eight," Claire replied. "He hadn't yet told me about his debt to the bookie and he didn't want me to find out. He knew quite well that if he was out when I got back I should want to know where he'd been and why—and that it wouldn't take me long to extract everything. As you've discovered for yourself, he's not a good liar."

A good spur-of-the-moment explanation, the Inspector thought, but not quite convincing. At that particular moment it was more important to Bertie to get some money for the bookie than to conceal the matter from Claire. "What time did you get back here?" he asked him.

"At half-past seven."

"Then you didn't walk?"

"I took a taxi."

"You had obtained some money then?"

Bertie hesitated, then looked Claire. Her face and her hopeless gesture said as clearly as words, "I've just done my best to get you out of this hole, but you've fallen straight back into it." The seconds ticked away until at last Bertie said, "I managed to borrow some."

"From someone who came to the flat or whom you met when you left?"

"From Netta." The seconds ticked away. "Must have taken an evening purse with her as her bag was in the sitting-room. I only borrowed a little. Ten pounds to keep the bookie quiet until I could raise the balance, and some silver for the taxi. I was going to tell her—but after we learned of Halberd's death I couldn't. And I didn't want anyone to know I'd been there that night in case they thought I'd had something to do with it." He passed the back of his hand across his brow. Sweat gleamed on the knuckles.

"I see." Whatever the Inspector was thinking did not colour his voice. "But you told your wife."

"He had to," said Claire bleakly. "His wallet was on the dressing-table. I picked it up and saw the notes. I thought up an alibi and rehearsed him until he knew it backwards."

"You believed that he had told you the complete truth?"

"I know when he's lying," she said brusquely.

"And you felt that the best way to protect him was for both of you to lie?" The deep voice held no criticism.

"It was the only way, Inspector. If what you now know were to get into the hands of the Press, do you think either of us would have any peace? Would anyone believe that Bertie had not arrived earlier and been caught by Halberd taking money from Netta's bag? I don't have to say any more, do I? But I want to say this. A wife will lie to protect her marriage. Ours is a poor marriage because I've always been master in the house. I'm not a nice woman. I have a sharp and venomous tongue and I can't stop myself from criticizing Bertie in public as well as in private. I don't have to tell you about Bertie's faults. You've heard enough to form your own judgment. Perhaps with a different marriage partner our faults might have been fewer and less uncontrolled. We let each other down—we let ourselves down. But we're

178

bound together by twenty-five years of shared experience, and basically each of us is loyal to the other. That's why I lied for Bertie—and for the same reason I have no doubt that he would lie for me, bitch though I am."

"That's right, old girl," said Bertie. "Trouble is, as you said, I'm not a good liar and I let you down. Never could talk my way out of anything. Used to get beaten at school once or twice a week. Managed better in the Army. Always carried out orders, so never got into a jam. Suppose I've got both of us into a jam now."

The Inspector remained silent while his eyes travelled from husband to wife. Was Claire sincere in what she said? Was her self-criticism really genuine? If not, then she had given an admirable performance of a wife who, despite shortcomings on both sides, remained faithful to her man. Could this performance have been intended to divert his attention from weaknesses in Bertie's revised account of his actions last Friday? If so, what were those weaknesses? Or could it have been designed to give such a picture of frankness and honesty that she would not be questioned about her own actions?

"Do you wish to amend your account of what you yourself did last Friday, Mrs. Summersby—apart, of course, from the telephone call which you did not make to your husband?"

"No, the rest of what I told you is the truth."

"You said you rang your friends about your lighter shortly before twenty-past six. Where was the call-box from which you rang?"

"Not far from Dolphin Square. I can't tell you the name of the street, but I can take you there. Of course, I realize that won't prove that I used the call-box." Her smile was nothing but a widening of the mouth.

"Then I have only two more questions. Colonel Summersby, were you anywhere near Euston Road this afternoon?"

"No. Been indoors since lunch. Claire'll bear me out."

"When you left Termini House on Friday—at seven-fifteen

179

I think you said—did you leave the side-door open as you found it or did you close it?"

"Closed it. Open door's an invitation to walk in." Bertie came forward a pace as the Inspector stood up. "What I've told you about borrowing a tenner from Netta—from her purse, I mean—don't have to tell anyone else, do you? Rather tell Netta myself if she has to know." He spoke with anxious rapidity punctuated by gasps. There was a plea for mercy in the watery eyes and self-abasement in the droop of the shoulders.

"If you have both told me the whole truth I shall not need to see either of you again, and there will be no reason for me to repeat any of this conversation." The Inspector left them looking at each other, and when he closed the door neither of them had broken the silence.

It was midnight before Anthea went to bed, leaving her uncle and the Inspector in the study.

"So the position is this," Sir Otto said. "You think that neither Mrs Ducayne nor Lennie had anything to do with Corsair's death. Minnie was, of course, in the lorry with her brother when he fell. Lennie confirms Julian Killigrew's alibi. Roddie is a 'possible' if we can accept that he was Netta's lover and that, thinking you had found out more than you had, he tried to push you under a lorry."

"If he hadn't held me up I should probably now be in a mortuary," the Inspector said lightly. "So I may be a trifle prejudiced in his favour."

"And not unreasonably," Sir Otto said with a smile. "As for Bertie, you feel he has now told you the whole truth—but you are uncertain about Claire."

"If she took a taxi after the bridge party she could have reached Termini House while Corsair was alive."

"And made the telephone call about the lighter on the way?"

"She may not have made it when she says she did. Would

her friends know whether the call came from a private telephone or a public one? And would they recall the actual time at which she rang?"

"Probably not within ten minutes either way."

"Then it's possible that she was in the flat when Corsair died, concealed herself until Netta went, and then telephoned from the study or Netta's bedroom."

"And departed, leaving the front door unlatched for Bertie when he turned up at twenty-five to seven. You know perfectly well that you're only putting up an Aunt Sally for me to knock down," Sir Otto said, tapping the ash from his cigar. "And now for Keith. It was he who wanted the inquiry reopened. Why should he want that if he had killed Corsair?"

"More than one murderer in the past has asked the police to investigate a death and offered his assistance—and been found out. Why did they do it?" The Inspector spread his hands. "Vanity? Paranoia? Challenge? Psychiatrists will give you a dozen more words. We know now that Keith did leave his suitcase in the lift; but his alibi is still unconfirmed and there is a certain amount of circumstantial evidence against him. But one could say the same of Netta and Claire—and for that matter of Lennie. The fact is that what I've found out amounts to almost nothing in the way of evidence of murder. If I can't find some clear evidence within the next twenty-four hours I'll have to admit defeat and tell Mallick so. But I shall still believe that Corsair was not alone when he died." He took a notebook from his pocket and opened it. "There are still two men connected with the case whom I haven't seen. One is Minnie's brother, Sid; the other is the man whom Roddie saw on the entrance steps when he drove away from Termini House shortly before Sid and Minnie came out into the courtyard."

"And you think Sid might have seen this other man?" Sir Otto stifled the birth of a yawn. He was too interested in the discussion to allow the late hour to terminate it.

"It's possible." The Inspector was looking at the notebook.

"I've made out a timetable from various witnesses' accounts. Certainly they may have misinformed me, but, as the times dovetail, I'm assuming they are reasonably correct. At approximately thirteen minutes past six Lennie heard the main doors close and presumed that somebody had just gone out. At about the same time Roddie saw a man on the entrance steps. A minute or two later Keith arrived in a taxi, went to the side-door, brought down the lift, put his suitcase in it, and, according to his story, went off at once to the Tube station. He had scarcely gone when Minnie and Sid came out to the lorry. Sid sat in the cab while Minnie went back to fetch some knitting. She was away for two minutes. Now neither Keith nor Minnie saw anyone on the steps. Whoever was there had gone—but he need not necessarily have gone far. He may, indeed, have been near at hand when Corsair fell. No-one has asked Sid whether he saw anyone while he was waiting for Minnie. If he did he may be able to give some sort of description. It's a slim chance"—the Inspector shrugged—"but it's a chance. It might enable us to find out who it was that left the office building, why he was coming out so long after office hours, and why he did not come forward to tell the police or anyone else that he had been there shortly before Corsair fell."

He closed his notebook and looked at Sir Otto for any comment. Sir Otto nodded—and nodded again. A faint snore broke the silence. Smiling, the Inspector picked up an ashtray and let it drop onto a table. When Sir Otto opened his eyes his guest was again closing his notebook.

Chapter Fourteen

THE sun was bright and the air pleasantly crisp as Anthea drove north against the Friday-morning traffic. The Inspector had been thoughtful during most of the journey, recalling the conversations of the past two days. He apologized for his silence as they walked across the farmyard and knocked on the door.

"Sid's round the back," said Mrs Butterworth when he had explained the reason for his visit. "You run along, Bill, and tell your Dad he's wanted," she instructed her son, who was staring with undisguised admiration at Anthea. "Come along in and have a cup of tea while you're waiting. The kettle's on and it won't take a minute. It's warmer in the kitchen, if you don't mind taking us as you find us. We don't hardly use the parlour," she explained, "unless we're expecting company, and I've got the dust-covers on. Sit down now and make yourselves at home." She put a plate of cakes on the table. "Just help yourselves. You must be hungry after that drive. Minnie was saying on the 'phone that you was trying to find out how that poor man came to fall to his death. Terrible, wasn't it? There's Dad coming. I'll leave you alone with him as soon as I've mashed the tea."

"There's no need for you to go," the Inspector assured her. "I just want to check some small points with your husband." He stood up to shake hands with Sid and smiled permission to Bill, who was fidgeting in the doorway in the hope of being allowed to stay.

"I can't tell you more than what I told the Sergeant," said

Sid a few moments later, putting his cup down. "But if you want to hear it, here goes." His story corroborated Minnie's in every detail. She had been with him for the full period of his visit except for the few moments when she took Lennie a cup of tea and when she went back for her knitting.

"When you parked your lorry on arrival, was there any other car in the courtyard besides the green Humber?"

"There was a van over in the corner, one of them little Austins."

"Was it still there when you left?"

"No, it had gone off."

"Did you see anyone in the courtyard while you were waiting for Minnie?"

"Not a soul. Remember looking round and wondering where everyone had got to. I asked Minnie, and she said it was like that at night when the people in the offices went home." Pulling a crumpled packet of cigarettes out of his pocket, he held it out to Anthea. The Inspector felt for his lighter, but Bill had jumped forward and was striking a match. When the cigarette was glowing the Inspector said, "May I see those matches, please?"

"There aren't any left now," said Bill as he handed over an empty book-match folder.

The Inspector bent the cover forward to disclose a gilded letter K. "Did someone give you this, Bill?" he asked.

Bill hesitated. A glance at the pleasant face assured him that he had done no wrong. "I found it in the yard," he said. "Last Saturday before all the policemen came. It was in the straw Dad took out of the lorry."

"There's no proof that those were Keith's matches," Anthea argued as they drove away, but even to herself her voice lacked conviction.

"No proof," the Inspector agreed. "But there is or was a box of similar booklets on his desk, and this booklet is identical with the one he gave you, which you've just put back in your bag."

"Other people have book-matches with their initial on the cover, and names beginning with K aren't so awfully uncommon. There's Kenneth and Kate and—I can't think of any others, but there must be some. And there are all the surnames like King and Knight and—what about Julian Killigrew?" Momentarily excitement lit her voice; then despondently she acknowledged, "I suppose people don't have the initials of their surnames put on things unless they're peers of some kind or Greek shipowners. But in any case Keith's not the sort of man who'd ever want to see his initial on anything. He's too modest."

"You mean he didn't buy these matches?"

"Good heavens, no. Someone sent him a box of them. He doesn't know who it was, as there wasn't any note or card in the parcel—just the firm's label on the wrapping."

"Did he tell you the name of the firm?"

"Yes, it was Shacklock's, the pipe-makers in Jermyn Street."

"Then we'd better go there," the Inspector said.

Shacklock's was—and is—one of the old-established London shops whose name is almost a household word, at least in those households where only the best is good enough and can be afforded. Their pipes, tobacco, and snuff are to be found wherever a well-shod British foot has trodden. The firm was founded by one James Shacklock in the year of the Great Plague when smoking was widely thought to confer immunity from infection. The original premises perished in the Great Fire, and a subsequent series of moves took the business to its present home during the nineteenth century. Now coat after coat of black paint has filled in the details of the carving of the timbered shop-front. Inside, the noticeably uneven floor has been covered with dark-red carpet under whose thick pile the boards creak rheumatically. An L-shaped counter and one or two discreetly lit display-cases are the sole signs that this is a retail business. The main area contains half a dozen low tables, each invested by three upholstered chairs, on which customers sit and chat as in a social club, while their orders of tobaccos are made up in the blending room at the rear. One or two of them glanced up as the Inspector and Anthea came in, returning immediately to conversation or meditation.

From behind the counter a young man recognized them as strangers and came forward to offer his assistance. A police inquiry? In Shacklock's? If they would wait for a moment Mr Shacklock himself would see them in his office.

Charles Shacklock, rubicund, portly, silver-haired, Savile-Row-suited, McAfee-shod, M.C.C.-tied, signet-ringed, and slightly pigeon-toed, received them genially, listened in silence, smiled, lifted the receiver of an internal telephone, spoke to Dispatch Department, jotted a note on his blotting-pad, and turned to the Inspector.

"Here we are," he said. "A box of twenty-five of our match-booklets was sent round by hand to a Mr Keith Antrim at Termini House last Friday morning. The cost was debited to the account of Mrs Netta Corsair. The assistant who attended to her was my son, Simon. He'll be with us as soon as he's finished with his present customer. Is there anything I can tell you meanwhile?"

"I noticed a tray of initialled booklets on the counter," the Inspector said. "They seemed to cover most of the alphabet. Is that tray always there?"

"Always. We give a folder to every customer—and quite a number help themselves." The rubicund face crinkled like a skin of a long-stored apple. "Our richest customers aren't above a little petty pilfering. It's mostly the women who take them. A few men help themselves—the kind who wear embroidered shirts. It's the women who buy them for themselves and as presents. The Christmas trade is substantial." He looked up as the door opened. "Come in, Simon." He made brief introductions and sat back while the Inspector explained what he wished to know.

"Yes, I remember Mrs Corsair coming in last Thursday," Simon said. "She had a friend with her." He gave a recognizable description of Claire. "She bought some cigars for this friend's husband and looked round for something to give to a nephew. I can't remember which of them suggested bookmatches. I asked Mrs Corsair if she wished to enclose a card, and she said 'no', she would tell him herself. When I said I would have to get a box from the stock-room she said she couldn't wait and asked me to send it round."

"Did you give Mrs Corsair a booklet when she made her purchases?"

"Yes, I knew her initial. Her friend said that she'd like one too, and took it before I could ask which letter she would like."

"Did you see which letter she took?"

"I'm afraid I didn't."

"Will there have been a booklet lettered K in the tray?"

"Several. It's one of my jobs to refill the tray every night when we close. The J's usually go fastest, and I make them up to twenty. The K's are made up to five. Last Thursday there were some K's left at the end of the day. I can't remember how many, but it was certainly more than one."

It was half-past one when Anthea and the Inspector reached Termini House. Julian, crossing the courtyard on the way to a late lunch, gave them a smiling salute. Keith and his secretary, Miss Bohun, were both out. The box of bookmatches was not on Keith's desk; it had been put in the bottom drawer of the pedestal. There were twenty-two booklets left. Replacing the box, they went out and had a quick meal at a near-by pub. Neither of them was inclined to be conversational. They were leaving when Anthea asked, "Should we ask Netta whether it was she or Claire who thought of sending Keith the book-matches?"

The Inspector shook his head. "You're assuming that one of them planned for a booklet to be found with Corsair's body and for the remainder to be traceable to Keith. If that is the case, isn't she going to attribute the purchase to the other one? All we can say at the moment is that this particular booklet may be one of the original twenty-five in the box or one that was picked up from Shacklock's counter. If it's the former, anyone might have gone into Keith's office and taken it, or Keith may have given someone a booklet just as he gave one to you. If it's the latter, the likely person is Claire. If Keith is back from lunch he can tell us what he knows."

But Keith was not in his office. "He's gone down to Wellclose Square to see a firm of packers," Miss Bohun told them. "He said he'd be back between half-past four and five to sign his letters."

"Wellclose Square." Anthea seemed surprised. "Isn't that off Cable Street?"

"Yes, it is—and it's not a very nice neighbourhood. But Watersons have been there for over a hundred years, and they've no intention of moving. It's handy for the docks, and there's no problem about getting local labour. You needn't worry." She smiled at Anthea. "I've been down there myself —and it isn't nearly as dangerous as Soho."

As they returned to the main hall the Inspector was thinking that circumstantial evidence was, as a Lord Chief Justice had said, often the best evidence. In a murder case it was often the only evidence. But when it was supported by tangible. . . .

"Is there anywhere you want me to take you?" Anthea's voice broke through his thoughts.

"Nowhere," he said. "I shall stay here."

"Until Keith returns."

"Yes, until he returns."

"Then may I leave you? I'll be back by five."

"Yes, do," he said absently. It was not until some time later that he recalled her smile and wondered what mischief she was up to. Now, walking across the hall, he asked the commissionaire, "Is there an unoccupied room which I could use for two or three hours?"

"Yes, sir. Mr Gray's away. You could use his room. I'll send a messenger with you to show you where it is." He beckoned imperiously at a blue-uniformed man. "Take this gentleman up to Room 820 and see that he has everything he needs." To the Inspector he said, " 'Fraid you'll have to wait a minute, sir. There's only one lift working. The gate's jammed on the other one."

A short distance along the corridor on the eighth floor the messenger opened a door and was moving aside to let the Inspector precede him when an inquisitive face peered out from the adjoining room. "You won't find Mr Gray in," said Miss Brind. "He's on holiday down at Brighton."

"Thank you, Miss Brind." The Inspector smiled warmly, so warmly that she returned to her typewriter convinced that she had been able to give him some invaluable information.

As the afternoon passed, the London sky began to disappear behind darkening clouds. Over the Atlantic, southwest of the Scillies, a storm gathered. Gulls flew inland and fishing-boats took in their nets and made for the nearest sheltered anchorage. From pavements outside second-hand shops dealers carried furniture, books, and other merchandise indoors. Meteorologists who had predicted continuing fine weather hastily revised their prognostications.

Minnie, coming into the sitting-room, picked up the tea-tray. "I've put your supper out on a tray," she said. "All you've got to do is to put a match to the ring to heat up the soup. If Mr Keith wants second helpings there's enough and to spare." She glanced at the window. "Looks as if it might come down hard."

Netta agreed that it did. "I think I've found another flat, Minnie. It's near the Albert Hall. If I were to move there, would you come with me?"

"Yes, madam, I'd come. Truth to tell, I'll be glad to get out of this place, and I expect you will." She paused before saying self-consciously, "I mightn't be able to stay long, though. You see, I might get married in the spring. If I did I've got a friend who I think'd suit you."

"I hope you do marry—and how nice of you to think about me." Netta looked at Minnie's buxom figure with a stir of envy. "I hope you'll have children."

"It won't be my fault if we don't. It's not much of a marriage without kids, is it?" She stopped, appalled by what she had just said. "I didn't mean that personal—it's just what I think for myself."

"So do I." Netta's head was bent. "Run along now and enjoy yourself."

When the door closed behind Minnie she switched on the television. I must make more friends, she was thinking. Claire isn't really a *friend*. I could never tell her anything that genuinely mattered. If I move to another flat I must do something useful and meet more people. I could address envelopes for charity. Her thoughts wandered on, leaping backward, forward, and sideways. When the clock struck five she was considering a winter cruise.

In a block of flats near the London Clinic in Harley Street, Roddie inserted a new cartridge fuse into an electric plug and screwed up the plug. Glancing up at the plump face hovering over him, he said. "Look, lady, you don't have to 'phone me every time a fuse blows. Costs you a quid or more each time. Mind you, I'm not saying it isn't easy money for me, but it ain't worth it to you. Supposing I was to leave you a dozen of these fuses, then your old man could do the job when he gets home." He rammed the plug into a wall-socket. "Was there anything else wanted doing?"

"The electric iron isn't working properly. Would you look at it? You'll find it on the kitchen table." She placed a multi-ringed hand on his shoulder.

Roddie rose swiftly, turning so that her hand hung momentarily in the air. "I'll give it the once-over," he said, and went down the passage to the kitchen. He heard her heels patter past as he tested the iron. Three minutes later he called out, "There ain't nothing wrong with this iron that using the regulator won't put right. You got it so low you couldn't hatch an egg under it."

"Oh, have I?" she called back. "Would you come here for a moment? I think I'd like a light over the mirror. I'll show you where."

Roddie walked along the passage, wrinkling his nose. Powerful sort of pong the old girl used. Must have put lashings of it on. At the bedroom door he stopped abruptly. Cor, stone the crows! he said to himself. What does she think she is? A ruddy Mata Hari? She was lying on the double bed completely nude, her arms raised in welcome, on her face an expression of simpering invitation. "Come here, Roddie," she murmured.

He leaned against the doorpost, fascinated by the expanse of quivering flesh. "Better get a hold of yourself, ducks," he said. "Put something on or pop between the sheets. I'm an obliging sort of chap, but I've got other calls to make." He backed a step as she showed signs of leaving the bed. "My missus is outside in the van. She can pick out a bedroom window from the rest, and if she sees a light on here she'll be up before you can say Lollobrigida." From the vantage point of thirty birthdays he regarded her with an objectively contemptuous pity. "If you want me again I'll come if you promise to be a good girl. If you try anything on I'll send along a pal of my dad's the next time. He can change a fuse as well as the next man, but he's topping seventy, and even dirty books don't interest him no longer." He stood up straight. "Ta for now, ducks—and don't trouble to see me out." Once outside the door he took a grubby handkerchief from his overalls and mopped the back of his neck.

"Shall I send the obituary of Mr Corsair to the printers, Mr Killigrew?" Miss Brind picked up the signed letters.

"Yes, send it down." Julian frowned. "No, it'll have to go

191

on Monday with the final copy. I promised Mr Wolfe to ask Mrs Corsair if there was anything she wished said."

"Would you like me to take it up to her?"

"I'd like it, but I think I ought to go myself." He signed the final letter and gave it to her. "That's the lot. You can don your roller-skates as soon as you've put the letters in the post-bag."

"My roller skates?" Miss Brind's face cleared as the penny dropped. "Do you know, I used to go roller-skating at Holland Park. That must have been more than thirty years ago. Doesn't time fly?"

"Relentlessly. Off with you before I find something else for you to do." Julian breathed relief as the door closed. During the last few days Miss Brind had shown a tendency to linger. He must discourage it.

Bertie flushed the tea-leaves down the sink and rinsed out the teapot. Claire had gone out after lunch, presumably to play bridge. She'd been nicer than usual today, he thought. Got up first and made the breakfast, gone shopping with him, cooked a damned good curry for lunch, and given him a quick kiss on the top of his head as she went off. Hanging up the tea-cloth, he returned to the sitting-room. That Inspector chap had been right about the bookcase. Claire had knocked another chip off the pedestal today with the carpet-sweeper. Be a bit of a job stripping the whole thing, though. Might strip the pedestal and paint it again—find out about that undercoat the Inspector had mentioned. He sneezed before he could get a handkerchief out of his pocket. Now why had he tied that knot in the handkerchief? Not much good tying a knot if you couldn't remember what it was to remind you about. He sat down and concentrated.

By jove, that was it. Return Keith's suitcase. The boy hadn't said how long he'd be staying in the flat, but now that Netta had the maid sleeping upstairs he'd probably be going back to his own place pretty soon. He looked at the clock.

Might as well walk there. Get a breath of air and stretch his legs. Have a chat with Netta, too.

Going into the bedroom, Bertie bent down and pulled the case from beneath the bed. Shortly, suitcase in left hand and walking-stick at the trail in right hand, he strode purposefully down the street.

Lennie sat at his table in the basement of Termini House. He had arrived much earlier than usual to carry out a special task. Learning from the commissionaire that the Inspector was in the building, he asked to be informed if the latter showed signs of departure; if so, Lennie wished to speak to him. On his way from his room in a near-by street he had bought some sheets of writing-paper and an envelope.

This would be the first letter he had written for a very long time, and he was finding it difficult to begin. Should he start with "Dear Sir" or "Sir"? Perhaps "Dear Sir" was a bit familiar for someone whom one scarcely knew. He dipped into a bottle of ink the fountain-pen he'd picked up in the street and found impossible to fill. Head on one side, in a sloping copybook hand he wrote "Sir". After a moment's thought he added a full-stop. The opening sentence proved elusive. Once he'd put that down on paper the rest would be easy.

Maybe a cup of tea would help, he said to himself and, getting up, filled his electric kettle from an enamel jug and plugged in. While the water heated he took from the cupboard a packet of tea, teapot, cup, and plate. From a net shopping-bag he had brought with him he extracted and unwrapped from its paper a slice of slab cake. The kettle boiled, and he made the tea and sat down.

Feet thumped along the passage, and the commissionaire appeared in the doorway. "Len, do us a favour," he panted. "The missus is on the blower and wants me to meet her at five before the shops shut."

"What time do you want to be off?"

"Ten to."

"That's O.K. I'll be up before then and take the keys off you?"

"And if one of the chiefs asks where I am?"

"I'll say you had such a thirst on you that you had to be at the boozer when it opened." Lennie grinned. "It's all right. I'll tell 'em your missus's has had an accident and you went off like greased lightning hoping to find she'd copped it."

"You're not so wrong at that," the commissionaire said and, with a word of thanks, lumbered off.

Finishing his tea, Lennie pushed the dirty crockery aside and, picking up the writing-paper, gazed at the single word at the top of the sheet. Five minutes passed before he dipped the pen into the ink-bottle.

The Inspector stood looking out of the window. The sky was now completely clouded over except for a small patch of pale blue across the river. In the courtyard below two errand-boys passed a ball of paper from one to the other until, reaching the street, one of them kicked it across the road. Immediately below the window a grey Rover had replaced Corsair's dark-green Humber. Idly he wondered where the Humber had gone. What more can I do? he asked himself. If Keith cannot explain away the match-booklet it is my duty to pass the evidence against him to Superintendent Mallick.

Turning away from the window, he went over to the desk and, picking up his notebook, put it in his pocket. Through the open window came the deep tone of a church clock striking the three-quarter hour. It was followed immediately by the sound of a car drawing up; then silence as the motor died. Looking out, he saw the familiar red Mini. Out of it came Anthea and Keith. So that's where she went, he said to himself. Has she told him about the book-matches? And what was his reply? He stared in astonishment. They were laughing. Happiness shone from Anthea's face as they walked towards the entrance. When they were out of sight he closed the window and walked down the stairs to the ground floor.

Already the staff were preparing to go. Before he reached Keith's room Miss Bohun flashed past him towards the cloak-room.

Keith was at his desk. Before him lay a pile of letters awaiting signature. "But he wouldn't have gone without leaving a message," Anthea was saying as the Inspector came in. "Oh, here he is." Jumping from her chair, she ran to meet him. "It's all right," she cried. "Everything's all right. Tell him, Keith."

"You remember," said Keith, "me telling you that during the breakdown on the Tube I shared a strap with a man whose face was vaguely familiar and who said something about a 'bloody awful crush'? Well, I met him today. He's one of the directors of Watersons. When I found Anthea waiting for me outside the packing-store I mentioned this, and she insisted on being introduced to him so that he could confirm he'd seen me on the train." Keith grinned. "I didn't realize until then that I hadn't an alibi."

"And the book-matches," Anthea prompted.

"I put a booklet into my pocket last Friday when I found I'd left my lighter at home. When Uncle Halberd asked me for a light I gave him the matches and he kept them. As soon as I came back to my desk I took another booklet. Here it is." He held out a partly used folder. "As you know, I gave Anthea one—and there are twenty-two left in the box." Half-seriously, half laughing, he added, "Anthea's counted them again. I hope I'm now in the clear."

"Of course you are," said Anthea gaily.

"Then as soon as I've got rid of these letters we'll go. Anthea says I'm dining with you at Sir Otto's." He leafed through the letters. "I should be through in about fifteen minutes. When I've put them in the pillar-box just up the road we can be off. If you'd like to look at a paper, Inspector, there's a fairly comfortable chair over there."

"I need some fresh air and exercise," the Inspector said. They'll be happier alone, he thought. It may take Keith a little longer to sign the letters, but what does that matter? "If I return before you're ready I'll wait in the car," he said as he went out.

Coming into the entrance hall, he saw that it was a minute to five o'clock. The hall itself was empty, but there was a feeling of waiting in the air, as if the staff were standing by their office doors poised for departure. Lennie was in the commissionaire's cubicle. His back was turned to the hall and he was licking an envelope. He did not see the Inspector's quiet exit.

"Shan't be long now." Keith signed another letter and added it to the pile by his left hand. "If you'd like to fold this lot and stick them in their envelopes it'll save a bit of time. Besides"—he looked up with a grin—"I don't like the taste of gum."

"Nor do I. However—" She came over to the desk and was about to pick up the letters when he said suddenly, "Good Lord, I haven't told Aunt Netta that I shan't be in to dinner. Could you ring her and explain? You'll have to use the 'phone in Wolfe's office. The red one is a direct line—you only have to dial."

"I'll go up and tell her. It's nicer—and I can see if she's all right, and tell her you won't be too late home."

"It would be nicer," he agreed. "You'd better take the keys in case she doesn't hear you ring. That's the side entrance—you'll probably find the door open—and that's the key to the flat. Don't let her keep you talking too long. I'll probably have posted the letters and be waiting by the car when you return."

She smiled at Lennie as he came from the commissionaire's box to see her out. "Is the Inspector still with Mr Antrim?" he asked.

"He went out just before five." Seeing the expression on his face, she said, "Did you want to see him?"

"Only for a minute, miss. It's nothing that matters." His

tone told her that, whatever it was, it was important to Lennie.

"He should be back in a few minutes. I'll tell him before I take him home. I shan't forget," she promised.

The Inspector, returning from his stroll, saw her going in the direction of the side-door. She did not see him but walked briskly round and went up in the lift. As she put the latch-key in the door she could hear a television or radio playing loudly. An orchestra was giving its rendering of the *Bolero*. She remembered with an inward smile what Keith had told her and wondered whether Netta was dancing round the room by herself. She was opening the door when the passage lights went out, but not before she had seen a hand in the act of taking keys from a hook on the wall. There was swift movement, and a handkerchief was thrust over her nose and mouth.

Chapter Fifteen

THE Inspector crossed the courtyard to the main entrance. He was angry, coldly and implacably angry, and the anger was directed against himself. It was inexcusable not to have realized it until now. It was obvious, so obvious that he had been blind to it. The fact that Superintendent Mallick had also been blind was no extenuation. As soon as Anthea returned they would go to Scotland Yard.

He peered through the glass doors. Keith should be coming out at any minute. Lennie came into the line of vision; he had a bunch of keys in his hand and was going in the direction of the Staff Door. Of course; it was approaching five-fifteen, the time at which the commissionaire locked that door. Where was the commissionaire?

Lennie stopped, surprise evident in his face; he cocked his head as if he were listening, glanced at the keys in his hand, stood indecisive for a moment, and then, moving fast, made for the lifts.

Mystified and curious, the Inspector went down the steps to the courtyard and, going a short distance from the building, looked up. Light poured from the Corsairs' sitting-room window, and he could hear the sound of music. Yes; it was Ravel's *Bolero*. A subdued illumination, probably from an internal passageway, lit a window on the floor below the flat. That must be Lennie. But what was he doing on a floor on which the rules forbade him to be? The Inspector continued to look upward. He could hear nothing except the *Bolero*.

The *Bolero*!

For reasons that he was unable later fully to explain to

himself—perhaps because the music had already figured in the case, perhaps because he sensed violence in the air, the Inspector ran to the side entrance. The private lift was not on the ground floor. Of course Anthea could have taken it up. Impatiently he waited for it to descend. It seemed to rise with funereal slowness. At the front door, finger about to press the bell, he saw that a latchkey had been left in the lock. Entering, he hastened along the passage and opened the sitting-room door. Netta sat before the television set, happily waving her hands in time to the music.

With a brief apology he turned off the sound. "Is Anthea here?" he asked.

It was apparent that she had not taken in the question. "Oh, it's the Inspector," she said in a pleased voice. "Have you caught those burglars yet?"

"*Please*, have you seen Anthea?"

"Not since she was here with Keith. Such a nice—"

"Hasn't she just been here?"

"No." She shook her head. "I've been alone since Mr Killigrew left."

"When was that?"

"Three or four minutes ago. He came to show me the obituary—" Netta blinked and stopped. The Inspector had gone.

He was about to look in the other rooms when he saw that the key-ring labelled FIRE—EMERGENCY EXIT was no longer hanging on its hook. The door itself refused to open to his urgent hand. Bending down, he could see that there was a key in the lock on the other side. To get into the building he would have to go down to street level. Lennie would let him in—if Lennie had returned to the hall. Wait a moment—unless he had misconstrued Lennie's actions the Staff Door was still unlocked. Tearing a sheet from the notebook, he wrote down a number and a name and, returning to the sitting-room, put the paper in Netta's hand. "Mrs Corsair," he said with quiet force, "this is a matter of life and death. I must go now. Please ring this number and ask for this man or one of his assistants. Tell him who you are and say that I need immediate help in Termini House. If Keith comes in before I return tell him that if the Staff Door is open it means that I am in the building and want him there as quickly as possible." He left her staring at the sheet of paper.

The lift took him slowly down. The Staff Door opened as he turned the handle and he breathed his thanks. The hall was deserted, and he noted that Lennie had not yet moved his work-table to its usual nightly position against the inner doors. Keith's room was in darkness. On the half-open gate of one of the lifts hung a printed card "Out of Order". If the other lift had been taken up to one of the top floors it would be time ill-spent to wait while it made its slow descent. He began to run up the stairs.

His heart was thumping as he reached the eighth floor. From the open doorway of Julian Killigrew's room came subdued light. On the desk an Anglepoise lamp shone on a scatter of page-proofs, but the room was empty. He raced to the next floor. A breeze from an open passage window chilled the sweat that was now trickling down his face. From behind him uneven footsteps approached and he pivoted. Towards him came Julian, carrying the motionless body of Anthea.

"Thank God you're here," Julian panted. "Open that door. There'll be something there I can put this girl on."

The Inspector opened the door of the directors' luncheon-room and helped Julian to lay his burden gently down on an upholstered settee. As he took the flaccid wrist and laid his fingers on the pulse he noted a bruise-mark on her cheek. Lightly he probed body and limbs, then, raising an eyelid, examined an unseeing eye.

"I'd better get a doctor," Julian said anxiously.

"She'll come round very soon." The Inspector spoke with reassuring certainty. "She's fainted, but I think she is unharmed. Until she can tell us what happened perhaps you will tell me what you know."

Julian slumped into a chair. "Give me a moment, please. I thought when I found her that she was dead. Who is she?"

"Anthea Merrow. The niece of a friend of mine."

"What on earth was she doing here?" Julian took out a handkerchief and mopped his brow. Then he said harshly, "There's a dead man along the passage."

The Inspector waited.

"It's the caretaker, Lennie." Julian balled the handkerchief and gripped it tightly. "I was in my room when I heard someone moving on this floor. I was thinking it was Lennie whom I hadn't seen in the hall when someone screamed. No, it wasn't a scream—but a sound as if somebody had started to scream and been stopped almost at once. Then there was a noise: it's hard to describe it but it seemed to me like someone drumming their heels against the floor. There was desperation about it. I ran towards the sound, which came from the stairs to the Emergency Exit. I'd nearly reached them when a man came falling down backward. I heard something snap as his head struck a stair. I'd just recognized Lennie when I saw the girl lying farther up the flight. He must have attacked her, and somehow she'd managed to trip or push him away." His eyes turned to the settee as Anthea stirred and opened her eyes to see the Inspector bending over her.

"Somebody hit me," she said, putting a hand up to her cheek.

"Don't move or talk if it hurts," he told her.

"It doesn't really hurt." She moved her head experimentally, and her gaze passed from the Inspector to Julian. "This isn't the flat, is it?"

"It's the office floor below the flat," Julian said. "I found you a few minutes ago on some stairs. Can you remember how you got there?"

"I remember going up to the flat and opening the front door. Then the lights went out and somebody put a handkerchief over my face."

"You don't know who it was?"

"I only saw a hand taking some keys from a hook on the wall. I think it was a man's hand. That's all I remember." Anthea raised herself on an elbow. "I feel better now. Is Keith here?"

Her question was answered by the sound of running feet and the eruption of Keith through the doorway. His eyes went from her to the two men and back to the pallid face. "What's happened? Are you all right?" He knelt and took her hand.

"I fainted, but I'm perfectly all right." She returned the pressure.

"Keith, will you please take Anthea back to the flat?" The Inspector's tone was quiet and firm. "Give her some tea with plenty of sugar and ask your aunt to make up a bed for the night. But before you go tell me where you were five minutes ago."

"I must have been at the end of Scott Street and on my way here."

"You'd been taking your letters to the post?"

"Yes. And I walked a short way with a man who wanted to find Harley Street. As neither of you were in the car I thought you'd probably both gone up to the flat, so I went up. Aunt Netta gave me your message and said she'd rung up the number you gave her, and I came here as fast as I could." He turned to Anthea. "You must have come through the Emergency Door if you were up in the flat seeing Aunt Netta. We'll go back that way."

"I'm afraid it's locked." The Inspector was thinking of Lennie's body, which Julian had said was on the stairs leading to the Emergency Door and the roof. "Will you take one of Anthea's arms, Mr Killigrew, and Keith the other?" Easily, unhurriedly, he shepherded them from the room and walked rapidly ahead, saying, as he steered Anthea and Keith into the lift, "Will you come back here, Keith, as soon as you've taken her up and seen that she's all right and being looked after?"

He waited until the lift was in motion. "And now, Mr Killigrew, we'll look at what you found."

Lennie lay on his back, his head on the bottom step, his heels on the seventh. As Julian had said, it needed no second glance to know that he was dead. He seemed shrunken, as if the life-blood had been drawn from him; but no blood was visible. His eyes stared upward, still and doll-like, and his face bore an expression of peacefulness as if separation from the living world had been no intolerable ordeal.

"He's lying as I found him," said Julian, "and the girl was up there. Her skirt was up to her thighs and one arm was trapped under her body. She was completely motionless, and it wasn't until I bent down that I could see she was breathing." He seemed to shiver. "What can we do about Lennie—about the body? Can we move it?"

"Not for the present, I'm afraid."

"We can at least cover him." Julian produced a handkerchief and, stepping in front of the Inspector, spread it over the face and stood upright. "There's something up there on the top tread." A few rapid strides and he shook his head. "Just dust. While I'm up here I'd better make certain that the door's locked. You don't want anything disturbed, do you? Yes, it's locked." He came down and handed the two keys on their labelled ring to the Inspector. "I expect you want to report what's happened and make arrangements about the body. There's a direct line in the commissionaire's cubicle."

"Mrs Corsair has already telephoned Scotland Yard. While we are waiting shall we sit down and see if we can sort out what happened?" The Inspector started off towards the directors' luncheon-room.

"Let's go to my office? I can give you a comfortable chair and, in any case"—Julian half smiled—"I've left my cigarettes there. I know I shouldn't smoke—but I must." Leading the way to his room, he waved towards a chair, sat down at his desk and, pushing aside the page-proofs, offered a cigarette, accepted the refusal, and lit one himself. "You know," he said, "it would never in a month of Sundays have occurred to me that Lennie could have killed Corsair."

"Is there any evidence that he did?"

"Evidence? No, I suppose not. But why should he have attacked Miss Merrow unless he thought that she had found out something, some sort of proof?" His fingers tapped the desk-top. "What could he have been doing in the flat?"

"And how did he get in?"

"How?" Julian looked surprised at the question. "With one of the keys I took out of the door and gave to you."

"Those keys were hanging *inside* the flat. You may have noticed them when you visited Mrs Corsair this afternoon."

"I don't remember seeing them." Julian thought for a moment. He was about to say something but stopped as the sound of lift-gates and a murmur of male voices came into the room.

The Inspector rose. "If you would please stay here, Mr Killigrew, I'll be back as soon as possible."

Julian was correcting proofs when the Inspector returned. With him were the Superintendent and a flushed and put-out Bertie. Introductions between Bertie and Julian were made and the former sat down, saying with some testiness, "Asked me to sit in at some sort of conference. Fellow dead somewhere here. Expect you know."

"I was just about to ask Mr Killigrew about his visit this afternoon to Mrs Corsair and what happened subsequently," the Inspector said. "Perhaps he will tell us now."

"Of course." Putting an elbow on the proofs, Julian explained succinctly about the obituary notice. "I left here shortly before five and went to see her. She had no suggestions to make, but I stayed talking to her for a time. It wasn't quite a quarter-past five when I left, and I hoped to find the Staff Door still open so that I could pick up these proofs and correct them over the weekend. It was open, and I walked up, as one of the lifts wasn't working and the other was somewhere up top. I'd only just switched on this desk-light when I heard someone moving about overhead—and then the scream." He glanced interrogatively at the Inspector and in response to his nod continued his story up to the time of the latter's arrival.

When he finished, the Inspector, turning to the Superintendent, asked if he required any further clarification. Mallick shook his head. "If you'll carry on, Inspector, I'll interrupt if I have any query."

"When you returned here, Mr Killigrew, after seeing Mrs Corsair, was there anyone in the entrance hall?"

"I didn't see anyone."

"Since the Staff Door was open, didn't you expect to see the commissionaire?"

"No. He was having an early night. I saw him from my window hurrying along the road at about ten to five."

"Did you happen to notice if there was a light in Mr Antrim's office?"

"I think I'd have noticed if there had been. You can see right down the passage from the hall, and Keith's door is one of those with a glass panel with his—" He broke off as Keith appeared in the doorway, curtly returned the Superintendent's nod, and looked with surprise at Bertie.

"Came along with your suitcase, Keith, found these chaps milling about and they roped me in. What's this all. . . ?"

But Keith was not listening. Anger was in his voice as he faced the Inspector. "Why the devil didn't you tell me that Anthea had been attacked? We might have caught the man before he left the building."

"I wished to prevent her knowing about, perhaps having to see, a dead man," the Inspector said. He summarized Julian's account. "You will agree that it was better she should not be told until later."

"Yes, I agree—and thank you. But"—Keith rubbed the back of his head—"Lennie—I can't believe it. I've known him for years. He was so quiet, so ordinary."

"So are most killers—until they kill," commented Julian.

"We are trying," the Inspector said, "to establish how Lennie got into the flat and why he was taking down the keys of the Emergency Door from their hook in the passage when Anthea arrived. What time did she leave your office, Keith?"

"Between ten and a quarter-past five."

"And you yourself?"

"As soon as I'd sealed the letters up. I looked at the clock as I went out. It was eighteen minutes past."

Julian leaned forward as if about to speak, caught the Inspector's eye, and stayed silent.

"And you'd heard nothing during the previous few minutes, no sound from the top floor."

"Nothing at all. My door was shut, of course."

"I see. Now, Keith, we agreed before you came in that Anthea was probably attacked because she had seen or found some evidence that connected her attacker with your uncle's death. Has she mentioned anything of the kind to you?"

"Nothing. She has no idea who attacked her—or why."

"Isn't it possible," asked Julian, "that Lennie knew she was going up to the flat and went up to lie in wait for her? He had only to take the lift up—the one that's working—to be well ahead of her. I know that doesn't explain how he got into the flat—but perhaps the Emergency Door had been left unlocked."

"He could scarcely rely on that if he intended to dispose of Anthea," the Inspector observed drily. "But I would like to go back to the problem of Corsair's death. I think the solution to that will also solve the present problem. You told me, Mr Killigrew, that you were in your office last Friday until you came downstairs and Lennie let you out at half-past six. What you can't tell us is what Lennie was doing in the preceding twenty-five minutes. According to Lennie himself, he let Corsair in by the Staff Door at about five-past six, waited while Corsair collected some papers from his office, and showed him out some two or three minutes later. What he did not tell me at first was that Corsair found him breaking the security regulations and sacked him on the spot. A little later Lennie saw that Corsair had left his brief-case behind and rang up to ask if he needed it over the weekend. When Corsair said 'yes' Lennie took the key of the Emergency Door from the commissionaire's cupboard, went up, opened the door, and tried to attract someone's attention. Unable, however, to make anyone take notice, he left the brief-case in the passage and returned to the hall in time to let Mr Killigrew out."

"And do you believe this story?" asked Julian.

"Don't you?"

"Of course not. Isn't it pretty evident that Lennie saw Corsair, that when Corsair confirmed the sacking Lennie saw red, and, in the ensuing struggle, Corsair fell or was pushed out of the window?"

"If this is so, what do you think was Lennie's reason for trying to kill Miss Merrow?"

"I don't suppose we shall ever know. She can't tell us, and he's dead. It seems to me quite likely that he was a pathological case." Julian leaned forward, suddenly excited. "We were wondering how he got into the flat tonight. I didn't know until you mentioned it that there was a key to the Emergency Door which Lennie could get at. Of course he must have used that one. It's obvious, isn't it?"

"It seemed so," the Inspector allowed. "Unfortunately that key is still in the cupboard. Superintendent Mallick and I found it there ten minutes ago."

"Then there must be some other explanation." Julian was disappointed but not deflated.

"I think there is. I believe we shall find it in the person whom Lennie heard leaving the building shortly before six-fifteen last Friday."

"Surely the person whom Lennie *said* he heard?" Julian said.

"Yes." The Inspector accepted the correction. "But there seems no reason for Lennie to have invented him. I think we may be able to identify him. But in order to avoid having to refer to him as the man who left the building before six-fifteen—"

"Let's call him Smith," Julian said with a smile.

"Smith it shall be. Well, Smith came out by the main doors, and immediately afterwards a man was seen on the steps by an electrician who was driving out of the courtyard."

"Seen and identified?" asked Keith.

"Not identified at the time," the Inspector replied equivocally. "Now from that moment there are no witnesses to Smith's actions, but there is certain evidence. This then is what I believe happened. Smith went round to the side entrance and took the private lift up to the flat. A minute or so later Keith arrived by taxi, took his suitcase to the side entrance, brought the lift down, placed the suitcase under the seat, and went off to the Tube station. At this moment Mrs Corsair was in her bedroom, varnishing her nails and listening to Ravel's *Bolero* on her radio. It's important to remember that her hearing is very slightly subnormal; consequently she sets the volume control rather higher than do most people. We must also remember that she left the television set on in the sitting-room though she had, at her husband's request, turned the volume down. When Smith rings the doorbell Corsair has just poured out some whisky and is about to add soda. The bell, actually a chime, is subdued, and Mrs Corsair does not hear it. Corsair puts down his glass, goes to the front door, and finds Smith there. We must assume that Smith is not a complete stranger since Corsair lets him in and, willingly or unwillingly, allows him to reach the sitting-room. He makes it quite clear, however, that he is not pleased to see him."

"Isn't that guesswork?" Julian coughed, patted his chest and, taking a pastille from the tin on his desk, looked round apologetically.

"He neither gives him a drink nor turns off the television, which he would surely do if he were ready to have a friendly chat. I believe that the conversation began on a sour note and that very soon Corsair lost his temper. He didn't shout—he wasn't that kind of man—but he started to push Smith out of the room. Smith struck aside his hand, knocking Corsair's cigar against his shirt and causing a slight burn. Only Smith can tell us what happened next—but some moments later Corsair staggered against the low windowsill, tried to save himself by bracing his knees against it, failed, and fell out. Smith, possibly horrified, looked out and saw that Corsair had fallen into the back of a lorry. Almost at once the lorry moved off. Smith watched helplessly. He was not to know until the following day that Corsair was dead. If he survived, then Smith would have to accept the consequences of his action. But if he were dead, which seemed likely in view of the distance he had fallen, then Smith might be able to escape those consequences by remaining silent. It was a difficult situation in which to find oneself." Turning to Bertie, he asked abruptly, "What would you have done, Colonel Summersby?"

"Me?" Bertie was startled. "God knows." He seemed about to add some comment when Julian interrupted, "Presumably Smith thought he was alone in the flat."

"I'm inclined to think that for a short time he did not realize that the radio playing the *Bolero* was actually inside the flat. He must have been in a mental state which sounds scarcely penetrated—and, of course, there was a background of noise from the television. Let's assume that for the moment he thought he was alone. But should that make any difference to his decision, Mr Killigrew?"

"None, of course. The right thing to do was to find a telephone and report everything to the police."

"Unfortunately Smith did not do that. Perhaps he thought that if Corsair were dead he would be charged with homicide. Perhaps he panicked—though I do not think so. What he did was to pick up a pair of opera glasses that Mrs Corsair had laid down and to throw them out of the window in the hope that people would conclude, as in fact they did, that Corsair had been leaning out to look at something and had over-balanced—to his death. Smith then had to get away without being seen. Going out into the passage, he not only realized that the radio was playing in one of the end rooms, but he heard it being switched off and knew that someone was likely to come out at any moment. Quickly he concealed himself in the study—just before Mrs Corsair left her bedroom and went into the sitting-room. Unaware of what had been taking place, she went to turn up the volume of the television. As she touched the control she heard someone cough. It was Lennie who had brought up Corsair's brief-case and was politely making his presence known. Realizing that he would not be heard over the now turned-up television, he put the brief-case down on a table in the passage, relocked the door, and re-turned to the hall. Two or three minutes later Mrs Corsair, having looked in vain for her opera glasses, went out to dinner."

"Leaving Smith alone in the flat?" asked Julian.

"Yes, he was now entirely alone. His problem was to leave without being seen. If he used the front door he might meet someone as he left the lift or came out into the courtyard. He had not, so far as I know, been in the flat before. He had however, passed the Emergency Door at least once before dur-ing a fire practice. He had also heard the cough which Mrs Corsair mistook for her husband's and knew the direction from which it came. When he went out of the study into the passage he looked in that direction and saw a pair of keys hanging on a wall-hook. At once he realized that there was an alternative and safe exit by the Emergency Door."

"Don't see how he could know that," croaked Bertie. "Sorry, throat's dry. D'you think I could have one of those pastilles, Killigrew?" He took the pastille which Julian put in the lid of the tin and passed across the desk.

"The key-ring was plainly labelled and the hook from which it hung was on the door-frame."

"I see." Julian was visualizing the situation. "So Smith put two and two together, let himself into the main building, and slipped out without Lennie's knowledge. But he must either have left the Emergency Door unlocked or taken a key to lock it."

"He locked the door after him."

"And no-one noticed that a key was missing? I thought there were police all over the place last weekend."

"There was apparently nothing missing when the police came. The split-ring with its label and two keys was hanging on the hook."

"You mean that Smith managed to replace the key he had taken? Then he must have been able to walk into the flat." Julian looked up sharply. "Did he have a latchkey to the flat?"

"Three people had latchkeys—Mrs Corsair, Minnie, and Keith Antrim. There was a fourth key, but it was in Corsair's pocket when he was found."

"You have called Smith 'he'." Julian's eyes flicked from Keith to the Inspector. He seemed about to speak when Keith forestalled him. "If Smith left the building without Lennie's knowledge he would have had to move the table which Lennie always put against the inner doors. He would have found it impossible to replace the table from the other side of the doors. Did Lennie say whether the table had been moved?"

"He said it had not."

"Feller could have got out of a window, couldn't he?" Bertie nodded, satisfied that he had made an intelligent contribution to the discussion.

"He preferred not to take the risk when there was a simple solution." The Inspector looked at his listeners, but no-one offered a comment. "Let us go back to the two keys which the police found hanging on a hook by the Emergency Door. One of them belonged to the mortise lock of that door, the other to some different lock. I assumed that these two keys had been on the split-ring for some time, and it did not occur to me to try to find the lock which the other key fitted."

"It did not occur to any of us," the Superintendent commented.

The Inspector smiled faintly. "My error was the greater because I had been told that three keys had been supplied with every lock in the building. One of the keys to the lock on the Emergency Door was on the split-ring and one in the commissionaire's cupboard. Where was the third key?" Momentarily he paused. "You will all know what Smith did. He removed one of the keys from the ring and substituted the mortise key to his own front door."

"Pretty smart, that," Bertie said appreciatively.

"But how did he get into his own home if he had left the doorkey behind?" asked Keith.

"By a window. His flat is on the ground floor, and there is no catch on one of the sashes." The Inspector looked round, inviting further questions, then resumed. "When Superintendent Mallick decided in the light of new information to reopen the inquiry into Corsair's death, Smith realized that for his continuing safety it was necessary to reverse the exchange of keys and so eliminate a damning piece of evidence. His problem was to find or invent some good reason for being in the flat without exciting suspicion. He found this reason, and this afternoon he was in the act of taking the keys from the hook when Miss Merrow came in by the front door. He had seen her with me sufficiently often to realize that she was assisting in the inquiry and would pass on to me whatever she saw. Although he had turned out the passage lights at once, he could not be sure that she had not recognized him. It was therefore necessary to eliminate her." He paused as the sound of indrawn breath indicated his listeners' reaction.

"D'you mean to say he was going to kill the girl?" Bertie croaked.

"She threatened his safety," the Inspector said bleakly. "He had to act quickly and silently. He clapped a handkerchief or some piece of cloth over her nose and mouth, opened the Emergency Door, dragged her through, and relocked the door with this key." Holding up the split-ring, he placed a finger on one of the two keys. "His next problem was how to dispose of Miss Merrow. He did not lose his presence of mind."

The listeners had long ago stubbed out their cigarettes. Bertie's mouth was slightly open. Keith's hands gripped his thighs. Julian stifled a cough and took a pastille. Mallick's face might have been carved in sandstone.

"Smith's solution was thorough. He left Miss Merrow, who had fainted, went to his office, put on a light to support the story he intended to tell and, going to the lift-shaft, called urgently for Lennie. When Lennie came up in the lift Smith efficiently broke his neck. His plan was, I believe, to kill Miss Merrow, perhaps to strangle her with Lennie's handkerchief or tie and so identify him as her killer. Then, as soon as it was dark—let us say now—to drop Lennie's body head-first from the floor above. When the bodies were found, would anyone doubt that Lennie had killed both Corsair and Anthea—and finally himself?" The Inspector's voice was completely devoid of expression. "Once Lennie's body was disposed of, Smith would be the only living person in the office building. He could then choose a suitable moment for going home to his flat in Wren Street."

"Wren Street?" Bertie cleared his throat. "Don't know it. Who the devil lives there?"

"This devil." Julian smiled and shook his head. "Inspector, why aren't you writing film scripts? A wonderful story except for the last two words." A mischievous glint came into his eye. "Where do you live, Summersby?"

"Me!" Bertie sat up with a jerk. Whatever words were in his mind stuck in his throat.

"There's a simple test we can apply to my reconstruction, Mr Killigrew." The violet eyes were no longer soft. "When I left you alone in this room I asked one of the Superintendent's men to ensure that you stayed in it. If we find in this room or in the courtyard near this window the missing key to the Emergency Door, or if the second key on this split-ring turns the lock on your front door, we shall know that you are Smith."

In the ensuing seconds everyone moved except Julian. The Superintendent reached the doorway, Keith the window. Bertie stood up, right arm at defensive level. The Inspector came to the desk. Julian looked amused. Putting a hand into his pocket, he pulled out two keys. "Here you are," he said calmly. "The missing key and a spare key to my own front door. I'm relieved to be rid of them. They've been burning a hole in my pocket for the past half-hour. Yes, I was responsible for Corsair's death. He told me with an air of insufferable arrogance that he did not wish to see my report; he had already decided to close down the Bookman's Weekly. When he began to push me out of the room I retaliated. He slipped, twisted, stumbled, and was out of the window before I could do anything to stop him. Then, as you said, I was faced with the problem of what to do. It's easy to say that I should have rung the police. But do you honestly think that in the circumstances they would have believed me? Whether they did or not, I should have had to stand up at the inquest and say what had happened. I would, I think, have escaped a murder charge, but not a lesser one. Do you imagine that when I came out of the courtroom—or out of gaol—my friends would have been waiting with outstretched arms to receive me? Would anyone be happy in a room alone with me? Would a kindly, smiling employer press me to remain in the editorial chair?"

The Inspector's eyes were glacial. "So to avoid discovery you killed Lennie and would have killed Miss Merrow if you had not been prevented?"

"I would have killed as many as necessary. In your case I was unfortunately not successful." Julian smiled bleakly. "I looked at the situation subjectively—how else could I have regarded it? As I told you the other day, a man with blood on his hands cannot afford to hesitate at the prospect of making them bloodier. Macbeth was wrong, you know. Blood washes off if the soap is more blood."

There are occasions, the Inspector was thinking, when blood calls for blood. But even for crimes such as this there is no rope, no chair, no garrotte, no guillotine. He looked at the faces of the other men and wondered what their thoughts were as Julian went on talking. He watched Julian put out a hand to the tin of pastilles and bring the hand up to his mouth and, though he knew what was about to happen, he did not try to stop it. He had seen death many times and in many forms, and the convulsive gasp, the cyanosed face, and the clown-like rictus did not move him.

Mallick swore quietly to himself. "I thought I saw something else among the pastilles, but I never thought—" He banged a fist into a palm. "Where the devil can he have got it from?"

"He was in Special Services during the War," said Keith, and met the Inspector's eye. There was no need for either man to speak. Each knew that the other could have stayed the dead man's hand. Each knew why he had not done so. No cataract of false idealism had blinded their eyes to the Spartan demands of life.

Indifferently, impassively, the Inspector watched the removal of the body. People spoke to him and he replied. Automatically he played the part that was his. As had happened before at the end of an inquiry during which an innocent person had died, he was censuring himself. Could he have prevented Lennie's death? Yes, he could and should have done so. One by one he went through the pointers that had led him to Julian. In retrospect it seemed that the path had been well-lit, the signposts clearly lettered. There had been possible motive. He had known that there were three keys to the Emergency Door, and that Julian's front door had a mortise

215

lock. There was Julian's request for the "exact time", so that the moment of his departure should be impressed on Lennie's mind. There was his use by association of the phrase "on the wing", an indication, however slight, of knowledge that Corsair was flying somewhere—information that only Corsair could have given him. Roddie mentioning that his glimpse of a man on the entrance steps had reminded him to post a letter was surely as good as saying that the man had an envelope in his hand—the report that Julian was about to take to Corsair. There was. . . . The Inspector sighed and banging a mental lid on clues and useless regrets looked round to find that he was alone.

The page-proofs were still on the desk, and he saw that Julian had corrected them as far as the penultimate paragraph. He read the final sentences and marked a letter transposition; then, going into Miss Brind's room, he laid the proofs beside her typewriter. Soon, switching off lights as he went, he made his way down to the entrance hall and going to the Staff Door found that someone had locked it. He returned to the hall.

On the table which Lennie had used for his work a whisky bottle lay on one dimpled side. Inside the bottle a jib schooner proudly sailed a painted plaster-of-paris sea. Black sealing-wax gleamed dully over the corked neck. Beneath the bottle lay an envelope addressed in a sloping copybook hand to "The Inspector". Opening the envelope, he took out a sheet of writing paper, unfolded it, and read:

Sir.
If I am not here when you come will you kindly accept this ship as a token of gratitude from yours respectfully,
Lennie

For a long time he stood holding the letter. Then, refolding it and placing it in his wallet, he found a discarded newspaper and wrapped the bottle neatly. Soon he let himself out, and the heavy glass doors closed behind him.

THE PERENNIAL LIBRARY MYSTERY SERIES

Delano Ames

CORPSE DIPLOMATIQUE   P 637, $2.84
"Sprightly and intelligent."
> —*New York Herald Tribune Book Review*

FOR OLD CRIME'S SAKE   P 629, $2.84

MURDER, MAESTRO, PLEASE   P 630, $2.84
"If there is a more engaging couple in modern fiction than Jane and
Dagobert Brown, we have not met them."   —*Scotsman*

SHE SHALL HAVE MURDER   P 638, $2.84
"Combines the merit of both the English and American schools in the
new mystery. It's as breezy as the best of the American ones, and has
the sophistication and wit of any top-notch Britisher."
> —*New York Herald Tribune Book Review*

E. C. Bentley

TRENT'S LAST CASE   P 440, $2.50
"One of the three best detective stories ever written."
> —Agatha Christie

TRENT'S OWN CASE   P 516, $2.25
"I won't waste time saying that the plot is sound and the detection
satisfying. Trent has not altered a scrap and reappears with all his old
humor and charm."   —Dorothy L. Sayers

Gavin Black

A DRAGON FOR CHRISTMAS   P 473, $1.95
"Potent excitement!"   —*New York Herald Tribune*

THE EYES AROUND ME   P 485, $1.95
"I stayed up until all hours last night reading *The Eyes Around Me,*
which is something I do not do very often, but I was so intrigued by the
ingeniousness of Mr. Black's plotting and the witty way in which he spins
his mystery. I can only say that I enjoyed the book enormously."
> —F. van Wyck Mason

YOU WANT TO DIE, JOHNNY?   P 472, $1.95
"Gavin Black doesn't just develop a pressure plot in suspense, he adds
uninfected wit, character, charm, and sharp knowledge of the Far East
to make rereading as keen as the first race-through."   —*Book Week*

Nicholas Blake

THE CORPSE IN THE SNOWMAN   P 427, $1.95
"If there is a distinction between the novel and the detective story (which we do not admit), then this book deserves a high place in both categories."   —*The New York Times*

THE DREADFUL HOLLOW   P 493, $1.95
"Pace unhurried, characters excellent, reasoning solid."
     —*San Francisco Chronicle*

END OF CHAPTER   P 397, $1.95
". . . admirably solid . . . an adroit formal detective puzzle backed up by firm characterization and a knowing picture of London publishing."
     —*The New York Times*

HEAD OF A TRAVELER   P 398, $2.25
"Another grade A detective story of the right old jigsaw persuasion."
     —*New York Herald Tribune Book Review*

MINUTE FOR MURDER   P 419, $1.95
"An outstanding mystery novel. Mr. Blake's writing is a delight in itself."   —*The New York Times*

THE MORNING AFTER DEATH   P 520, $1.95
"One of Blake's best."   —Rex Warner

A PENKNIFE IN MY HEART   P 521, $2.25
"Style brilliant . . . and suspenseful."   —*San Francisco Chronicle*

THE PRIVATE WOUND   P 531, $2.25
[Blake's] best novel in a dozen years . . . . An intensely penetrating study of sexual passion. . . . A powerful story of murder and its aftermath."
     —Anthony Boucher, *The New York Times*

A QUESTION OF PROOF   P 494, $1.95
"The characters in this story are unusually well drawn, and the suspense is well sustained."   —*The New York Times*

THE SAD VARIETY   P 495, $2.25
"It is a stunner. I read it instead of eating, instead of sleeping."
     —Dorothy Salisbury Davis

THERE'S TROUBLE BREWING   P 569, $3.37
"Nigel Strangeways is a puzzling mixture of simplicity and penetration, but all the more real for that."   —*The Times Literary Supplement*

THOU SHELL OF DEATH P 428, $1.95

"It has all the virtues of culture, intelligence and sensibility that the most exacting connoisseur could ask of detective fiction."
— *The Times* [London] *Literary Supplement*

THE WIDOW'S CRUISE P 399, $2.25

"A stirring suspense. . . . The thrilling tale leaves nothing to be desired."
— *Springfield Republican*

THE WORM OF DEATH P 400, $2.25

"It [The Worm of Death] is one of Blake's very best—and his best is better than almost anyone's." — Louis Untermeyer

John & Emery Bonett

A BANNER FOR PEGASUS P 554, $2.40

"A gem! Beautifully plotted and set. . . . Not only is the murder adroit and deserved, and the detection competent, but the love story is charming." — Jacques Barzun and Wendell Hertig Taylor

DEAD LION P 563, $2.40

"A clever plot, authentic background and interesting characters highly recommended this one." — *New Republic*

Christianna Brand

GREEN FOR DANGER P 551, $2.50

"You have to reach for the greatest of Great Names (Christie, Carr, Queen . . .) to find Brand's rivals in the devious subtleties of the trade."
— Anthony Boucher

TOUR DE FORCE P 572, $2.40

"Complete with traps for the over-ingenious, a double-reverse surprise ending and a key clue planted so fairly and obviously that you completely overlook it. If that's your idea of perfect entertainment, then seize at once upon *Tour de Force.*" — Anthony Boucher, *The New York Times*

James Byrom

OR BE HE DEAD P 585, $2.84

"A very original tale . . . Well written and steadily entertaining."
— Jacques Barzun & Wendell Hertig Taylor, *A Catalogue of Crime*

Henry Calvin

IT'S DIFFERENT ABROAD   P 640, $2.84

"What is remarkable and delightful, Mr. Calvin imparts a flavor of satire to what he renovates and compels us to take straight."

—Jacques Barzun

Marjorie Carleton

VANISHED   P 559, $2.40

"Exceptional . . . a minor triumph."

—Jacques Barzun and Wendell Hertig Taylor, *A Catalogue of Crime*

George Harmon Coxe

MURDER WITH PICTURES   P 527, $2.25

"[Coxe] has hit the bull's-eye with his first shot."

—*The New York Times*

Edmund Crispin

BURIED FOR PLEASURE   P 506, $2.50

"Absolute and unalloyed delight."

—Anthony Boucher, *The New York Times*

Lionel Davidson

THE MENORAH MEN   P 592, $2.84

"Of his fellow thriller writers, only John Le Carré shows the same instinct for the viscera."   —*Chicago Tribune*

NIGHT OF WENCESLAS   P 595, $2.84

"A most ingenious thriller, so enriched with style, wit, and a sense of serious comedy that it all but transcends its kind."

—*The New Yorker*

THE ROSE OF TIBET   P 593, $2.84

"I hadn't realized how much I missed the genuine Adventure story . . . until I read *The Rose of Tibet*."   —Graham Greene

D. M. Devine

MY BROTHER'S KILLER   P 558, $2.40

"A most enjoyable crime story which I enjoyed reading down to the last moment."   —Agatha Christie

Kenneth Fearing

THE BIG CLOCK   P 500, $1.95

"It will be some time before chill-hungry clients meet again so rare a compound of irony, satire, and icy-fingered narrative. *The Big Clock* is . . . a psychothriller you won't put down." —*Weekly Book Review*

Andrew Garve

THE ASHES OF LODA   P 430, $1.50

"Garve . . . embellishes a fine fast adventure story with a more credible picture of the U.S.S.R. than is offered in most thrillers."
                                                —*The New York Times Book Review*

THE CUCKOO LINE AFFAIR   P 451, $1.95

". . . an agreeable and ingenious piece of work." —*The New Yorker*

A HERO FOR LEANDA   P 429, $1.50

"One can trust Mr. Garve to put a fresh twist to any situation, and the ending is really a lovely surprise." —*The Manchester Guardian*

MURDER THROUGH THE LOOKING GLASS   P 449, $1.95

". . . refreshingly out-of-the-way and enjoyable . . . highly recommended to all comers." —*Saturday Review*

NO TEARS FOR HILDA   P 441, $1.95

"It starts fine and finishes finer. I got behind on breathing watching Max get not only his man but his woman, too." —Rex Stout

THE RIDDLE OF SAMSON   P 450, $1.95

"The story is an excellent one, the people are quite likable, and the writing is superior." —*Springfield Republican*

Michael Gilbert

BLOOD AND JUDGMENT   P 446, $1.95

"Gilbert readers need scarcely be told that the characters all come alive at first sight, and that his surpassing talent for narration enhances any plot. . . . Don't miss." —*San Francisco Chronicle*

THE BODY OF A GIRL   P 459, $1.95

"Does what a good mystery should do: open up into all kinds of ramifications, with untold menace behind the action. At the end, there is a bang-up climax, and it is a pleasure to see how skilfully Gilbert wraps everything up." —*The New York Times Book Review*

THE DANGER WITHIN   P 448, $1.95
"Michael Gilbert has nicely combined some elements of the straight detective story with plenty of action, suspense, and adventure, to produce a superior thriller."   —*Saturday Review*

FEAR TO TREAD   P 458, $1.95
"Merits serious consideration as a work of art."

—*The New York Times*

Joe Gores

HAMMETT   P 631, $2.84
"Joe Gores at his very best. Terse, powerful writing—with the master, Dashiell Hammett, as the protagonist in a novel I think he would have been proud to call his own."   —*Robert Ludlum*

C. W. Grafton

BEYOND A REASONABLE DOUBT   P 519, $1.95
"A very ingenious tale of murder . . . a brilliant and gripping narrative."
—*Jacques Barzun and Wendell Hertig Taylor*

THE RAT BEGAN TO GNAW THE ROPE   P 639, $2.84
"Fast, humorous story with flashes of brilliance."

—*The New Yorker*

Edward Grierson

THE SECOND MAN   P 528, $2.25
"One of the best trial-testimony books to have come along in quite a while."   —*The New Yorker*

Bruce Hamilton

TOO MUCH OF WATER   P 635, $2.84
"A superb sea mystery. . . . The prose is excellent."
—*Jacques Barzun and Wendell Hertig Taylor, A Catalogue of Crime*

Cyril Hare

DEATH IS NO SPORTSMAN   P 555, $2.40
"You will be thrilled because it succeeds in placing an ingenious story in a new and refreshing setting. . . . The identity of the murderer is really a surprise."   —*Daily Mirror*

DEATH WALKS THE WOODS P 556, $2.40

"Here is a fine formal detective story, with a technically brilliant solution demanding the attention of all connoisseurs of construction."

—Anthony Boucher, *The New York Times Book Review*

AN ENGLISH MURDER P 455, $2.50

"By a long shot, the best crime story I have read for a long time. Everything is traditional, but originality does not suffer. The setting is perfect. Full marks to Mr. Hare." —*Irish Press*

SUICIDE EXCEPTED P 636, $2.84

"Adroit in its manipulation . . . and distinguished by a plot-twister which I'll wager Christie wishes she'd thought of."

—*The New York Times*

TENANT FOR DEATH P 570, $2.84

"The way in which an air of probability is combined both with clear, terse narrative and with a good deal of subtle suburban atmosphere, proves the extreme skill of the writer." —*The Spectator*

TRAGEDY AT LAW P 522, $2.25

"An extremely urbane and well-written detective story."

—*The New York Times*

UNTIMELY DEATH P 514, $2.25

"The English detective story at its quiet best, meticulously underplayed, rich in perceivings of the droll human animal and ready at the last with a neat surprise which has been there all the while had we but wits to see it." —*New York Herald Tribune Book Review*

THE WIND BLOWS DEATH P 589, $2.84

"A plot compounded of musical knowledge, a Dickens allusion, and a subtle point in law is related with delightfully unobtrusive wit, warmth, and style." —*The New York Times*

WITH A BARE BODKIN P 523, $2.25

"One of the best detective stories published for a long time."

—*The Spectator*

Robert Harling

THE ENORMOUS SHADOW P 545, $2.50

"In some ways the best spy story of the modern period. . . . The writing is terse and vivid . . . the ending full of action . . . altogether first-rate."

—Jacques Barzun and Wendell Hertig Taylor, *A Catalogue of Crime*

Matthew Head

THE CABINDA AFFAIR P 541, $2.25
"An absorbing whodunit and a distinguished novel of atmosphere."
—Anthony Boucher, *The New York Times*

THE CONGO VENUS P 597, $2.84
"Terrific. The dialogue is just plain wonderful."
—*The Boston Globe*

MURDER AT THE FLEA CLUB P 542, $2.50
"The true delight is in Head's style, its limpid ease combined with humor and an awesome precision of phrase." —*San Francisco Chronicle*

M. V. Heberden

ENGAGED TO MURDER P 533, $2.25
"Smooth plotting." —*The New York Times*

James Hilton

WAS IT MURDER? P 501, $1.95
"The story is well planned and well written."
—*The New York Times*

P. M. Hubbard

HIGH TIDE P 571, $2.40
"A smooth elaboration of mounting horror and danger."
—*Library Journal*

Elspeth Huxley

THE AFRICAN POISON MURDERS P 540, $2.25
"Obscure venom, manical mutilations, deadly bush fire, thrilling climax compose major opus.... Top-flight."
—*Saturday Review of Literature*

MURDER ON SAFARI P 587, $2.84
"Right now we'd call Mrs. Huxley a dangerous rival to Agatha Christie." —*Books*

Francis Iles

BEFORE THE FACT   P 517, $2.50

"Not many 'serious' novelists have produced character studies to compare with Iles's internally terrifying portrait of the murderer in *Before the Fact,* his masterpiece and a work truly deserving the appellation of unique and beyond price."   —Howard Haycraft

MALICE AFORETHOUGHT   P 532, $1.95

"It is a long time since I have read anything so good as *Malice Aforethought,* with its cynical humour, acute criminology, plausible detail and rapid movement. It makes you hug yourself with pleasure."
                              —H. C. Harwood, *Saturday Review*

Michael Innes

THE CASE OF THE JOURNEYING BOY   P 632, $3.12

"I could see no faults in it. There is no one to compare with him."
                              —*Illustrated London News*

DEATH BY WATER   P 574, $2.40

"The amount of ironic social criticism and deft characterization of scenes and people would serve another author for six books."
                              —Jacques Barzun and Wendell Hertig Taylor

HARE SITTING UP   P 590, $2.84

"There is hardly anyone (in mysteries or mainstream) more exquisitely literate, allusive and Jamesian—and hardly anyone with a firmer sense of melodramatic plot or a more vigorous gift of storytelling."
                              —Anthony Boucher, *The New York Times*

THE LONG FAREWELL   P 575, $2.40

"A model of the deft, classic detective story, told in the most wittily diverting prose."   —*The New York Times*

THE MAN FROM THE SEA   P 591, $2.84

"The pace is brisk, the adventures exciting and excitingly told, and above all he keeps to the very end the interesting ambiguity of the man from the sea."   —*New Statesman*

THE SECRET VANGUARD   P 584, $2.84

"Innes . . . has mastered the art of swift, exciting and well-organized narrative."   —*The New York Times*

THE WEIGHT OF THE EVIDENCE   P 633, $2.84

"First-class puzzle, deftly solved. University background interesting and amusing."   —*Saturday Review of Literature*

Mary Kelly

THE SPOILT KILL　　　　　　　　　　P 565, $2.40

"Mary Kelly is a new Dorothy Sayers. . . . [An] exciting new novel."

　　　　　　　　　　　　　　　　—*Evening News*

Lange Lewis

THE BIRTHDAY MURDER　　　　　　　P 518, $1.95

"Almost perfect in its playlike purity and delightful prose."

　　　　　　　　　—Jacques Barzun and Wendell Hertig Taylor

Allan MacKinnon

HOUSE OF DARKNESS　　　　　　　　P 582, $2.84

"His best . . . a perfect compendium."

　　—Jacques Barzun & Wendell Hertig Taylor, *A Catalogue of Crime*

Arthur Maling

LUCKY DEVIL　　　　　　　　　　　P 482, $1.95

"The plot unravels at a fast clip, the writing is breezy and Maling's approach is as fresh as today's stockmarket quotes."

　　　　　　　　　　　　　—*Louisville Courier Journal*

RIPOFF　　　　　　　　　　　　　　P 483, $1.95

"A swiftly paced story of today's big business is larded with intrigue as a Ralph Nader-type investigates an insurance scandal and is soon on the run from a hired gun and his brother. . . . Engrossing and credible."

　　　　　　　　　　　　　　　　　—*Booklist*

SCHROEDER'S GAME　　　　　　　　P 484, $1.95

"As the title indicates, this Schroeder is up to something, and the unravelling of his game is a diverting and sufficiently blood-soaked entertainment."　　　　　　　　　　　—*The New Yorker*

Austin Ripley

MINUTE MYSTERIES　　　　　　　　P 387, $2.50

More than one hundred of the world's shortest detective stories. Only one possible solution to each case!

Thomas Sterling

THE EVIL OF THE DAY　　　　　　　P 529, $2.50

"Prose as witty and subtle as it is sharp and clear. . .characters unconventionally conceived and richly bodied forth . . . . In short, a novel to be treasured."　　　　　　　—Anthony Boucher, *The New York Times*

Julian Symons

THE BELTING INHERITANCE   P 468, $1.95
"A superb whodunit in the best tradition of the detective story."
                              —August Derleth, *Madison Capital Times*

BLAND BEGINNING   P 469, $1.95
"Mr. Symons displays a deft storytelling skill, a quiet and literate wit,
a nice feeling for character, and detectival ingenuity of a high order."
                              —Anthony Boucher, *The New York Times*

BOGUE'S FORTUNE   P 481, $1.95
"There's a touch of the old sardonic humour, and more than a touch of
style."   —*The Spectator*

THE BROKEN PENNY   P 480, $1.95
"The most exciting, astonishing and believable spy story to appear in
years.   —Anthony Boucher, *The New York Times Book Review*

THE COLOR OF MURDER   P 461, $1.95
"A singularly unostentatious and memorably brilliant detective story."
                              —*New York Herald Tribune Book Review*

Dorothy Stockbridge Tillet
(John Stephen Strange)

THE MAN WHO KILLED FORTESCUE   P 536, $2.25
"Better than average."   —*Saturday Review of Literature*

Simon Troy

THE ROAD TO RHUINE   P 583, $2.84
"Unusual and agreeably told."   —*San Francisco Chronicle*

SWIFT TO ITS CLOSE   P 546, $2.40
"A nicely literate British mystery . . . the atmosphere and the plot are
exceptionally well wrought, the dialogue excellent."   —*Best Sellers*

Henry Wade

THE DUKE OF YORK'S STEPS   P 588, $2.84
"A classic of the golden age."
   —Jacques Barzun & Wendell Hertig Taylor, *A Catalogue of Crime*

A DYING FALL   P 543, $2.50
"One of those expert British suspense jobs . . . it crackles with undercur-
rents of blackmail, violent passion and murder. Topnotch in its class."
                                              —*Time*

Henry Wade (cont'd)

THE HANGING CAPTAIN   P 548, $2.50

"This is a detective story for connoisseurs, for those who value clear thinking and good writing above mere ingenuity and easy thrills."

—*Times Literary Supplement*

Hillary Waugh

LAST SEEN WEARING . . .   P 552, $2.40

"A brilliant tour de force."   —Julian Symons

THE MISSING MAN   P 553, $2.40

"The quiet detailed police work of Chief Fred C. Fellows, Stockford, Conn., is at its best in *The Missing Man* . . . one of the Chief's toughest cases and one of the best handled."

—Anthony Boucher, *The New York Times Book Review*

Henry Kitchell Webster

WHO IS THE NEXT?   P 539, $2.25

"A double murder, private-plane piloting, a neat impersonation, and a delicate courtship are adroitly combined by a writer who knows how to use the language."   —Jacques Barzun and Wendell Hertig Taylor

Anna Mary Wells

MURDERER'S CHOICE   P 534, $2.50

"Good writing, ample action, and excellent character work."

—*Saturday Review of Literature*

A TALENT FOR MURDER   P 535, $2.25

"The discovery of the villain is a decided shock."   —*Books*

Edward Young

THE FIFTH PASSENGER   P 544, $2.25

"Clever and adroit . . . excellent thriller . . ."   —*Library Journal*

If you enjoyed this book you'll want to know about
THE PERENNIAL LIBRARY MYSTERY SERIES
Buy them at your local bookstore or use this coupon for ordering:

Qty	P number	Price
	postage and handling charge	$1.00
_____ book(s) @ $0.25		
	TOTAL	

Prices contained in this coupon are Harper & Row invoice prices only.
They are subject to change without notice, and in no way reflect the prices at
which these books may be sold by other suppliers.

**HARPER & ROW, Mail Order Dept. #PMS, 10 East 53rd St., New
York, N.Y. 10022.**
Please send me the books I have checked above. I am enclosing $_____
which includes a postage and handling charge of $1.00 for the first book and
25¢ for each additional book. Send check or money order. No cash or
C.O.D.s please

Name_____

Address_____

City_____ State_____ Zip_____
Please allow 4 weeks for delivery. USA only. This offer expires 6/30/84.
Please add applicable sales tax.

—